T0156772

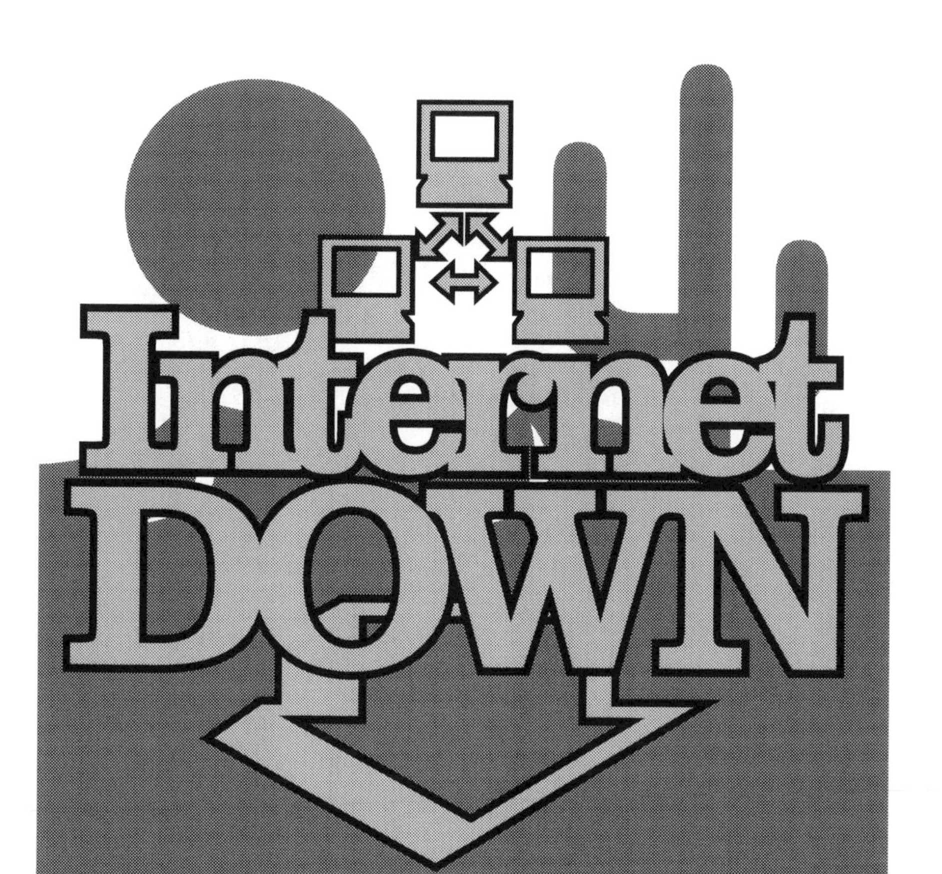

...A Modern
American Western

by

**R. R.
Hultén**

AuthorHouse™
1663 Liberty Drive
Bloomington, IN 47403
www.authorhouse.com
Phone: 1-800-839-8640

Published by AuthorHouse 11/2/2012

ISBN: 978-1-4772-8286-1 (sc)
ISBN: 978-1-4772-8323-3 (hc)
ISBN: 978-1-4772-8285-4 (e)

Library of Congress Control Number: 2012919712

PART ONE

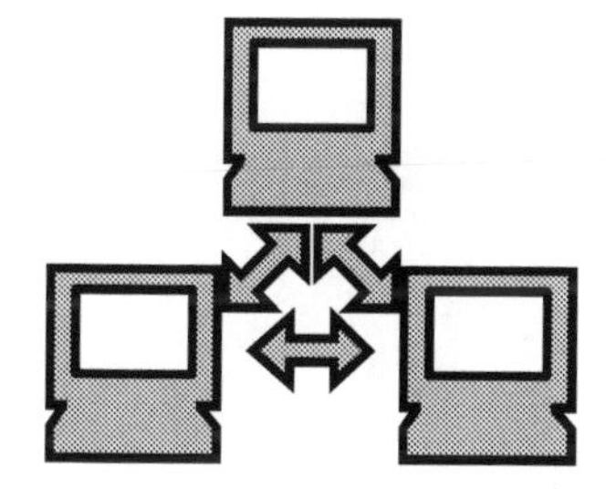

Chapter One
Reflections

The slow rise and fall of the ocean around the oil platform sounded like someone slowly snoring. The gently rising swells filled an empty chamber with a shuddering slurp and emptied back through the clumps of seaweed and barnacles with a sigh as the wave passed. An employee of the oil company, obviously driven by the company's productivity benchmarks, had haphazardly refastened the now lost inspection cover.

The warm night had a waning moon with gauze-like clouds obscuring all but the brightest stars. A light, offshore breeze carried with it a hint of the spicy South American cuisine. Chris Nelson was dozing on the sea side of the mud house thirty feet above the waves. This retreat kept him away from the pounding noise of the powerhouse and the whine of the pneumatic tools at the heliport. He leaned back on an old, wooden ladder back chair that he had braced against a bulkhead wall, and by hooking the heels of his work boots over the middle cable on the safety fence, he was securely anchored. This was his personal quiet time; he let his thoughts drift where they may.

His thoughts drifted back in time to when he graduated from the Colorado School of Mines. Four years ago, the job market had been poor, and the future didn't look any brighter than it had before he began college.

The Chilean government had seen that privatization was beneficial to both business and government, and with that realization, many companies were started on the road to private ownership, a board of directors, and stock market offerings. Career advertisements started to appear in the North American newspapers. They were looking for new talent educated in the United States and offered many benefits and hiring bonuses as inducements. His geology degree, plus a kind word from a former professor, had gotten him in the front door. Eco-oil had used a European model for their company, so the obvious choice for a new hire was to monitor his progress by starting him at the bottom of the ladder as a welder and pipe fitter. Eco-oil wanted well-rounded employees with management potential that could mesh in any work or social strata.

Putting his water bottle next to a leg of the chair his thoughts turned to the dangerous things happening around the world since the attack on the World Trade Center. The growth of global terrorism was becoming exponential since 9/11. Not only had terrorists become bolder, but they had learned to enlist others from both sexes and at all levels of society, including well-educated computer geeks. Their low tech schemes seemed to continually trump the high tech, expensive precautions.

He felt isolated and exposed away from his home in Colorado. The eastern half of Colorado lies in the Great Plains, often referred to as "flyover country." Most airline passengers look out their windows and see a vast openness, which translates mentally into desolation, since many are conditioned to the compactness of the larger cities. Chris chuckled as he thought of the Homeland Security measures taken back east. Government buildings were surrounded with concrete bollards along with anti-aircraft guns and rockets at the White House and other Washington icons. This might have made sense on the coasts, where the "teeming masses" came in all shapes and sizes. Profiling might be politically incorrect there, but it worked out west, where a stranger was quickly noticed.

Before many of the communication links and backup routes had been systematically sabotaged throughout the world, Chris had been in touch with Marcie, his girlfriend since college, during his stay in Chile. The company was very generous with the use of company communications for keeping in contact with friends and relatives. She was his source of information for local news in Colorado and what was happening around the rest of the world.

What Chris had learned from Marcie was that the societal fabric was slowly being torn apart by random terrorist activity, extremist groups with an agenda that was known mostly to themselves, weakened and bankrupt governments, drug cartels with many gangs becoming "security" for them.Surprisingly, many people were finding ways to keep their communities together and functioning while all hell broke out around them.

When Chris went to college, he minored in Criminal Justice. This helped him to enter law enforcement as a reserve deputy. After completing the sheriff's nighttime police academy, he was commissioned as a deputy and assisted full-time deputies with their work, learning much about the inner workings of law enforcement. Many times, he saw a lesson from the classroom being reinforced in the field. Chris found a lot of common sense in the thinking and actions of his fellow officers. He observed and absorbed the games played by citizens, felons, and cops.

He took an interest in firearm training and soon found himself under the wing of an instructor. He enjoyed the tactical training and proved himself creative in his approach to the various scenarios presented. He was thoroughly coached by two veteran instructors and, after much practice, entered competitive matches. After several years of competing, he had a number of trophies from the state, regional, and national matches. The protégé of the old-timers had learned well. Chris loved the work, and many times, he thought of doing it full-time instead of geology. Chris's good friend at the Colorado School of Mines, Bob Nelson, he'd known since the beginning of college. They shared the same last name but were not related. It made for some interesting conversation and confusion. They hung out at a local flying club in Boulder. Bob tried to educate Chris about Marcie and mentioned that she was close to her dad and not interested in Chris. If anything, she was using him to keep other suitors at bay. A cock blocker, if you will. Chris, of course, thought he was tight with Marcie and wouldn't listen to anything contrary to his belief. Still, Bob and Chris enjoyed their time together, flying to far-flung airports for the sheer joy of it or for an early-morning breakfast. Chris occasionally asked Bob what he was going to do after graduation. Bob's answer was always, "Haul ass!" Chris assumed it was a smart-ass answer and quickly dismissed it even though the answer tickled him. He thought about Bob's family of mule skinners and breeders. It was obvious that they would all have to "haul ass" after school.

He was getting anxious since he, along with his coworkers, had been isolated from the rest of the world on this steel island. His replacement couldn't get there soon enough.

Chapter Two
Don't Inhale!

During the odd breaks in the cacophony on deck, Chris thought he heard the sound of a small watercraft engine and the drumming of its hull. He lingered in that space between sleep and awareness, and his subconscious sent a message to him that a motorboat, at this time of the morning, was very odd. His eyes snapped opened, and he looked into the darkness toward shore.

He couldn't imagine his replacement showing up at this time in the morning. If it was the Management Team, he'd just keep his comfortable seat and see who came aboard the rig this early in the morning. He dozed off again.

Being inside a blast is rarely something not remembered. For one to survive the searing heat while being pushed overboard is beyond belief. The painted side toward the blast was instantly blistered and pocked by shards of metal, solid and molten blasted against the opposite side. A quick thought came to mind that was shared by an old fireman. *When in intense heat, do not inhale!* The esophagus will instantly blister and close, suffocating the victim. This may be good information to know while being burned at the stake and wanting to end the agony. This thought occupied his mind on the way to the water below. *Don't inhale! Don't inhale!* The trip was short and numbing. Surprisingly, he was thrown clear of the protective steel building during the explosion. Regaining the surface of the water, he was shaken but quickly regained his bearing and looked around for other survivors. Seeing none in his immediate area, he decided, *So much for this job.*

Alongside the tubular leg, he looked across the brightly lit surface of the water and saw three motorboats idling behind the east caisson. The sole guard was anxiously looking toward his co-conspirators dogpaddling the hundred years back to the three boats, yelling in some Middle Eastern tongue. It seemed quite humorous that a mission at sea would require people with better swimming skills. Chris swam, somewhat impeded by his heavy work boots, the fifty feet to the boat closest to him while minor explosions reverberated above him, sending more of the superstructure into the water.

After sliding over the transom of the empty boat and quickly crawling toward the helm, Chris clicked the gearshift of the idling boat into reverse. It slowly tracked straight back. Just as it was about to pull the slack in the rope from the guard's hand, he threw the wheel over and gave it full power. The armed guard immediately realized he had a conflicting problem and knew he had to stay with the second boat, but he managed to snap off a stream of ineffective automatic fire toward the quickly disappearing boat. The sound of the roaring engine and gunfire signaled the others that they now had a big, unforeseen problem, and they redoubled their efforts. Chris with a hundred-yard lead motivated the saboteurs to not waste any more time getting in the two remaining boats. Another one tried machine-gunning Chris in the darkness. His shots were too high and went overhead, making a deep droning, buzzing sound. The oil rig was quickly coming apart. The explosions were farther apart. As the floating rafts of oil closed into each other, similar to mercury attracting other drops of mercury, they would catch the unburned floating puddles afire.

As Chris headed toward shore a thousand yards away, the darkness helped to conceal him. He made a ninety-degree turn to the north, ran a few hundred yards, and shut down the engine. In the humid darkness, he heard the booming of the approaching hulls. Chris wiped the fear-caused sweat that was pouring from him and noticed that his legs had become still and his hands started to shake. The unknown men motored past his position and suddenly stopped their engines. Their double wake rocked his boat. It was obvious that they were listening for his engine. What seemed to be an eternity for Chris ended when they ran out of patience and restarted their engines, heading for the shore. One of the engines started to miss, changing to rough running and then stopping. The other boat went to idle, most likely to pick up the stranded men in the stalled boat. While they machine-gunned the abandoned boat's hull to scuttle it, Chris saw the muzzle flashes and involuntarily crouched in his boat. They were much closer than he had guessed.

Peering through the darkness at the unknown foe, Chris waited until he could no longer hear their engine and then restarted his engine and slowly headed north. Staying on course for five minutes, he shut down the engine and listened again. When he felt secure he had no followers, he restarted and headed for shore.

Closer to the coast, he saw parts of Valparaiso in flames, as was Vina del Mar to the north. Staying on course, he avoided the two large cities, hoping for a safe haven further north. The GPS on board showed his position as being just south of the thirty-second parallel. This put him on a line with a resort town called Pichidanqui. Not much was happening in that direction, so his choice was obvious. The sun was just beginning to lighten the eastern sky. He didn't like the thought of being a sitting duck. From what he saw along the coast, there wouldn't be any flights leaving soon. Now he needed another way back to Colorado. His wallet, credit cards, passport, even the little money he had were now at the bottom of the Pacific.

In the gathering morning light, the coastline jungle gave birth to thick tendrils of fog, creating a picture worth remembering some other time. Quietly motoring along the coast, he looked for a place to beach. A sandy, brush-covered outcropping offered itself as a hiding place. Heeling the boat around, he drove the craft up onto the beach. As he reached to shut down the engine, he heard it cough, sputter, and quit. Mostly out of curiosity, he looked in the tank. It was dry! That was much too close.

He pushed his way through the brush to see the surrounding area. While doing so, he came across a pile of suitcases, attaché cases, and various odd-sized cases that were in various stages of having been vandalized. Hearing retreating footstep on the concrete Chris peered through the brush catching a glimpse of a couple of men looking back over their shoulders as they walked quickly in the direction of the hotel. He was south of a resort, which the marquee proudly announced as *Cabanas Del Sol.* It was obviously a resort for the well to do. The three-story building had recently been painted white with coral trim. Stucco finish was evident. The roof covered with clay tiles was typical in the tropics. The upper balconies sported wrought iron trimming, and all the windows had colorful awnings. The front entrance columns betrayed the colonial background of the area. Palms, ferns, and grass were kept immaculate with constant attention.

Dressed in his blue work shirt and jeans, he was oil soaked and looked like a refugee from an industrial accident. Perhaps if he took a look through the bags, he could find something usable. With some soap from one and a towel along with some very nice clothing from another, he headed back to the beach for a quick bath. After stripping off his clothes, he lathered himself to rid himself of the stink of fear and oil. So far, not even a maintenance employee had noticed him. He chose a tan pair of slacks with a matching light, straw-colored shirt. The clothing fit him well. Smiling to himself, he thought he should fit in well at the resort. The worn work boots didn't go with the clothes. For now, he would play the part of a barefoot hotel guest just off the beach from an early morning stroll.

Getting back to the pile of luggage he started where the two thieves left off. One attaché case yielded a large quantity of American cash. In a smaller suitcase, a roll of money was tucked in a stretch pocket along the side. He didn't think twice about putting that in his pocket. The other items in there were feminine, including the negligee that looked like it was straight out of a Victoria's Secret catalog. Another attaché case was a quality built, dark leather case and more difficult to open. Finding a screwdriver in one of the boat storage bins, he used it to force open the latches. Inside the case were bundled twenty-, fifty-, and hundred-dollar bills that were all American green backs. Thoughts ran wild in his mind. This could be from drug people, business hijinks, or a swindle. Whatever the reason or source, he was now in line, with the rest of the world, to salvage what he could. While walking to the opposite side of the parking lot, he found an innocuous place to hide the case and work boots. With that done, he walked along the beach and found the breakfast buffet being set up.

Chapter Three
La Palmeda

Not many people were present at this early hour. Picking up a plate, Chris paused to look at the beautiful and intricate design while he moved along the buffet choosing small quantities of various foods that caught his attention. Retreating to a table away from the buffet and closer to the water, his solitude was short lived.

"Excuse me, Señor. May I breakfast with you?" asked a gentle female voice.

Chris quietly regained his thoughts and stood pulling out a chair for the lady to sit. "I'd be delighted. Please, have a seat." *I must have been on that rig too long or she is the absolutely most gorgeous woman I've ever seen or imagined.*

Chris looked again and caught his breath. Never in his life had he seen an exotic beauty like her, at least not this close. They were about the same height, and Chris quickly noticed she was also shoeless. Her light brown, wavy, shoulder-length hair looked heavy and thick. The light green summer dress complemented her eyes. The plunging neckline stopped just before her navel and exposed her flat belly. The rising sun, backlighting her, shone through the diaphanous summer dress, creating myriad hues within the fabric and revealing a body that defied description. He caught a hint of her perfume. It was magnetic, and it was working. Her green eyes caught his as he was taking inventory. They both blushed, averting their eyes from each other. When Chris mustered up his courage again, he saw the total lack of makeup. It was obvious she didn't need any. Her eyelashes were wickedly long, the eyebrows arcing perfectly above her eyes as two bird wings. Her cheeks glowed with health, and her lips held a hint of a permanent smile.

"I haven't seen you before. Are you a new arrival?" she asked while motioning to a waiter that she'd like a cup of coffee.

"Yes. I just got off the boat, so to speak."

"There aren't any boats docking here." She paused a bit, thinking. "Oh! That must be an American phrase."

"Yes, it is. I arrived early this morning."

He thought he should add a bit more to his lie.

"I planned this vacation for three months. I work for an oil company and just wanted to forget about the pressures of the job. Now, looking around, I have to wonder if I made the right decision." He hoped it sounded like he was a typical American on vacation. Wanting to continue the conversation, he said, "Do you know who or what is responsible for what's going on around here?"

"Please call me Sarita. How shall I address you, sir?"

"Chris will do. It's short for Christopher."

"Chris, I've been reading a copy of some news that has been posted on the Internet. It is from the Free Republic. This may help you understand what is happening here." She handed the four sheets to Chris. Chris read the news article with interest. A Lebanese businessman was arrested and charged with money laundering and software pirating. The Chilean government had found money transfers to Canada, Chile, Lebanon, China, North Korea, Russia, and the United States. Following his release on bail, he disappeared and was believed to be in Syria.

The area around Bolivia, Nicaragua, Columbia, and Brazil was well known as a resting spot for local drug traffickers and terrorists, such as the Revolutionary Armed Forces of Columbia, also known as FARC. During the past decade, it had changed to a hotbed of extremist Islamic terrorism.

The area currently provided housing to 25,000 Arabs or those of Arab descent. The original immigrants came from Syria, Lebanon, Jordan, Egypt, Iraq, and Palestine. Members of international terrorist groups were frequenting the area.

The nexus between Islamic terrorists and drug trafficking was under investigation by regional and US agencies, and they were finding considerable corruption at all levels of government. The international crackdown on terrorist activities caused many of these groups to revert to drug money for funding. The Taliban had earned an estimated $40-50 million dollars per year from taxes on opium production in

Afghanistan. This was according to the website TerrorismAnswers.org, produced by the Council on Foreign Relations. Cocaine was smuggled from South America to Europe and the Middle East. In 2002, the Drug Enforcement Administration had arrested 136 people for drug smuggling in the United States. Further investigation found that there was a direct link between terrorists and drug money. Also discovered by other agencies were links between charitable groups and Islamic terrorists.

The article also mentioned statements made by various American politicians. Hezbollah had been seen as a main threat to American interests and Americans in general. The spokesperson for the extremist group emphasized that any threat to the Lebanese people would be defended.

Chris finished the article and looked out to sea. This is what he had learned in school. Under whatever guise, religious, terrorist, or business, it was another version of organized crime. How far it would spread and how long it would take could be anyone's guess. Poor, undeveloped countries can profit most by hosting terrorists. The rich, developed countries would, of course, weaken their economies by spending untold billions of dollars trying to end terrorism and increase their security. Taking a broad view, Chris saw the "have-nots" had indeed found a way to get to the "haves."

"I learned about terrorism in college, but I hadn't any idea that it had spread this far." Chris had always wondered why news from South America and other countries was minimal at best.

She told him about how the governments of Chile and surrounding countries were starting to lose control of their citizens. The local gangs had been easily convinced to ally themselves with the terrorists. The terrorists had supplied the organization and training, while the gangs supplied the labor and security. Valparaiso and Santiago had many public and private records. By destroying the public records in these cities, they hoped they would erase information about citizens, property, and finances. The gangs went along, thinking they would be creating a new form of freedom for the citizens by ending government control. It was obvious the terrorists, for now, were out to create havoc. Eventually, they would graduate from mundane bombings to the more sophisticated cyber-terrorism. It was just a matter of time. Many were, after all, going to American colleges and universities.

Chris was thinking ahead of Sarita. He was sure that some students majoring in business weren't there just for bettering business back in their home countries. They were learning all they could about international computer networking, Domain Name Systems or DNS, routing, security, backup files, and the ease of stealing those files. Chris was sure that viruses, Trojan Horses, misdirection of domain addresses, and worms were on their minds. It sounded like the bunch in Florida that had learned to fly large commercial aircraft and crash them were just the tip of the iceberg. It seemed that a question would have arisen when the "student pilots" weren't interested in learning about landings. Chris wasn't so much as amazed as he was angered by the amount of damage that could be caused by someone getting his or her palm greased or looking the other way.

"So, here we sit, acting like there isn't a care in the world. Why doesn't anyone seem too concerned about the goings on?"

Sarita went on, "People aren't in a panic, just yet, but there is a deep concern about their future. Many are not sure what to do. As of this morning, money transfers were not completing for the hotel. Some are finding out their credit cards are useless." Her English was perfect, and Chris was drawn to the sound of her voice.

While she was talking, Chris thought it wouldn't be long before terrorists gained access into the bank and credit computers, if they hadn't already. In an effort to massage stockholders, American companies were using tech companies in India to service their customers and thereby showing a reduction in the cost of doing business. One had to question the intelligence of letting American personal information loose on an international scale. He asked himself, *What would happen if someone were to get hold of all that information about American citizens?* There would be the possibility of global financial destruction. Cash would again become king. Chris could very easily imagine a future with good guys, bad guys, con men, stickup men, and just about anyone with an eye toward crime and the ever popular "opportunity." Terrorists will have created chaos. They will have accomplished their goal, the financial crippling of Europe, Asia, and both Americas into something short of a financial Stone Age.

"Excuse me, Sarita, I was just thinking about the possible problems that may come from all this."

"I've been thinking about that all night too, Chris."

She was taking notice of the clothes he was wearing. For the first time in his life, he felt that he was being undressed. The odd feeling was replaced with a need to leave quickly.

Chris politely excused himself from Sarita, mumbling something about seeing a plumber about a leak, and left the table, heading for the front door of the resort. *Jeeeesh, I've turned into a true knuckle dragger with cute sayings like that.* As Chris went through one entrance door, a man about his height and weight, but built much stronger, entered the door next to him. He stood stiffly and rolled his shoulder as if to be getting ready for combat. He flexed his fingers and looked along the buffet tables. He had a white streak in his coal-black hair and the largest hands Chris had ever seen on a man.

Nick, "La Palmeda", was in a foul mood after discovering this morning's parking lot theft from the hotel's management.

Nick had earned the "La Palmeda" nickname from his method of dealing with his reluctant "customers." Those that both feared and respected him used the nickname behind his back. His novel method of encouraging individuals that had fallen short of his expectations or those of his employer at the time, either on a deal or loan, was to hold one of the "associate's" arms while slapping the back of the victim's head while they ran in a circle trying to outrun that punishing hand. The translation was literally "palm," as in slapping one on the back. Nick just aimed his hand a bit higher. Occasionally, one suffered a brain hemorrhage or went unconscious. Nick loved his work immensely. At times, it was his entire reason for being. He was successful and respected and even feared by employers around the world. He was a very handsome Italian that loved women, and when the occasion arose, men.

"Sarita, I just found something out," Nick said while giving Chris a double take as they passed.

Chapter Four
New Wheels and a Close Shave

Chris picked up a lever-type corkscrew while passing the bar. At some other time, it would have been a great bar to meet women. It was tastefully done in ultra-masculine, dark hardwood, trimmed with brass. The kind of bar many middle-income men dream about having in their basements but could never afford.

He walked out the front door toward the bush where he had hidden the leather case. Without breaking his stride, he stooped to pick it up along with the well-worn boots. Walking among the parked cars, he noticed a clean black Cadillac. It was locked, and a flashing red LED on the dash informed him it had an active alarm. Passing the Cadillac, he saw the top of a short black car. Curious, he walked around some other cars and found one of the Chrysler ME Four-Twelve prototypes. This was Chrysler's first-ever mid-engine super car. Chris walked up to it and carefully looked inside for any winking lights or obvious alarm switches. Seeing none, he reached for the door handle next to the window. Slowly he pulled up the small handle and heard a subtle click. The door gently opened. No alarm screamed that the car was being violated. Emboldened, Chris climbed aboard and closed the door. He pushed the seat back and slid down. The new car smell was still there. The ignition switch was typical and easy to defeat since manufacturers thought it nice that the key fit in both ways. What they didn't foresee was that they inadvertently created an internal weakness. He pulled the corkscrew out of his pocket and screwed it into the ignition switch. It was hard going until the tip of the screw found the tumbler. Then it plowed its way through the small pins in the thin brass barrel. When the corkscrew was deep enough into the switch, he forced the raised arms down. He heard the pins shearing from the tension. The core of the switch pulled free. Tossing the corkscrew and lock on the floor next to the passenger seat, he noticed that he was dripping sweat on the upholstery—it was not from the heat. His nervous energy and male need to succeed were in high gear. He looked around for something to turn the ignition switch. He retrieved the corkscrew and tried one of the paddle levers into the keyless hole. He sat up in the seat, looking around for anyone close to the car. No one had yet noticed him. He started the car, and it came alive as a civilized beast. He eased the car out and headed toward the exit. He looked into the rearview mirror out of habit and saw Nick standing by the front door. Sarita was pointing in Chris's direction. His blond hair stood out in a sea of black.

Chris knew his welcome had been worn out, and he wheeled the car onto the street, forcing himself to stay calm. He managed to rein in his fear. He quickly found a highway or something resembling a major road with a sign pointing ahead with "Norte" on it. That was good enough for Chris. Settling into the seat, he continued his journey.

He was wearing a seatbelt, but something kept nudging his hip. He ran his right hand between the seat and console. His fingers found something that felt like more leather, and he pulled it out. Thumbing through the wallet, Chris found about $2,000 in American bills, a California driver's license belonging to Philipé Bouchét, a few credit cards, and a company ID from an American corporation. The picture of Philipé looked like he was sneering at the photographer. The wallet was well made and relatively new. Chris flipped Philipé's things in the glove box. He tried adding the cash from the vanity to the wallet. It was getting thick. He changed his mind and took the bills out and folded them in half, placing the cash in his pocket and the billfold in his back pocket. It was a start. If an official asked for his identification, he'd show them a picture of Jackson, Grant, or Franklin. If the official demurred, he'd have to show him twins or triplets. Chris was starting to understand how to play the game in South America. A quick thought went through his mind again about corruption in government. It was just a matter of who benefited from the transaction.

Chris hoped he could put a very large distance between him and Nick. He pressed harder on the gas pedal. The needle passed one hundred and headed toward 150. He had heard this car was good for another hundred miles per hour, so he wasn't too concerned about the "Boris and Natasha" duo tailgating him.

Part of his morning's conversation with Sarita came to mind. If civilization were coming apart, what would it take to stop the pending destruction? People, having seen the rapid changes in their lifetime, might be reluctant to rebuild back to the previous level. Chris knew that many, including him, preferred the country and thought of large cities as being unavoidable but necessary. America was well past the Industrial Age, and in the twenty-first century, most city dwellers faced danger, at their jobs, equal to an infected paper cut. "Outsourcing" was responsible for many jobs leaving the country. Farming, ranching, and construction seemed to be the only things left that required muscle and couldn't be sent overseas. Still, he had to question the North American Free Trade Agreement (NAFTA) and the rapid influx of products.

It was too quiet in the car. Even the air conditioner was quiet. Chris thought he'd try the radio for an English-speaking station. The sound system was the best he had heard in any car. Eventually he found an English-speaking station broadcast from Santiago. The announcer spoke of the fires in the city, damage to government, the demands on the police and fire departments, and how dangerous his job was becoming. Later, there would be a guest speaking about the data that was being lost. Chris waited patiently during a commercial for a local pest control company. Afterward, the guest was introduced. He spoke of the importance of keeping paper records. Chris imagined a whole new crop of counterfeiters. Would the banks take the word of a stranger? Chris didn't think so. Most likely, the dollars, rupees, lire, pounds, pesos, francs, and any other form of money would disappear down a computer wormhole. Bonds and securities may stand a chance. He envisioned a surge in safe manufacturing.

Chris made wonderful time. The drive through La Serena, Vallenar, and Copiapo was a breeze. Chris thought of using Mr. Bouchét's credit card but then thought better of it; he didn't want to victimize anyone else. The rich and harmful were fun to screw with; the everyday working stiff, he preferred to leave alone.

Chris noticed a slight pull in the front end that was becoming more pronounced. A front tire was going flat! He quickly found a small side road leading into the trees. He turned the car off the main road and down the small road. Even with a flat tire, it handled well. It was a very well-designed car, the best he had ever driven. It was a bit stiff, but who was he to complain? He looked at the soft tire and noticed a line of nails running across the tread. It was obvious that someone had set them in the road as a way to stop a car.

He opened the trunk and pulled out the spare. Searching around, he found the jack, jack handle, and lug wrench. As he was loosening the lug nuts, he heard a car moving slowly along the gravel shoulder of the highway. It coasted to a stop, and a door closed as if someone was trying to be very quiet. Footsteps slowly crunched the gravel. He stood behind a large tree to see who it was.

A man was moving from tree to tree, trying to be quiet. It was not Nick, and Chris was glad of that. This fellow was dressed shabbily and had a wicked machete in his hand. Obviously this wasn't Mr. Bouchét trying to reclaim his car. He had to be the one that had set the trap. Chris was still holding the tire iron and maintained his position. The stranger, seeing the car, walked toward it. He noticed the flat tire and mumbled something unintelligible. He started to search through the bushes going away from the car. Chris waited until he was out of sight and went back to the car, quickly replacing the tire. He had put the flat in the trunk and was tightening the lug nuts when the sound of a sharp inhale caught his ear. He turned. The man was running toward him, arm held high, machete in hand and ready to swing the evil blade. Chris threw the tire iron underhand, mostly by reflex in a feeble effort to slow him down. The spinning tire iron struck the man and wedged tip-first in the hollow of his neck. It had hit just behind the point of the jaw, entered the trachea, and obviously tore a major artery. The man was choking on his own blood. The quickly forgotten blade fell from his hand. Lack of blood to the brain quickly gave way to unconsciousness.

Chris was shocked, relieved, and scared at the same time. Intellectually, he knew this day would have come sometime. He just wasn't prepared emotionally for it. He was relieved he had won this contest but was pissed off that a total stranger had tried to kill him. Helping the man along on his personal journey to oblivion, he pulled the iron out of the man's throat. A final twitch, and the body lay still. The iron would be needed in the future; this guy wouldn't. Wiping the tire iron with the man's shirt, he threw it into the trunk and slammed the lid. Back in the car, he drove out to the main road. He didn't bother to look back. Both his hands and legs were trembling from the adrenalin and fear.

Chapter Five
Here's Looking at You

The restaurants were still open and doing business. He didn't know if word had spread about credit becoming an instant modern dinosaur. Perhaps many were used to dealing in cash and saw nothing out of the ordinary. He was getting more than nervous about being in a hot car and loaded with money. He'd feel safer in a nondescript vehicle.

After having lunch at an out of the way restaurant, he pocketed some of the money from the case and looked for an auto dealership. A few blocks later, he found what he was seeking. Ten minutes after that, Chris emerged from the dealership driving a white Ford Taurus. The sales clerk was wearing the broadest grin of his life, possibly comparable to when he lost his virginity.

In his new and somewhat used set of wheels, Chris continued on to his next destination, Lima, Peru. While he was driving along trying to look like a tourist, he noticed that many vehicles were trucks filled with armed men. As Chris approached the first group, he glanced over and saw the uniformed men in the back of the truck. A few idly looked his way, and Chris nodded, smiled, and waved casually at them. They returned his nod, and some even smiled back. They must have had a list of things to do, and thankfully he wasn't on it. Maybe, they were just "going to town." Chris was getting closer to the center of Lima and saw a pall of smoke over the downtown area—apparently the troops were "going to town" in more ways than one. Driving through town, he watched the sudden change from one area to another. Some were untouched while other neighborhoods were the scene of human rage brought on by a broken society. He preferred to keep a low profile while he continued on to the next town of Pasto, Columbia. Keep a low profile? Ha! He'd like to disappear.

Chris had been watching the rearview mirror intermittently. A black Mercedes Benz had caught his attention. After a while, it was obvious it was following him. It was just a bit too far away to see the individual occupants, but he did see the outline of two in the front seat. He tried losing them on the side streets. When that didn't work, he reverted to the busier streets again. He was really starting to miss the speed of the Chrysler. He thought changing cars would throw Nick off his trail. Nick must have spotted the Chrysler at the dealership and "encouraged" the salesman to tell him about the driver of the Chrysler.

Chris headed out of town. The black Mercedes was still a quarter mile behind him. East of the city, it was flat; the side roads were a combination of gravel and dirt. At the next side road, Chris started to push the Ford. The wind was calm and the road dry. The dust cloud behind the Ford was tremendous. He had to roll up his window to keep from choking. Chris would find out if the heavy Mercedes could stay on a dirt road. He went east about a mile and slid around a corner to the north. He looked over his left shoulder to see if he was still being followed. Nick was just behind the Ford's dust cloud. Another ten miles they drove; the two men would play this deadly game until one or the other would run out of gas or crash.

As he sped over the crest of a hill, Chris saw an opportunity. A farm vehicle, moving slowly toward him, was coming to an intersection. If he timed it just right, he could make a left turn in front of the truck. He hoped the driver would react like most drivers, slamming on his brakes while cussing a blue streak. Chris powered around the turn, fishtailing and leaving a dust cloud. His timing was almost perfect. He heard a "ting" as his right rear bumper met the right front fender of the truck. Nick couldn't make the turn; he had to slam on his brakes. The Mercedes stuttered to a stop. A grapefruit-sized rock dislodged from the roadbed, bounced up, and lodged between a cross member and the tie rod. The farmer had gotten over his fit and moved his truck clear of the intersection.

As Chris came around the next turn, looking over his shoulder, he checked the position of the Mercedes. It was about a half-mile behind and gaining. The rear started to slide left, and he had to ease off the gas to keep the slide under control. The washboard surface was too much for the shocks and springs. The Mercedes was traveling too fast for the next turn. A combination of the heavy weight, momentum, and the inability to turn right were causing major problems. The Mercedes slid sideways across the road, the tires catching on the rough surface of the road, flipping the Mercedes on its top, while the momentum caused the car to roll over in the gravel and come to a stop in a ditch.

Chris quickly stopped the Ford. Looking through the dust-covered rear window, he saw the immense dust cloud. The Mercedes wasn't emerging from it. He waited while the cloud cleared enough to see the Benz. It looked like an overturned turtle. He had won the competition, but something made him pause. Was it curiosity or maybe one more look at Sarita? He drove back to the overturned Benz, warily watching it through the lingering dust. Pulling alongside the car, he saw no movement from within. Getting out, he saw Nick and Sarita hanging by their seatbelts. The torn dress revealed her upper torso and those goddess-like long legs. He crawled through the broken window glass and gently released her belt. As he carried her to the shade of a nearby tree, Sarita regained consciousness and clung to Chris.

"Thank you." Visibly shaken, Sarita was obviously at a loss for words.

Still curious, he asked, "Why?"

"We were after what you stole from the car," she said, dumbfounded at his question.

"Sarita," he said, as if talking to a slow child, "I saw two hotel employees running from the pile of luggage just off the beach and it seemed obvious they had taken them from the cars in the parking lot."

"You had nothing to do with the theft?"

"I had just arrived in a motorboat."

Chris didn't want to admit that he had "appropriated" an attaché case that may or may not be theirs. He knew that he had a great distance to travel, and the money was security. Sarita never did tell him what they had been missing other than some clothes.

He impulsively kissed her before leaving. Sarita looked shocked and bewildered. Nick was starting to moan while he was helplessly suspended. Sarita noticed a good-sized rock lying next to the Benz. As fate would have it, the same rock that was wedged in the steering gear had come free. She held the rock in her hand, staring at Nick.

He soon left the accident scene and found the main highway. Sarita looked fine, but he wasn't too sure about Nick. He had seen that look before on certain women when faced with similar options. He wondered if she had the courage.

At the Chilean checkpoint, there was an obvious lack of guards. He didn't think about it while driving around the red and white wooden gates. Pasto looked like its ancient heritage. The old buildings looked well cared for, and the streets were impossibly narrow. The people were dressed in clothes that hadn't changed in hundreds of years. Culture shock hit him when he saw an ATM at a corner bank. Chris had gotten used to modern dress farther south in the larger communities. However, even in this faraway community, once in a while, he would see someone dressed in newer clothing. Tradition was the word here. This was a town of living history.

He had heard about the Galeras Volcano erupting a few years ago, killing three of the six students studying the volcano. That was one fieldtrip Chris was glad he was not invited to attend. It must feel eerie living five miles from a sleeping dragon. The mountains were covered with an impossible green foliage, and the geological history was unique to this area. Chris was half-expecting Juan Valdez to show up doing a Folger's coffee commercial.

Chris saw more Cash Only signs starting to appear in English, Portuguese, and Spanish. He drove out of town and headed toward Cali and Medellin, and the quality of homes dramatically improved. Over the next hill, Chris saw some larger homes that had just started to burn. Beyond them, flames had engulfed several other homes. He didn't see the local fire department, or anyone else for that matter. Looking closer, he saw litter and broken furniture. Those on the bottom of the totem pole may have decided that they had a chance to raise their standard of living. This scene was becoming more common around the newer parts of the larger cities.

Chapter Six
The One and Only...

A young woman standing alongside the road was waving at traffic. Next to her were two Briggs and Riley suitcases. It was obvious she wanted a ride out of town. Chris pulled over, sliding the attaché case under his seat with his heel.

"Can I help you?" he asked in English.

She responded in very good English, "I'm heading back to my family in Nicaragua."

"I'm going that way. If you want a ride, hop in. I certainly could use the company."

She tossed her two suitcases in the backseat and sat in the front seat. Chris pulled back onto the road. She thanked him for stopping. He asked her why an obviously good-looking, young woman like her wasn't being helped. Her wavy blonde hair fell below her shoulders. Chris hardly noticed the beginning of the dark roots. Her summer dress was not too modest; he thought the hemline a bit too high. She looked like she was in her mid-twenties.

"No one would pick me up. I'm glad you stopped," she said in a lilting voice. "My old boyfriend was a drug hot-shot," she continued.

Chris felt a little nervous. She must have seen the look on his face because she quickly added, "Oh, don't worry about him. When the banks started to fail, many of his so-called friends wanted their money immediately. When he couldn't pay them, they cut him up in small pieces and burned his house. I think they thought it was a 'good enough' kind of cremation."

"How did you get out of that mess?" queried Chris.

"Oh, they thought they owed me for some small favors I did for them in the past." She smiled and looked out her window, licking her lips at some random thought.

"Senor, what is your name?"

"Chris."

"Chris, my name is Evelyn, and I'm glad to meet you." As she turned in her seat, Chris noticed from the corner of his eye that she had let the dress ride a bit too much up her leg. He was starting to wonder what he had gotten himself into.

"If you don't see cars coming toward you on this road, pull over and stop," Evelyn told Chris.

Chris looked at her questioningly.

She replied, "There would mostly likely be a roadblock ahead. There's been a constant war going on between the FARC and the ELN." She went on to explain that the two factions were a pain in the ass for the Constitutional government of Columbia, which was constantly trying, with the help of the United States, to end the drug trade and warring factions. They weren't shy about killing anyone for just about any reason that came to mind. It was too common.

Evelyn ended with the advice, "The best time to travel is morning. Never travel this road when it is late afternoon or raining."

Chris promised himself that after this trip, he would never again venture out of the United States.

They arrived at the Panama Canal and saw a long line. Many people were loaded in cars, trucks, and buses. Chris took his place at the end of the line. It seemed to be moving well. When they neared the head of the line, he saw why they were moving as quickly as they were. The guards weren't inspecting vehicles or checking passports. Many were being waved through. There were two men dressed as Panamanian military. Their unshaved faces did not fit the picture of a typical military man. Chris quickly noticed that they were randomly "collecting fees" from the people. He pulled out his wallet and fished out a load of fifty-dollar bills. When they approached the Ford, Chris held out the money. The guard swallowed hard, looked up at his partner, and quickly slipped half the money into his pocket. His partner was unaware of the subterfuge since he was obviously enraptured with Evelyn's bosom. Both men smiled their guilty, toothy grins and waved for them to proceed. Each had received what they expected and was pacified. One of them must have said something rude because Evelyn flipped them the finger. They both laughed at her defiance. Everyone seemed to be enjoying the goings on. Chris heard different voices in Portuguese and Spanish. Here and there, he picked up a familiar word.

The capitol of Panama, Panama City, looked the same as the other large cities he had passed. The drive westward, along the southern coast of Panama, was beautiful. The modern buildings mixed well with the older, colonial architecture. While driving, Chris still felt like a tourist. Evelyn was constantly finding new sights and pointing at them. When she pointed to the left, her arm was in Chris's field of vision. He tried to explain to her how unsafe that was on the curving road. She mumbled something in Spanish and pouted. If Chris had a watch, he would have seen that in exactly two minutes, she would be over her pout and back to normal.

The city of Penonome had archaeological sites that Evelyn begged him to stop and see. Chris finally relented. He looked for a place to hide the car, out of sight from the main road. They walked hand in hand to the ruins—Chris, rather stiffly, and Evelyn, like a puppy on a leash. Chris found the site interesting, and Evelyn did the translating for him. When they walked, Chris became aware of Evelyn bumping into him more often.

When they stopped at a marker to read it, Chris was so engrossed he failed to notice the look on Evelyn's face. When he turned to ask her a question, she threw her arms around his neck and French-kissed him. Chris thought about pushing her away. *What's the harm?* he then thought. He briefly returned the kiss. Then, feeling self-conscious, he quickly separated from her. She looked at him questioningly. She raised her arm and sniffed her armpit. Her eyebrows jumped, and she told Chris to stay in the area. She would be right back. She disappeared into the lush forest.

Chris, curious about where she went, walked into the thick foliage and saw a small trail. It was quiet, even this close to the road. The trees were covered with thick moss and hanging vines. The constant mist made the air heavy; the growth rate of plants was phenomenal. He followed the sound of running water and came to the edge of a clearing. Evelyn was in a pool of water at the base of a small waterfall. A random thought passed through his mind about how she had come to know about this place. As he walked toward her, Evelyn saw him and waved hello. Chris walked over and sat down next to her hastily tossed clothes. Evelyn, nonplussed at his sudden appearance, continued to bathe. Her nakedness did not seem to bother her. When she glanced at Chris, her movements became more provocative. Chris, feeling a bit like a voyeur, noticed the physical effect it was having on him. He told her they were leaving. Evelyn proceeded with her two-minute pout. Just then, it dawned on him. He was the innocent! She was playing a game with him and enjoying it.

"Chris. Don't you like me?"

"Evelyn, I hardly know you."

"We could be very good friends," she said with a sly smile.

Chris looked at her, picked up her clothes, and started to walk away. Evelyn giggled as she jumped out of the water, grabbing her clothes from Chris's hand. She wiped the water off with her hands and dressed. She twisted her hair and held the impromptu ponytail with a simple twisted knot. They walked back to the car. Chris was leading, and Evelyn following, with a smile.

Chris drove straight to the capital of Costa Rica, San Jose, all the while angry with himself. He was hungry and asked Evelyn if she wanted something to eat. It was obvious she was not a morning person. She nodded her head. Chris drove around Costa Rica looking for a place to eat. Spotting an open-air café, they parked across the street. They walked across the street and found an unoccupied table. Chris sat in a chair facing the street watching the crowd. Evelyn sat next to him, also watching the people.

When the waiter arrived, she did the ordering for both of them. She spoke Spanish. The waiter, apparently distracted by Evelyn's cleavage, forgot to retrieve the menus and left them on the edge of the table. Coffee came, and Chris thought it the freshest he ever had. Then he realized where he was. Breakfast arrived soon after. Chris wasn't sure what it was. He certainly could not pronounce it. He tasted it and was surprised. It was delicious.

He was just about to ask Evelyn what it was when he sensed, more than he saw, the Mercedes slowly driving down the street. He reached for the menu and held it up, blocking his face. He watched from the corner of his eye until it passed. The Mercedes looked like a rolling wreck. He couldn't see who was driving it. No doubt it was Nick back on his trail. Chris decided not to bolt. With Nick dogging him constantly, he wasn't sure how many days he had left on earth. Eventually, Nick or one of his connections would catch Chris. He kicked back and watched people on the street.

Chris's hair hadn't grown much longer, but his face was in need of a shave. Across the street, he noticed a man with longish, blond hair. He looked like he had walked off the streets of Los Angeles. Mr. LA was walking along the street, talking to different people. The man made his way toward the cafe. Seeing the used-car-salesman smile,

Chris knew the man had spotted Evelyn. For that matter, everyone spotted Evelyn sooner or later.

"Excuse me. Do you speak English?" asked Mr. LA.

Evelyn slowly turned her head toward the man. "*Si.*"

"I'm new to the area, and I'm looking for an old friend. You may have seen him. He's a tall North American driving a newer car, a white Ford," said Mr. LA. His attention was solidly locked on Evelyn, along with his rather high testosterone level, and Chris was someone he was obviously overlooking.

Chris looked at him through slit eyes. He quickly noticed that he was missing both earlobes. Some weird fashion trend he missed or an equally odd accident. He sat back in his chair and put his hand up to his face. His thumb was underneath his jaw, with two fingers next to his ear and two fingers at the corner of his mouth. His eyes were on Evelyn, but he was watching Philipé and he looked very much like his drivers license photo. He seemed the type that was capable of shamelessly insulting a vegetable by calling it a "veggie."

Evelyn looked toward Chris. Philipé was too busy trying to look down Evelyn's cleavage to notice Chris slowly twist his head no. She looked back at the man and waited until he self-consciously looked back into her eyes. Pulling up her neckline, making it plain that she did not appreciate his attention, she said, "No. I do not like to associate with Americans. Most of them look and act like you." She dismissed him, turning in her chair.

Philipé turned to Chris, "Sir, can you help me?" His hormone levels still obviously high and his brain overloaded.

"No English," said Chris convincingly.

Mr. Bouchét said thank you and continued down the street. When he was out of sight. Chris let out his breath. With a personality like that ...

"Do you know that man?" asked Evelyn.

"I never saw him before."

"He sure has busy eyes. Do you think some woman pinched off his ears?"

Chris chuckled at that thought.

The mismatched twosome left town, northbound on the Pan-American Highway. The next stop was Nicaragua, where he would gratefully deposit Evelyn. It was late afternoon, and the sun was starting to set. Chris caught a fleeting glimpse of people along the beach. Evelyn had grown tired and sprawled across the front seat. They drove along the shore of Lake Nicaragua. It didn't look like they would make it to Managua that night. He was too exhausted.

There were many parks and places to hide the car that night. He chose a spot that looked secretive. He pulled in, changed his mind, and then backed in. He would be able to watch for Nick. He partially rolled up the windows and locked the doors. He pushed back the front seat, stretching out diagonally. Chris looked out the window awhile. He couldn't remember when he fell asleep.

There were fingers moving on his chest. His shirt was open. Evelyn was quietly humming. He just lay there quietly. She seemed harmless—this time. Chris lay there enjoying the sensation, listening to the wind blowing through the trees. Her hand slid down his hip and rested on his inner thigh. Chris found the sensation pleasurable and responded with his own hand lightly stroking her shoulder. They lay there quietly, lost in their own thoughts hanging on the edge of wakefulness.

Chris heard the rev of an engine. He sat up, looking out the front window. It was a powerful sounding engine in a dark car heading straight toward him. Chris sat up in a hurry. He tried the starter. It barely caught before he slammed the car into drive. The cold engine groaned as he sped away in a hail of gravel. The other car fishtailed into a turn, trying to catch up.

Chris floored the little Ford along the side streets, alleys, and main thoroughfares trying to get that car off his ass. Nick was a good driver. Evelyn asked what was going on. Chris told her it was just an old friend wanting to talk business. He just wasn't in the mood at this time. Evelyn looked at him, shook her head, rolled her eyes, and pouted exactly two minutes. Chris had a full tank of gas and could keep this up for some time, at least until the engine or the tires failed.

They entered a highway. The traffic was nonexistent this late at night. Chris stayed in the right lane and let the other driver start to ease up on his left side. When it was about halfway up the left side of his car, Chris turned hard right to an off ramp. The other driver couldn't make the turn and tried to get back on the highway but missed by an inch. The right side of the car caught against the retaining wall, and then the car continued down the highway. Chris could have sworn he saw Bouchét.

He kept looking in his rearview mirror, thinking that somehow word must have gone out to find him, which couldn't have been too hard since there was only one highway going north.

Breathing a temporary sigh of relief, he turned to Evelyn. "Where did you want me to drop you off?"

He followed her directions to her aunt's house. He didn't know what to say. On one hand, he was glad to get rid of her. Walking around the car, he opened the door for her and waited as she retrieved her suitcases from the backseat. He turned to watch her walk away, but she pushed him against the car, overwhelmed by a sudden gush of passion. Her hands started to go south. Chris grabbed her arms, put them behind her back, and hugged her. He held on a bit longer than planned.

Chris whispered in her ear, "Evelyn, you are a special woman, and I've enjoyed the time spent with you. I'm sure that you will find a man that deserves you." He took a deep breath, "I'd love to spend more time with you, but I need to be going. As you've noticed, there is someone that would like to talk to me." She seemed to accept his partial lie.

She looked like a sad puppy. Chris hugged her briefly again and released her. He watched her walk up the stairs to the front door. When she turned to wave good-bye, she was halfway into a two-minute pout.

Chapter Seven
A Fall from Grace

After refueling the Ford, he drove around the southern shore of Lago de Managua. It was picturesque along with a lakeside, general aviation airport. Pulling off the road, he parked alongside the fence, remembering when he was a pilot in Boulder. Those were good days. He had made many friends back then. Some of them would go off to flying careers, while others would fool around as general aviation pilots. Chris wondered what had happened to his flying buddies and their dreams. They, like Chris, may have realized that it was just an itch in need of a scratch.

A few thoughts occurred to him. From what he'd seen in the recent past, why not shorten his exposure in Central America and fly to America? After all, he was sitting next to an airport, and he certainly knew how to fly. While these thoughts were forming, it also dawned on him that he was out in the open, did not look like a local, and from his loitering, it was obvious that he was planning something. It was also time for him to be less conspicuous. Slipping the Ford into gear, he tried to be as innocuous as possible and drove to a side street, parked, and walked the two blocks back to the airport.

Walking along the chain-link fence, he let his little finger bounce along the links. It felt good to be out of the car and walking. After rounding the corner, he walked up the drive and stepped into the small Fixed Base Operations (FBO) office. Looking around, he saw no one, and without stopping, he went to the pilot briefing room in the corner. It looked like every briefing room he had seen in the United States. The only difference was that this one had a large map of northern

South America, all of Central America, and the southern half of North America on the wall, covered with plastic. A tape, graduated in kilometers, was hanging from a star indicating the airport. A grease pencil hung by a string alongside the map.

Picking up the tape, he ran it to the center of Colorado. Trying to remember the formula for converting kilometers to miles, he stumbled through and figured it would be roughly 2,000 statute miles to Colorado. Much of that was over the Gulf of Mexico. He didn't have the physical endurance to cover over 2,000 miles nonstop. He would have to resign himself to a two-day flight, possibly longer. There were some sectional charts on the table. They covered the area to the north. Chris picked them up and put them in his back pocket. He walked out of the office, across the street, and around the corner to a restaurant to think this out.

He ordered what looked like a sandwich, corn chips, and a Coke by using the language of the linguistically challenged, otherwise known as pointing and smiling. Opening a sectional chart for the local area, it was quite obvious that he'd have to fly west to the Pacific coast. Putting that thought on hold, he pulled out all the charts showing north of Nicaragua. Organizing them in order, he saw he needed to continue along the coasts of Nicaragua, El Salvador, and Guatemala, then east across Mexico to the Gulf side—his final leg, north along the east coast of Mexico to the United States. To make the trip, he needed an airplane that could do 200 MPH and have the endurance of about five hours. Most high-performance twin-engine aircraft fell into that range. It was late afternoon, and he needed to clean up. After his meal, he used the men's room to take a fast sponge bath. He was getting rank in the tropical air.

As he walked back to the FBO office, he kept expecting someone to show up. Still, there was no one in sight. He went out the rear door and onto the flight line. He looked around, and seeing no one, he walked along three rows of aircraft trying to look like he belonged there. At the end of the third line, he found a likely looking candidate. A newer looking Piper Seneca II that had enough muscle to do the job. He tried the door latch and found it secured. He looked around the tie-down area for a number designating what spot this was. In the dim light, he found the number 36 painted on the asphalt under the nose wheel.

He walked back to the briefing room. Just as he got to the door, he saw through the window someone in the office. Slipping out of sight, he watched the window for the occupant to reappear. He didn't have long to wait. Bouchét! He ducked back around the corner of the attached hangar, making his way back to the street. He thought about the attaché case in the backseat of the Ford. He quickly went to the car. Walking up to it, he saw the broken side window. The case was gone. If the Californian had retrieved the case, then there was only one reason why he wanted Chris. He threw the ignition key on the dashboard. Someone else could have the car. His boots were in the backseat; he retrieved them. On the way back, he saw the Chrysler. It was interesting that Philipé had gone through all this trouble to find it and had gotten this far north. Then again, that was one fast car.

Another blond-haired man exited the car and walked toward the FBO. He could have passed for a twin to Bouchét, but this guy was missing only the right earlobe. There definitely was something odd about these two. When the twin with the missing earlobe walked around a corner, Chris boldly walked up to the car, opened the passenger door, and saw the attaché case on the floor. He quickly grabbed it. Going to the far end of the hangar and around the corner, he continued out to the flight line and tried to position himself to see through the window of the briefing room. He tried different angles to see if anyone was in the building. None worked. He moved closer to the door and looked through the window—still, no one.

He was starting to sweat from the anxiety. He slowly turned the knob, easing the door open, and there was a faint creak from a hinge. He stopped. No sound from inside. Moving toward the front desk, he spotted the box of keys on the wall. Just as he was reaching for the door, the sound of a flushing toilet came from the men's room. Chris pulled open the door, trying to remember the key number. In his near panic, it finally came to him. Thirty-six! He grabbed the keys, closed the door, and walked quickly and quietly out the line door. There was a light breeze outside, and Chris opened his shirt to try to cool himself down. He ran to the third line of airplanes and waited behind the Seneca.

From Chris's hiding place, he could see both office doors. Watching, he saw one of the men looking out the flight line window. They may have figured out that Chris was going to try to make a break for it in an airplane. One of the Bouchét twins walked across the parking lot to the car and looked in the back seat area, obviously checking to see if the case was still there. Chris could tell by his stiff-legged walk back to the FBO that the missing attaché case was quickly noticed. Chris had no time to waste nor to reflect on the carelessness of these two idiots.

He tried the key in the door lock. It popped the handle free. He eased the door open and climbed in. Lying down in the seat, he felt around and found a small pen light with a red lens. Cupping the light, he felt around the expandable pockets and found the checklists for pre-flight, run-up, and pre-departure. Another set of checklists produced the en-route settings and pre-landing checklists. Chris took a quick look out the window. One of the twins had a flashlight and was starting to check the aircraft along the flight line. It was good to see that he was being methodical and working up the line away from Chris.

Chris eased open the small side window to listen for anyone approaching. He heard Bouchét's high pitched voice berating his brother for the missing case. Chris pulled the control yoke lock free and checked that the rudder pedals were unlocked. He found the inspection drain cup in another expandable pocket. Opening the side door, he slid off the wing to the ground. He crawled under the airplane to the left engine nacelle and felt around in the darkness for the sump drain fitting. The plastic inspection cup had a center post that fit into the drain. He pushed up on the cup to release fuel into the cup. When filled, he held it up to the available light and saw no sign of water in the fuel. Crawling to the center of the airplane he did the same with the opposite sump. In his haste he had forgotten to untie the tie-down on the left wing. Moving back to the left wing, he quietly untied the chain and slid the chock away with his foot. On the way back to the right wing, he paused at the nose gear and pulled the front chock to the side. He checked the fuel on the right engine nacelle, releasing the chain, and pushed that chock free. He looked around to see if anyone was close. With no one in sight, Chris moved to the tail and untied that chain, checking the elevator and rudder for movement. He climbed back into the cabin and carefully closed the door.

He knew that he had to calm down. He couldn't expose himself on top of the wings to check the fuel and oil levels. He had to rely on the fuel and oil pressure gauges. He couldn't start the engines not knowing where the two men were. Again, Chris got out of the airplane. He caught a glimpse of movement six airplanes away, moving in the opposite direction toward an amphibious aircraft. He lay there and waited while forcing himself to calm down since his next effort would require all his wits. Chris spotted his boots under the wing of the Piper—too late now.

He watched one of the men working his way along the line of airplanes. He was being very thorough and getting closer to the Piper and Chris's boots. He had been using the flashlight enough that its dry cells were starting to run down. He shook the flashlight and realized his problem. He hadn't noticed the boots, since the flashlight had preoccupied him. He walked back to the office in search of fresh batteries or another light. Chris knew this was his chance and made his way back into the Piper, grabbing his boots.

Inside the aircraft, he forced himself to concentrate. The attaché case was in the backseat. He pulled the fuel-sampling cup from his pocket, putting it back in the expandable pocket. He picked up the flashlight and found the pre-taxi checklist. He checked each item twice since he had minimal time in a twin-engine airplane. His license was for a single-engine land aircraft. When he turned on the instrument panel lighting, he turned down the rheostat to the dimmest intensity he could see. The controls were free and clear. The gas gauges showed full. The electrical gyros in the artificial horizon started to spool up. The turn and bank coordinator was electrical, and that was running. The vacuum gauges wouldn't work until the engine was running. He would save those for a fast check while he was taxiing. He remembered a joke about checking the instruments while taxiing to the active runway as being a "commercial pilot pre-flight." He still didn't see Bouchét or his partner. The winds were negligible, so any runway would do. The blue taxiway lights led to a runway on his right. His escape plan made, he needed to get his ass in gear.

With the key in the "on" position, the radio stack lit up. He turned the radio power switch off. The propeller pitch was set to fine. He cracked open the throttle lever and primed the engine with three quick pumps of the primer. Leaving the exterior lights off, he looked around the nose of the airplane for anyone near the propellers. Out of habit and as a joke to himself, he whispered, "Clear." Chris saw no one. He turned the key to the "start" position. The propeller slowly turned, and the engine coughed a few times and stopped. Chris quickly pumped the primer five times. He tried restarting the engine. The engine fired up, and he pulled the throttle out to keep the engine running at 1200 rpm. Keeping his heels on the floor and toes off brakes, the airplane started to move slowly.

He quickly started the other engine while he was taxiing. He added more throttle to get the ship moving and pushed the right rudder pedal. From the corner of his eye, he saw a flash of reflected light from the pilot briefing room door's window. *Shit! Here they come!*

Chris added more throttle to get the airplane moving at a good running speed. As he was taxiing to the runway, he leaned the mixture and set the flaps ten degrees. This would get him off the ground sooner. Chris looked to his right and could see the running man yelling and waving his arms as be got closer to the airplane. It was obvious that secrecy was no longer an issue, and with that, Chris turned on all the navigation lights and strobe lights, along with the taxi light. With his left index finger, he rolled up the rheostat to half brightness for the panel lights.

When he turned onto the runway, the man had caught up to the airplane in mid-turn. He grabbed the boarding handle above the door and tried to run alongside the airplane. Chris increased the throttle to full. The engines roared to life. The propellers blew with hurricane force, picking up small stones and sand from the vacuum created beneath them. The strange man tried to get his foot on the entrance step and made a grab for the door handle while being pelted with sand and gravel. The airplane accelerated. Chris could feel the airplane getting light on the gear, causing the reality to decrease the man's testosterone level. He was starting to look nervous. His sweaty hand was loosening on the stainless steel handle. Chris quickly glanced to his right and saw the man's face in the window. The blond hair and tan looked almost exactly like the original Bouchét. A fucking twin with one intact earlobe and a crazed look that went beyond anything Chris had ever seen or imagined.

The airplane had just come off the ground and was still in ground effect, riding on a cushion of air. He pressed the control yoke forward and released the yoke pressure as the gear hit the asphalt. The airplane was still accelerating, and the twin was still at the window, but this time his face was contorted from insanity, fear, and screaming. Chris tried bouncing the plane twice in a row. It had the effect he wanted, just not quite the way he wanted. Instead of bouncing down and away from the airplane, he was bounced up and along the fuselage, landing on the horizontal stabilizer. His right hand grabbed the vertical stabilizer while his upper torso bent over the horizontal stabilizer. His heels dragged along the runway before the airplane lurched into the air.

Chris immediately felt the heavy weight on the tail and compensated by applying pressure on the control yoke. He kept the airplane in a shallow climb and retracted the flaps and landing gear to decrease drag. The air speed continued to climb, and he gave it a bit of left rudder. This centered the ball on the turn coordinator. A little more left rudder would put the twin in the full force of the slipstream.

The reluctant passenger's hands were getting numb in the cold air, and the force of the air was pushing his body away from the fuselage. Sliding further from the airplane, his grip was lost, and his numb body slid along the leading edge of the horizontal stabilizer, falling free of the airplane. Chris felt the loss of weight and corrected for it. The airborne twin became "one with the earth" exactly 826 feet later. To say that the resident of a mobile home was amazed when he dropped in would be an understatement. In a way, it could have been a blessing. But for whom?

Chapter Eight
Slipping the Surly Bonds...

Since Chris rid himself of the dead weight, he had climbed to 2,000 feet above ground level. He set his course to the Pacific coast and watched the autopilot engage. The throttle, propeller, and trim were set. He turned his attention to the sectional charts. He failed to notice the faintly blinking red LED on top of the instrument panel.

Continuing west, he reached the Pacific coastline. Changing course, he followed the coastline on a northwest heading. When he reached the Gulf of Fonseca, he again changed his heading to fly along the coast of El Salvador. Passing over the cities of Puerto El Triunfro, La Libertad, and Acajutla, the three major coastal cities looked serene nestled among the dark green foliage. The majestic mountain backdrop completed the picture.

He continued heading along the coast of Guatemala. As he passed the major cities of Monterico and San José, he saw fishing boats out at sea with their tiny navigation lights blinking in the vast inky blackness. Guatemala City was off his right wingtip, fifty miles away. He turned to a northwest heading and re-trimmed the airplane. Off in the distance, to the east, he could just make out the southern end of the Sierras. North of his course was the peak of Tajmulco, all 12,000 plus feet of it. He was getting close to the border of Mexico, which was the end of Central America and the beginning of North America. He had traveled quite a distance and considered himself quite lucky. His fuel looked good. He had enough to make it to Veracruz.

His eyes focused on the top center of the instrument panel.

Manufacturers always fasten a placard showing the registration number of the airplane in this spot. Chris was expecting an XA, XB, or XC, followed by a series of numbers. This was how Mexico would require aircraft to be registered. In the United States, the letter N preceded aircraft registration numbers. Chris was looking at an airplane registered in the United States. He was flying some American's airplane. His curiosity motivated him to search for the registration. He found it in a small plastic pocket near his left calf. He pulled the papers out, retrieved his flashlight, and paged through the papers until he found the registration. The world had just become smaller for Chris. The registered owner was Philipé Bouchét!

He winged westward along the coast of Mexico, and two peninsulas, one from the west the other from the east, announced his next turn. He arced northward over the eastern peninsula next to Laguna Inferior, turning over Santo Domingo and above Highway 185. The ground was rising with high mountains on both sides. Chris climbed a bit to 10,000 feet. To his left was the ancient volcano, Volcan Pico de Oriba. The highest point in Mexico, 18,410 feet. He was over the Sierra Madre del Sur mountain range. The ancient volcanic activity was evident even at night. As he flew over the highest point of this valley, he saw lowlands ahead. He turned northwest at Oluta and stayed inland to Veracruz. The early rising sun nearly blinded him, which brought forth a thought about the Mexican Air Force and if their curiosity was aroused by his sudden and unannounced appearance.

As he began his descent, Chris reduced power and closed the cowl flaps. He had been watching the fuel gauges en route. It was going to be close. Then it hit him. He was low on fuel because he had not changed the prop pitch to coarse and lessened engine speed. He heard a miss from one of the engines and immediately banked the plane to line up with a road out of Tantoyuca. To make up for lost fuel, he leaned the mixture and changed the prop pitch to coarse. It put one hell of a load on the engines. Well, he would not be the one having to pay for an engine overhaul, he thought. Good thing it wasn't his airplane.

He scanned both sides of the road, looking for a safe place to land. Passing over another town, he saw low mountains ahead. The engines were missing more frequently. He nursed it along. The airspeed looked good. He made it over a small notch in the mountains. After crossing over an old dirt road, he saw a highway running parallel with him, with an airport to the left of it. The fuel gauge needles were no longer bouncing off the pegs. He was dry as he was approaching the airport. Using altitude and airspeed to his advantage, he made it over the airport and glanced at the windsock to determine wind direction. It was east along the runway. He lowered the landing gear and pulled the throttle to idle. He ran the flaps down to twenty degrees, pushed in right rudder, and banked the airplane left. He slipped his turn, keeping the nose down to keep his airspeed up. The descent was a graceful arc. He rolled the aircraft level over the numbers. Running the flaps to full down, he pulled the yoke back for a full stall landing. At the turn off, he headed for the parking area, pushing on the toe brakes just as he crossed the tie-down wires. The propellers had already stopped.

Chris exited with the keys, attaché case, and his boots. While standing at the tail, a very excited man ran up to him. He was telling him something in Spanish. Chris couldn't understand a word. He stood there, his hands in the air using the universal sign of surrender. With a broad smile, he held out the keys. The man didn't know what to expect, but held out his hand. Chris dropped the keys into the man's hand. He picked up the attaché case, slung his boots over his shoulder, and slowly walked away before the old man could speak.

Chris walked out of the airport and crossed the main road. Walking along the dirt road, he saw some houses in the distance. It was a typical real estate development. If he didn't know he was in Mexico, he could have pictured himself being in any housing development in the United States. People do the same things around the world. Some even worked out of their garages. Chris saw the garage door open at one house. The resident working on a car's fender with a grinder was too intent to notice Chris. He walked around the side of the house and took a drink from the spigot. He was hungry, exhausted, and stunk from the hours in the airplane. He walked around the back of the house toward some trees on the side of the hill. He found a place to sleep in the shade of some low bushes.

Chapter Nine
Footloose

The vision of a Bouchét twin outside an airplane window woke Chris. He opened his eyes and lay still. He listened to the relatively quiet night air. The sound of crickets was a welcome relief from the unrelenting drone of the aircraft engines. He rolled over to the edge of a bush and watched the neighborhood.

The man was still working on the car. The house interior was dark. It was past sunset, and the twilight ushered in the cool night air. He needed clothing more substantial than what he was wearing. Chris looked around to see if anyone was around other than the man working in the garage. Seeing no one else, he walked down from the hill to the backyard of another house that was also dark. There were clothes hanging on the clothesline. He saw a pair of jeans that might fit him, along with a colorful shirt. He included a pair of white socks and a T-shirt. He stopped short at the underwear. He looked around the back of the house for a bucket, which he filled with cold water, and with a little luck, he spotted a bar of soap in a dish alongside the sink.

Gathering up his collection, he headed back to his hiding spot, but not before pausing to grab a towel from the clothesline. Up the hill, he stripped down and washed himself. The change of clothes did wonders. He enjoyed the feel of the stiff jeans and the familiarity of the work boots.

He waited until the man quit working in his garage and turned off the lights. The overhead garage door was left open, obviously to let the dust clear. Chris walked along the side of the garage, leather case in hand, and slipped through the open door. Silently, he stepped to the inner door leading into the house and listened. He could hear the muted sounds of a television set. The man inside was preoccupied watching the set. Chris hoped he would not hear any sound in his garage.

Chris pulled the small flashlight from his pocket, and stepping over to the workbench, he looked for a certain type of body work tool. A few minutes later, he found it—an old-fashioned auto body dent puller. It was very simple tool that was known by car mechanics and auto thieves around the world. On one end of the round bar was a screw, and above that a flange, or stop. The sliding weight was stopped at the other end by a larger flange and handle. The point was screwed into a dent, and sliding the weight hitting against the end flange pulled on the dented metal. It was also a great tool for popping ignition switches and similar to the way he had used the corkscrew at the resort.

With the flashlight and dent puller in hand, he went to the other car in the garage. It was a newer model Chevrolet that was well cared for. The door locks were in the unlocked position. He opened the door and got in. He reached overhead, took the lens off the dome light, and pulled out the small bulb. In the darkness, he quickly screwed the end of the tool into the keyhole. After two tries with the tool, the core pulled out. He felt for any parts left in the cylinder with his little finger. Finding none, he put the tool back on the workbench and searched for a screwdriver. He found a wide flat-tipped screwdriver with a short shank. Perfect!

Back inside the car, he opened the driver's side window to cool the interior. He was proving himself a fine thief. Obviously, the police academy had served him well. His nerves were getting to him, and he felt his bowels getting loose. The screwdriver slipped out of his hand and fell to the other side of the car. He bent over to retrieve it, and just then the overhead garage door started to close. Chris froze on the seat. When the door was closed, he heard the house door close and the turning of the dead bolt. Chris lay on the seat waiting until he thought the man had gone to bed. The Chevy was backed into the garage, and the driveway descended away from the house. He got out of the car, found the release cord for the big door, and pulled it. He slowly opened the door, being careful not to let the rollers make noise in the tracks. He went back to the car and waited.

He had fallen asleep and woke up with a start, feeling vulnerable.

He got the leather case and placed it in the car. Very slow and cautious were on his mind as he pushed the car out of the garage.

The tires made a popping noise as the tires ran over small stones. The sound seemed magnified in the still evening air. He slid into the driver's seat and released the steering wheel lock with the screwdriver. He gave the car a heave to start it downhill. The car gathered speed on the driveway. It wasn't traveling fast enough to use the brakes. The Chevy had power steering; without the engine running, the steering wheel was hard to turn. Chris coasted past two houses and rolled to a stop. He rolled down the window, listening for someone to sound an alarm. When he felt no one had seen him, he started the car.

He drove along the dirt road until he came to the main road. Turning on the headlights, he drove north. After a few more turns, his confidence started to return, and he started to relax. Chris was starting to feel like a tourist, again. The countryside seemed to put him in the mood. It was different than Colorado but in many ways the same. He passed by a lake on his right, with an island in the center. There were still a few people in small boats enjoying themselves, fishing late into the night. At the north end of the lake was the town of Ebano.

Chris checked the gas gauge and saw it getting low. He wasn't about to stop for gas this close to the neighborhood he left. People would be familiar with this car and start to ask questions. He drove out of town on a hilly, curving road to the next town, wherever that might be. He had forgotten the charts in the airplane.

It was obvious that continuing north he would eventually end up at the United States border. The next town on his route, Estacion Manuel, had an open gas station. He pulled the car next to a pump. He flipped open the filler door and put the nozzle in the neck of the gas tank and squeezed the filler handle. Nothing happened. He looked over his shoulder at a handwritten sign in Spanish. He couldn't read the language, but he was sure it said, Cash First. He put the nozzle back in the pump and started to clean the windows, thinking over what to do next. He saw the cashier watching him. Others joined the cashier in a heated discussion. A few pointed in Chris's direction. They either recognized him or the car. The time to hit the road had arrived.

The customers were starting to pile out the door. Chris got in, started the car, and headed back along the northbound highway. Four of the men ran for their truck. They were going to try to catch Chris. The term "illegal alien" was starting to have a very personal meaning for him. Chris floored the gas pedal. The rear tire slid off the asphalt onto the shoulder, leaving a massive dust cloud. Ahead, he saw Highway 180 curving to the right. A dirt road going straight north branched off from the main road. He went for the dirt road; his pursuers were right behind him. Continuing along the winding road, he slowly gained distance. The end of the road was quickly approaching, and he prepared to bailout. Reaching over the seatback, he grabbed the attaché case and put it on the seat.

He turned off the headlights and drove off the end of the road and into the cactus. He turned the engine off and let it coast to a stop, fearing the use of brakes would signal his position. He looked out the back window to locate his followers. They were a quarter mile behind him following his tire tracks; so much for his worrying about giving away his location. He ran northeast through the cactus and around a large group of sage bush, trying to keep it between him and his pursuers. Without looking back, he heard the truck in the distance. If he looked back at the truck's headlights, he'd ruin his night vision. He slid to a stop at an arroyo. He quickly found a cow path leading down. He ran down to the bottom and continued a few hundred yards farther along until he felt there was sufficient distance. Then he climbed back up and looked over the edge. His four pursuers had stopped the truck. They were quite a distance away, and Chris could tell by the angle of the headlights that one of the front wheels was in a ditch. In the still night air, he could plainly hear their voices. He didn't understand the language, but the tone of their voices told that they were venting their wrath on the driver.

The sun was just starting to lighten the eastern sky. He had to find a place to hide and get a drink. Chris followed the meandering of the arroyo. Higher elevation was behind him; eventually it would lead to flatter ground and possibly water. He used it to distance himself from the others. The arroyo passed under a road, continuing toward a lake alongside a road. Part of the lake's south end was underneath a side road. That's where he spent the rest of the day to keep out of the sun.

During the day, he saw one auto and a fuel truck. While a herd of goats was being driven across the road farther north, a pickup truck stopped on the bridge. He heard the occupants talking. They were the four men still looking for him. They were arguing, most likely about where they would find Chris.

Chris was glad he had brought his boots with him. Prickly pear cactus was more than plentiful, and he had to stop more than once to remove an offending spine. Chris watched as the four men searched for his trail. At times they were close, and at other times they hadn't a clue. He watched them working toward a predetermined center by eliminating the obvious. They were starting to concentrate their effort toward his location. He hadn't left many footprints. They had to be looking for crushed plants and loose rocks. This was work for the skilled eye of a professional. The sun was setting. He felt like a fugitive on the run. He was now gaining firsthand knowledge how the "illegals" crossing into America felt, and he didn't like it one bit.

He crawled up the spillway, looked back to see if he was noticed, and ran across the road. There was a power line running north. Under the pole line was an access road for use by the utility company. He followed the old road, trying to keep low. A half-mile later, he stopped to see if anyone was following him. No one was. He came closer to a small town, moving away from the power line and deeper into the bush. He reasoned that the power line would end at a power station. He noticed the diameter increasing on the main run while the lateral runs stayed the same.

It was difficult traveling through the numerous cacti and thick brush but easy across the hard pan. He was making good time. A lone truck stopped on the road. Chris flattened immediately. A bright spotlight shone across the desert—searching. He watched as the light swung across the desert on either side of the road. The light went out, and they continued their search farther down the road. Chris saw that he was very near a town. He crossed the road next to a small airport. A sign read: San Fernandez. Chris remembered seeing this town on a sectional chart. He was relieved at being this close to Reynosa. He had a short distance left.

The east side of the street was more populated than the west side. Chris stayed on the sparse west side and kept to the poorly lighted areas away from the roadway. He watched the occasional pedestrian for sign of someone becoming too curious. The sky was starting to lighten; Chris had to find a place to stay and something to eat.

He turned away from the road and spotted a small store on the edge of the neighborhood. He went to the back of the building and listened at the door. There was no movement within. A quick tap on the door produced no reaction from within. He tried the obvious, turning the doorknob. It was locked. He pushed on the door and heard a creak. He pushed harder, and it creaked louder. He put his shoulder to the door and pushed. It opened.

He walked inside and looked around. The cooler was full of soft drinks and dairy products, while the shelves had just about what you would find at an American 7-Eleven. Chris took a paper sack from behind the counter and filled it with whatever came to mind. Leaving the store, he closed the door behind him.

Along his path, he came across an abandoned blanket. He slung it over his shoulder. He followed a dirt road toward a highway into Reynosa. A small overpass should give him cover until the next evening. He found a place to sleep in the ironwork and concrete. He wrapped himself in the blanket. The leather case was behind his back next to the concrete wall. He ate as good a meal as he could expect.

He slept most of the day. A pigeon tried to land near him, the noisily flapping bird disturbing his sleep. A large truck passing overhead forced him into consciousness. One time, he thought he had heard voices. His fatigue was too great, and he fell back asleep.

Chris slowly awoke. He opened his eyes and saw a group of men below him. He was watching some soon-to-be illegal aliens, or as the "enlightened" North Americans called them, "illegal immigrants," which he thought sounded a bit pretentious. Breaking the law of another country would get you arrested. Mexico was notorious about their lack of human rights. The United States, on the other hand, was going through some tough times, and he wanted to stay as far away as possible from government officials, Nick, Philipé, and whoever else was hunting him. Marcy was first and foremost on his mind.

The leader he thought of as "El Coyote." Everyone was speaking at the same time. Chris watched as one of the men pointed at him. All eyes turned toward him. "El Coyote" walked toward Chris. His English was understandable.

"My name is Paulo. Who are you?"

Chris nodded and said nothing.

"Senor, it is obvious that you are not a Mexican."

"Yes."

"Are you a government agent? A tourist? A criminal?"

"None of the above."

"So, why are you sleeping in this place?"

"I was tired."

Someone in the group understood English and chuckled.

"Sir, my friends and I are curious why an American is under a Mexican bridge."

Chris was silent.

"I have heard there are some men, with some French sounding name, looking for an American. Both of them look the same and have strange looking ears. The word is that they wanted to see this

American about a car and an airplane." Paulo sighed. "I have also heard that there is a big reward for the American."

Well, down to two of those assholes?

"I'm going back to the United States. I have no money for transportation, and I've walked a great distance. I'm very tired, and I don't know anything about some guy's car and airplane. Do you think that if I had some other form of transportation, I'd be here?"

"You sound like you have a lot in common with us."

If he only knew the truth.

"We are on our way north. If you come with us, we could help you over the river. On the other side, you could help us?"

Yeah, whack me and have fun spending the money. As soon as these Mexicans see the case, I'm history.

Chris kept his hand behind his back, attempting to make it look like he had a gun. Chris said he would be going solo, at sunset, and he wanted to take his chances alone. Paulo thought about this, shrugged his shoulders, and walked back to the group. There was murmuring among the men. Some looked back at Chris. A short time later, they walked up the slope and onto the road. Chris gave a heavy sigh. He stayed in his secure place and waited awhile longer. For once, he was glad the Mexicans had strict gun laws.

It was well after sunset before Chris moved. He walked down to what passed as a creek and pissed. As he walked back up the hill, he kept his head below the street level. Chancing exposure, he glanced over the edge of the road, looking for traffic and the group of men. He still felt that he'd be jumped for the reward. He had the case in his left hand and a candy bar in his right. He was ready. He thought these men, being Mexican, would be more familiar with the area. In that case, he would move more cautiously.

He sprinted across the street. North of the road was a field covered with low brush and the prickly pear cactus. He walked slowly through the field, listening carefully and avoiding making any noise in the darkness. He could see the lights from a house in the distance. He walked toward it, knowing if anyone were going to ambush him, he might stand a chance of waking up the neighborhood or at least someone's curiosity. The thought comforted him somewhat, but he knew the truth was quite the opposite.

Chris made it between two houses. He was getting close to the border. He came to another highway that he assumed was running along the border. He continued along a small dirt road leading under the highway. Leaning against a concrete support, he saw the group of men huddled together under the highway. They were going to make their way across the river when they felt the time was right and they had screwed up their courage. Chris had a ringside seat, and he'd watch the action.

They took off in single file heading for the water. Chris could hear them splashing. They ran up the bank and over the other side. Three US Border Patrol vans loomed out of the darkness, their overhead lights blazing. The band of now very illegal aliens was quickly put in the vans. They disappeared east toward the port of Reynosa. If those men had thought of Chris as just another wandering soul, and not as a possible reward, then he quietly wished them luck.

Chris pushed himself off the pillar. Walking down to the water, he quietly waded across the river. He sat down on the sandy bank, pulling the last candy bar out of his shirt pocket. He savored every bite. When he was done, he turned and walked away from the river. He failed to notice two men in a Cadillac Escalade SUV watching him from the elevated portion of the Mexican highway. They were screaming at each other like they had missed winning the Lotto by one number. By the time they drove down to street level, Chris was gone. The Californian, Bouchét, and his second brother, had come so close after all this time.

Chapter Ten
Josh, Dan, and Cy

He walked three miles to Mission, Texas. He walked into the first restaurant he found, the Longhorn. He smiled at another customer, the only one, and sat down. He looked through the menu and felt secure that he was reading English again. He looked up as an unsmiling and unattractive waitress arrived at his table.

"Made up your mind yet?"

"A hamburger, fries, and a large Coke."

"Mister, excuse me, but where have you been? You reek to high heaven."

"I was walking along the river, and I fell along the bank," which was true—to a point.

"You're lucky Homeland Security didn't catch you fooling around there!" She had a very serious look about her. "They've been building a fence all the way from California and are getting close to being finished. Then again, maybe it will never get finished, seeing that the new part has holes in it already."

She took his order for a hamburger and Coke and quickly departed. It had been a long time since his last American meal. When he was finished, he left a hefty tip and headed for the door.

Once outside, he looked around for a motel. Down the street, he spotted one that seemed nondescript, and perhaps he could slide by the requirement for identification. He certainly didn't want to call attention to himself. It was reasonably priced at $49.95, so he headed for it. He checked in, and when asked for identification, the placing of two hundred dollars on the counter quieted the clerk, and he was quickly handed the key. Looking over the clerk's shoulder, Chris spotted a sign, No Refunds After Ten Minutes. Along the way, he spotted a newspaper machine and picked up a paper to catch up on American news.

In the room, he looked around and noticed the usual table and chair didn't match, and the surface had been repaired more than once with wood filler and roughly sanded. It struck him as a work in progress. Such is the way of the world where the successful sell to the new immigrants who have shown imagination and resourcefulness in keeping a once failing enterprise from completely failing. Perhaps it was just a matter of degree in how this was observed.

He tossed the paper on the bed, put the attaché case under the bed, and stripped. He wasn't sure how long he was in the shower, but he was definitely fascinated by the different forms of mold and mildew stains. He really couldn't complain since he had slept in some very different surroundings. The water started to cool, signaling the hot water tank was about to give up its entirety. The Made in India, tiny soap bars could hardly stand up to use in the shower. There was no shampoo or rinse, and even the drain stopper was missing.

The room was a double. He took the pillows from the other bed and surrounded himself with plush comfort. Before he fell asleep, he noticed a fine dried blood stain in the shape of a fine spray on one of the pillow cases. He traded pillows and was fast asleep.

When he awoke, it was midday. With everything taken into account, the $49.95 experience wasn't too bad. He dressed in his old clothes and reached under the bed for the attaché case. Opening it up, he took out a few hundred dollars and placed it in his wallet. He took the case with him, heading out the door. Out on the street, he looked for a place to shop for new clothes. He saw a Wal-Mart down the road with an empty parking lot. It had to be open since he saw people walking in and out.

As he walked around inside Wal-Mart, he felt like a kid at a toy store. He pushed a large basket around, finding jeans, shirts, socks, underwear, toilet articles, and a smart-looking ballistic nylon bag that he'd use in place of the leather case. He found a backpack, hunting knife, waterproof matches, and a nifty, little bag full of fire-starting material. Another aisle produced a very decent flashlight that used diodes and could be charged with a hand crank, a good piece of rope, some MREs in assorted entrees, and a collapsible water bag called a Camelbak that would fit inside the backpack. Heading for the checkout line, he picked up a few other small items that caught his attention. He moved along the short line and paid the cashier in cash. He really had no other choice; there were signs everywhere announcing Cash Only. No Credit! He'd save the leather case transfer for the privacy of the motel room. The blue plastic bags he put in a pocket of the bag.

In the motel room, he stripped down for another shower. When he walked out of the small bathroom, he quickly became aware of the smell coming from his old clothes. This was why the waitress and some individuals at Wal-Mart had avoided him. The front desk motel employee had looked at him like he had been sprayed by a skunk. It was quite apparent Chris had gotten used to his own stink. His clothing reeked from the desert and the Rio Grande.

Chris took one of the blue bags from the backpack and put the dirty clothes in it. He opened the motel room door and put the bag outside. He turned up the air-conditioning to high and opened the window to air out the room. He cleaned himself up before he dressed. He sat on the edge of the bed and turned on the television set. Flipping through the channels, he looked for a news station. While he was doing that, he thought of calling Marcy and grabbed the bedside telephone. No dial tone. *Shit!* He found the Fox News channel and turned up the volume.

The announcer talked about the president's emergency plans. Banks were having a difficult time maintaining liquidity because customers were withdrawing their savings, home foreclosures were at a high that exceeded the thirties, companies were shutting down, and food lines were becoming commonplace in the cities. Many people had tried to get out of the city. The rural people would have none of that since they would take care of their own first.

The National Guard had started to set up camps for the homeless in designated areas within the cities. New York found a new use for Central Park. This new fad swept the East Coast, and California was quick to adopt this plan and refined it to include the county-owned areas around the airports that were used as buffer zones. Water was a big issue until the fire department came up with a quick fix using fire hydrants. Sewage was also another major concern that was solved by draining the human waste into the storm sewers. Still, it sounded like the government was having trouble keeping many citizens in the camps. It was similar to the old problem of keeping the Indians on the reservations. Many of the higher-income people had fled or barricaded themselves in their homes. They were occasionally under attack by those trying to move up the human food chain. The lower income people saw an opportunity to improve their standard of living by moving to the abandoned homes in the suburbs. Chris thought of it as a very adult version of musical chairs. Many left their old homes in flames, never to return. The middle-class suburbanites saw this as an excellent opportunity to get out from under their heavy mortgages, many of which had refinanced to keep up with inflation. This seemed to be as good a time as any to abandon ship.

From the information that Chris gathered, it sounded like the larger cities were imploding. The smaller, rural communities considered themselves self-sufficient if they didn't have to rely on too many products from the larger cities. Small communities had proved themselves, through their years of existence, to be able to go it alone. Their strength came from the surrounding agricultural areas and a very strong sense of community. There was a high level of distrust for the "city folk."

Chris was aware of the underlying dislike and distrust felt toward government interference and at times complete incompetency. He had seen it before in other places. All had watched the stumbling of the government after Hurricane Katrina, an oil accident in the Gulf, and the last time the Mississippi River flooded. It would be interesting to watch future happenings.

Chris switched the channel and stopped at a news show called *Dateline*. He was fascinated when he learned about an underground network using American citizens as phony, name only, spouses for illegal aliens. Some Americans were cashing in to the tune of anywhere from $5,000 to $30,000 for marrying a total stranger. The Immigration Service was aware of the severity of this problem. Chris could only imagine how many terrorists had infiltrated the United States and to what extent. The latest problem was the bribing of Border Patrol agents by the Mexican drug lords.

Chris turned off the television and opened the newspaper. A couple of articles caught his attention. The first was a $2.5 billion settlement between the three major credit reporting agencies or CRAs. They had been accused of violating the Fair Credit Reporting Act (FCRA) by failing to maintain a toll-free number that would allow customer's access to the companies. The companies did, in fact, have toll-free numbers in place since Congress had amended the FCRA. The problem was that the customers calling these numbers received a busy signal or recorded message telling the customer to call back because all representatives were busy. Since many customers had changed telephone service to cell telephones, the cost of waiting on hold became too expensive. The companies were well aware of this, and it was indeed a very clever way to skirt the new law. The article went on to explain the details of the settlement.

Two other articles caught Chris's eye. One was about identity theft, and another how errors had crept into various credit reports. The first article on identity theft dealt with the practice of dumpster diving and stealing personal information from garbage and the less obvious method of retaining copies of the credit card receipts at the point of purchase. Some entrepreneurs went so far as collecting the mail from outside mailboxes. Another was the increasing use of video cell phones to look over another's shoulder during ATM transactions. Other swindles were mentioned that Chris had either read about or learned in school.

The next article caught Chris by surprise. An investigative reporter had learned that terrorist hackers had secretly breached many banks and mortgage companies, along with many records available to the offshore companies operating in India and other Asian areas. Eventually a "spybot" was found hiding in the backup files. Virus protection programs hadn't found it because the spybot was over twenty years old and didn't fit into a modern virus profile. As programs were rewritten through the years, no one had thought about checking the backup files of the credit reports.

It was transmitted between primary and secondary computers as part of the data. This went on before the fiber optic boom of the eighties when security was starting to become more aggressive. During the change from dial-up lines to dedicated lines and then the more secure T-1s and finally fiber optics, the progress of virus protection had become almost perfected. This spybot was programmed to morph from the original and hide in the different operating systems, thereby avoiding detection, and encrypting the wanted information. When the spybot was remotely queued by the originator, it was retrieved along with whatever data was wanted. The ensuing panic by the company, when they finally found the spybot, caused them to contact Homeland Security (Internet) and make a deal with the government. The $5 billion settlement was struck as a way for the CRAs to save face and not have to admit, publicly, that their system had been in jeopardy for over twenty years. There were too many errors for the company to check, so it was deemed reasonable by the company, and government, to have individuals check for the accuracy of their credit reports. Things seemed to have heated up since he was in South America.

Checking his pack, he made sure it was filled. He looked around the room and added one washcloth and bath towel. He put the money from the case into the zippered, ballistic nylon bag, and it went inside the backpack. Feeling all was right with the world, he left a $50 tip on the bed. Once out of the room and heading for the front office, he threw the case and bag of dirty clothes into a dumpster.

"Have you enjoyed your stay?" asked the front desk clerk.

"Yes," said Chris. He added, "Do any of the telephones work around here?"

"Not since last year. The telephone company hasn't the parts, men, or trucks to fix the problems. But the phones do add a nice touch to the rooms. Wouldn't you agree?" he said wistfully.

The clerk looked like he suddenly remembered something and asked, "Are you from around these parts? You looked so worn out last night."

"No, I'm not from here. And I was very tired," said Chris.

"Got far to go? Things have been getting slow around here. We get a few folks hiking these days."

"Not too far."

"Bye, y'all."

Chris waved a hand over his shoulder on his way out the door.

Out on the street, he looked north and saw a row of car dealerships. He headed that way. He slung his backpack over his shoulder. At the first dealership he came to, he noticed the cars were not as clean and shiny as they could be. In fact, the closer he looked, there was quite a bit of road dust on the cars closest to the street. He walked back to the office, at the rear of the lot, and tried to open the door. It was locked. He peered through the glass at the dark interior and didn't see anyone. He knocked on the door. He waited awhile longer and knocked again. He started to walk away toward another dealership when he heard someone call out.

"Can I help, y'all?" asked an elderly man standing behind the building. He was wearing coveralls, a wide-brimmed hat, and the obligatory cowboy boots. The bushy white mutton-chop sideburns bordered on the theatrical, and Chris had to control a giggle. The man looked, spoke, and sounded like a Texan through and through.

"Yes, I was thinking about buying a car."

"Come on over here, sonny, and have a sit down out of the hot sun. Let's talk," the old guy said, chuckling under his breath.

He sat down with his elbows on his knees and leaned forward. He waited for the man to speak.

"What are you gonna do with a car?"

The old guy was going somewhere with this. Chris answered, "Drive?" He was starting to relax, and a broad smile crept across his face. He was starting to enjoy this conversation with the old fart.

The old man chuckled. "How far do ya think you'd get without gas?"

Chris's jaw dropped. He vaguely remembered the thin traffic along the road the last two days. While he was under the bridge, he heard only a few trucks. In addition, the near empty parking lot at Wal-Mart.

"That's right, bud. The government has stopped the flow of gas to civilians. They're worried that people will start migrating like they did back in the thirties during the Dust Bowl. You can buy all the cars you want, if you could find an open dealership. Even if you could buy a car from a private party, it wouldn't go any further than the gas in the tank. All these cars on the lot have had their tanks drained. The few cars you see on the road won't be running much longer, once the owner's stash of gas is gone. Truckers that use diesel are regulated by the government and watched continuously. They're considered essential, and all are equipped with GPS and data transceivers. The rest of us, well, you get to figure it out for yourself."

Chris thought about it for a while. A slow smile came over his face. He was, after all, in Texas. He looked up from the ground to the old man. The old man looked back, and he too started to smile. Chris looked at the old man and asked, "Okay, what horses do you have for sale?"

"Boy, you've come to the right place!" said the old guy. "By the way, my friends call me Josh. What's yer name?"

The two men, one with a backpack, and the other with a limp, walked over to the old man's house and corral. Chris looked over the stock and found a good, strong bay gelding. Chris looked at his teeth and knew that the horse was about five or six years old. He asked Josh about the horse's age to see if he was trustworthy. The old man said he was about five, maybe six years old. When Chris asked the man the price, he was surprised that he wasn't going to be gouged. Horse prices in Texas were lower than he remembered in Colorado. The old man could be taking advantage of the situation, but he was more concerned about making ends meet. He asked a fair price.

Chris told the man, "He looks like a good horse, and he's been well kept. Now I need to find a decent saddle and some other things."

The old man understood what Chris meant by "other things" and said, "My brother, Dan, lives a short distance from here. He can take care of the other things. My other brother, Cy, lives only a couple of blocks away. He can take care of the bridle, saddle, and blanket. Maybe he'll come up with some stuff you didn't think of yet." He gave Chris the addresses of his brothers and told Chris to tell them the better-looking brother sent him. While he was away, Josh would look after Chris's new horse. Chris walked around the corral toward the front of the house; he looked back and saw the old man starting to feed the horses.

Following Josh's directions, Chris easily found Dan's house. The garage door was open, and a man was working in the back. He was larger than his brother and looked a good deal younger even with the handlebar moustache. He was wearing a worn baseball cap with a big blue star—an obvious Dallas Cowboy fan. Chris continued up the driveway. He introduced himself and said that the "good-looking" brother, Josh, sent him. The man laughed heartily and asked Chris what he could do for him. Chris told him he had just bought a horse from his brother and would be traveling up to Colorado. Together they scrounged what Chris would need. Chris felt lucky when he saw a Wade design, which was a high-backed saddle. He knew the low-backed saddles used today were a fashion perpetrated by Hollywood ignorance. The Old West men knew that a high back or cantle would keep a man on a horse. Chris asked Cy if it was for sale. They talked about the importance of a good saddle that many overlooked today. Cy felt it would do a good job for the right man. He added the saddle to the growing pile.

Cy looked at Chris's work boots and shook his head. "When was the last time you rode a horse, Chris?"

Chris looked at his boots, shrugging his shoulders. He looked sheepishly at Cy. "I think we can find some spare boots in the tack shed. It seems that quite a few cowboys have been 'contributing' lately."

They found a decent pair that fit Chris well. At least he wouldn't have to worry about breaking in a new pair of boots. It felt strange wearing a dead man's boots. He wondered where Cy got his boot collection but didn't want to ask. He tied the laces of his old boots together and added them to the pile in front of the garage, silently saying good-bye to a different life he had so long ago. When both men were satisfied with the results, Chris paid Cy. "There's something else you'll need. I'll get it." Chris stood there, looking at the mound of equipment. He couldn't think of anything he had forgotten. Cy came around the corner with an old rifle scabbard in his hand.

"Where you're going, it's a fair bet that you'll need this for one reason or another. Your next stop will be at my other brother's. Dan is a handy man with a firearm, and he should have something you can use." The two men shook hands, looking each other in the eye, neither one knowing what the future held for the other.

Saddle slung over his shoulder, Chris was starting to look like a cowboy. Wearing the dead man's boots, he was starting to develop the typical rolling gait of a cowboy—not from riding, but from the load of the saddle and the heels on the boots.

Chris showed up at Dan's house and knocked on the door. When Dan answered, they introduced themselves. When he heard the line about the "better-looking brother," he also laughed. Chris imagined him to look like an old-town marshal would look, complete with a thick mustache, sunburned cheeks, and a permanent squint. His grip was as firm as his old firearm instructor was, and just as steady.

"Come on inside, and we'll figure out what you need. It looks like you're going to do a bit of traveling. And, by the sound of you, I'd bet somewhere up north." He looked at Chris.

Chris nodded and said, "Colorado."

"Going up through the center of Texas will run you through the Big Thicket for sure. There would be bad dudes hiding out there. Going east will get you in trouble around Dallas-Fort Worth. I wouldn't suggest anything along the Rio Grande. That area will get just as rough as it was a hundred years ago. The whole world is going to be rough in a few more weeks if it hasn't started already. Some people will get away with whatever they can. Others will try to keep society orderly. I'd suggest, young dude, to keep an eye peeled and your backside covered. I noticed that saddle scabbard. I have a Winchester Model 94 in .30-30 caliber. I'll look around for the rifle, and you think about what kind of sidearm you'll need. You might want to ponder a knife and something small like a derringer." He rolled up his sleeves as he walked to the rear of the house.

He would be prepared for this trip. When Dan came back, Chris agreed with the Winchester and added a nice .32 caliber, two-shot derringer with the rifle. He looked around and found a Colt, model 1911, .45 caliber auto-loader. He had had the same model gun when he was a reserve officer and was comfortable with it. Dan reached behind the counter and found four magazines. He paused, thinking, and grabbed two more. Chris decided a shoulder holster would fit him better. They added two of the modern "quad style" magazine holders that police had been using. Dan did some quick mental math and added three more magazines. Chris decided those four boxes of .45 ACP, one box of .32, and four boxes of 30/30s would be enough. Dan stood there and looked at the pile of hardware and ammo.

"I could say something like 'looks like you're going to a war,' but that would be lame. My only hope is it that you arrive at your destination with as much ammunition as you leave with. The truth will probably prove to be much different." He tossed a nice double-edged knife and sheath on the pile. "Boot knife" was all he said.

The two men shook hands, holding on to each other's hand just a moment longer than they would have a few months earlier. Chris paid Dan his price and loaded up his equipment for the trip back to Josh's house.

When he got there, he saw that Josh was sitting on his front porch surrounded by a stack of newspapers.

Josh looked up, his reading glasses on the end of his nose, and asked, "What is cyber … cyber …"

"Cyber terrorism?" volunteered Chris.

"That's right," said Josh. He looked at Chris, waiting for more information.

"That's when someone sends out code to another computer that will cause it to send errors, false or imbedded information. People can also gain access into different computers to find out information or corrupt existing information. I know what you're going to ask by the way you're looking at me.

"People, mostly tech geeks still in school, or just out of school, will try to circumvent security measures in different computers. It's just a game for them. Other people around the world don't see it as a game. Some will corrupt files in airline computers, large financial companies, and just about whatever they find access to. Still others have serious ideas about destroying a world they don't understand."

Josh sat there, trying to take it all in. "So, all this talk about how great the Internet is and how it can simplify life is just a bunch of hooey. It seems like it's just a passing fancy like the hula hoop."

"It's not that simple. Many people have made a lot of money from it. Many more have their entire careers based on it. Industry, commerce, the airlines, government, and just ordinary people have come to depend on it for banking, entertainment and gathering information or knowledge that wouldn't be accessible to them otherwise. It would be a shame to go backward since we've come so far forward." Chris was getting a wistful look on his face.

"We'll just have to see how this plays out," said Josh. They both walked out to the corral to get Chris packed up and ready to go. He still had enough daylight left to get clear of town.

Chris was saddled and down the road within an hour. Josh had given him two new canteens full of bottled water; he thought it was a nice touch. He also gave him a "bedroll," which was a fancy way of referring to two heavy, wool blankets. As a last thought, Josh added a detailed road map of Texas. He had used a yellow highlighter to mark the best route for Chris to travel.

Chris was glad he was on horseback. The weight of his equipment, if it were inside the backpack, would have had him whining after a few miles of walking. The large saddlebags were made from ballistic nylon and carried everything he would need. The map showed that there were a few wayside parks ahead. Chris would travel along Highway 281 and stop to rest his horse at each park. Whenever it was getting close to sunset, he could make camp. That, in itself, sounded strange. When he was in South and Central America, he hadn't thought of camping as camping. Now, in the United States, he felt at home, and the phrase fit perfectly. Perhaps he never was much of a traveler. Maybe he should have stayed in Colorado with Marcie.

Chapter Eleven
The Neighborly Thing to Do

It was now May, close to the end of spring in the northern hemisphere. He had just gone through that cycle in the southern hemisphere. It felt odd to have missed the fall/winter part of a year. This entire trip was odd, and Chris could not believe how lucky he had been in his traveling when it was quite obvious that he could have been dead in some jungle far from home.

Chris stopped just north of the town of Red Gate to water the horse and ease his yet-to-be-toughened-up rear end. He had passed through a few residential neighborhoods on his way. North of Linn, the homes were beginning to thin out. The total absence of cars and an occasional truck with the obvious white GPS dome over the cab was indeed eerie. Occasionally, he saw a resident, working in his or her yard, silently pause to watch him pass. Some even ventured a wave. Chris could easily tell that it was a perfunctory gesture and not an invitation to stop and chat.

That evening, he made his first camp at a roadside park. It wasn't much, but it was off the road, and his horse had grass. He wasn't alone. There were four other riders in the area. They kept to themselves, and Chris thought it best that he did the same. He watched them out of the corner of his eye. In another time, they'd be called saddle tramps. Hell, he was one too. He stripped the saddle and blanket off his horse. He knew they would be his pillows for some time. He separated his "bedroll" from the saddle, along with the backpack. He searched around in the backpack and found his toothbrush. He put it in his shirt pocket with a small tube of toothpaste. He pulled the

Winchester from its scabbard and walked over to the rest stop. He thought the rifle would signal to the others that he wasn't interested in having company. It did.

He came back to his cold campsite and saw nothing disturbed. With his horse tethered near him, he rolled out the blanket and made himself as comfortable as possible. With the rifle muzzle down along his right leg, his .45 in hand on his belly, he fell asleep.

Later that night, or it could have been closer to morning, a quiet nicker from his horse woke him. He opened his eyes and listened. He sensed someone moving in the darkness. Whoever it was, he was still some distance from Chris. Chris listened to the sound of halting, quiet footsteps moving slowly toward him. He waited. The footsteps stopped a short distance from him. The late-night visitor was apparently deciding what to do.

Chris, moving quietly, pulled the .45 off his belly and out from under the blanket. Pointing it in the direction of the noise, he slowly thumbed down the safety. The faint click caused a sudden reaction. The stealthy footsteps were transformed into a louder retreating run. When Chris woke up the next morning, the four men were gone.

The beautiful sunrise found Chris south of the Nueces River. He had passed by a number of ranches earlier that morning like a ghost in the dim light. He heard the sound of a gunshot and immediately nudged his horse in the direction the sound had come from. He was traveling through a small grove of trees when more shots were fired. Getting closer, he got off the horse, flipped a rein around a small sapling, and pulled the rifle from the scabbard and the bandoleer from the saddle horn. He quick-stepped along a dry ditch and slowly looked over the top of a berm. He saw a ranch house and barn. Some men were behind the trees along the river. He didn't have to wait long before he heard a female voice inside the ranch house.

"The next one that shows his face gets it." The voice had a tired waver to it. "This is the last time I'm telling you to get off my property!"

"Jenny," the male voice mockingly implored as it resonated through the trees with its strong bass tone. "We just want to help you."

"I don't need your kind of help."

"Okay, Jenny. We'll be waiting out here when you change your mind. But sooner or later, you'll have to come out of that house!"

Chris didn't need to know anymore. He saw, and understood, that these men were going to do whatever they wanted, and there was no one else around to stop them. Chris kept behind the berm and crawled along the ditch to the river. He spotted a fallen tree and crawled under it to get a better look at who was threatening the woman. He saw two, maybe three, men. He had a clear shot at two. He wasn't sure about the third. He lined up on the farthest man and squeezed off a shot, levering in another round. The bullet hit the farthest man. The man closer to Chris saw his friend fall, and thinking the threat was from that side, retreated around the tree with his back toward Chris. The next shot hit the man at the base of the skull. Chris was retreating from under the trunk when he heard a bullet hit over his head. Keeping low, he ran along the ditch, levering another round. He was moving toward the ranch house. Taking a quick look over the top of the ditch, he saw the shoulder of the third man, sticking out from behind the trunk of a cottonwood tree. He lined up on the man's shoulder and changed his mind. He aimed for the man's boot and fired. The man spun sideways, screaming in pain as he fell. The next shot entered the man's mouth and exited the back of his skull. With another round in the chamber, Chris waited in the silence.

"You over there, the one behind the ditch. Are you with those men?" a female voice asked from inside the house.

"No. I was passing by and heard some shots. I thought you might need some help," answered Chris.

"You came at the right time. I'm much obliged," she replied. "Were you walking by?" she questioned.

"No. I have a horse about fifty yards to the east," he answered while standing up.

She walked out the front door of the house. "Get your horse. By the way, my name is Jenny. What's yours?" She started to smile, a hopeful smile. As if she was waiting for something.

When Chris returned, Jenny greeted him at the door and asked him to have a seat on the patio. She had put together a meal of sandwiches, fruit, and lemonade. As they talked, she asked him what a Yankee was doing this far south. He told her a brief version of what had happened since the incident in Santiago.

Changing the subject, Chris asked, "Why are you all alone out here?"

"My husband works for the Border Patrol and is stationed at the Laredo Toll Bridge. We've been working to save enough to buy a piece of this ranch as our own. A very nice doctor owns it, and we'd been working with him until all this terrorism stuff started. Then paperwork started to get lost, and we sort of put it on the back burner, so to speak. Now he's been gone for close to two weeks. The telephone doesn't work, and his spare radio must be broken. I can't get hold of anyone. No other officers have stopped by, like they usually did." Jenny shrugged helplessly.

The men that Chris had shot were three brothers living in the next ranch to the west. They must have realized how badly things were falling apart and decided to have a fling at being what they really were. She always thought the three men were strange. In the future, she would reacquaint herself with her neighbors, those she knew could be trusted. Chris suggested that since her neighbors to the west no longer needed their ranch, she could use the land for grazing. If they had cattle, those would also need to be tended to.

Chris and Jenny dragged the three corpses off the property and used a tractor with a front loader to dig the hole. The bodies were wrapped in a tarp along with their weapons. Chris wanted to include the evidence if there was a future inquiry. Forensic experts would be able to determine the veracity of what had happened. They left the grave unmarked, not so much as to hide the evidence, but out of disrespect. The world would be a little better without those three. If there were any questions in the future, which Chris highly doubted, her explanation should be enough to justify his shooting them.

Back at the house, Jenny showed Chris a picture of her husband and asked if he ever came across him in the future, to let her know. Chris put her address in his wallet. He slept in the barn that night. He was gone before dawn.

Chapter Twelve
One's Duty Can Stink at Times

Chris rode away that morning thinking that there would be more widows like Jenny in the future—women not knowing what happened to their men. His only hope was that they could piece what was left of their lives back together. It would be much worse for those with children in this wide-open country. The farming communities were always close. Ranching was a bit different, mainly because of the vast area between neighbors. Thoughts swept through his mind from the early accounts of the settlers in America. Loneliness was the biggest heartbreaker and cause for suicide.

Farther away, Chris stopped his horse and felt around in the saddlebag for a map. He was somewhere in the center of Webb County and traveling west. Soon he'd be crossing Interstate 35 and be north of Laredo and just a bit farther north of the toll bridge where Jenny's husband worked. The three brothers had strongly advised him against going near the river. His curiosity and some far-flung idea about a sense of duty drove him on.

In this area, the land was mostly dry grass with an occasional tree thrown in. The prickly pear cactus was sparse in areas. The dried manure in many of the pastures told a story of past large herds, with the remnants being a Hereford or Brahman here and there. In the low-lying areas along the creek beds, he spotted where deer had bedded down. There was a fine mist of rain and wind blowing from the Gulf. The deer wouldn't be moving about today.

He was starting to feel like a twenty-first-century cowboy wearing his fashionable sunglasses, wide-brimmed hat, and serape. He laughed as he thought about the old frontier men, crow's feet permanently etched in the corner of their eyes. They looked at the world through a permanent squint. Well, at least he was cool looking. He took one of the canteens and had a drink of de-bottled water. He was sure he would soon find out what the water tasted like over a hundred years ago. He didn't want to be reduced to a tough Texan and "drink water from a muddy hoof print." He chuckled at that thought. He had heard that line in the movie *True Grit*, starring John Wayne. Glen Campbell played the role of a Texas Ranger who uttered that immortal line.

He knew he was getting close to the river; he could smell it. He sat on the horse, looking south from behind a small rise. Watching the toll bridge for any sign of movement, he saw no one crossing it. Nor was there any foot traffic or vehicles. He rode closer, stopping a quarter-mile away. From behind another small hill, he continued to watch.

A bite to eat was in order. He fished around in the bag and found a ham sandwich given to him by Jenny. He finished the meal by washing it down with a long drink from the canteen. Another hour passed. There was still no movement around the booth on the American side, and the Mexican side looked just as deserted. He spurred his horse around the hill and headed that way. Pulling his rifle out of the scabbard, he set it across his thighs while he scanned the edge of the river, half-expecting a surprise. He stopped the horse a hundred feet from the tollbooth and waited. Nothing was stirring. He now felt secure enough to get off. He left the horse standing in the open. He knew if the horse saw something, his head would go up, and he'd look in the direction of any perceived threat or stranger. As he walked closer to the booth, he smelled death.

Chris walked through the open door and saw three dead men. They had been dead for some time. All three had been shot-gunned at close range. The smell was horrendous in the enclosed space, and the humidity and flies added to the physical revulsion. He quickly searched for wallets and found them thrown in a corner. Identification and anything else of value was missing. As close as he could tell, none of the men looked like the picture of Jenny's husband. The hair on the head of one did not match, and the other two were in different stages of balding. All firearms and ammunition were gone. The building had been ransacked.

Chris left the building as the first wave of nausea hit. Out in the clear air, he breathed deeply, trying to rid himself of the smell. He walked from the building and took off his shirt, shaking it. He tried to get the stink off. He remembered when he was a deputy, and they had given his partner a "call for service" about an elderly woman that couldn't be reached by her daughter. When they knocked on the front door, there was no answer. They had walked around the house looking for an open window or door. His partner, a full-time deputy, stopped at a window and said, "Oh-oh," and immediately went to the back door and forced it open. Chris was right behind him, and when they entered the small kitchen, the smell of putrefaction was overwhelming.

At the autopsy, the coroner spoke for the woman after her death. The widowed, elderly woman had died while sitting on the toilet. While straining to move her bowels, she had ruptured an artery in her brain. The hemorrhage immediately shut down her brain, and she was, most likely, dead before she hit the floor. The woman had lain on the bathroom floor for over a week before they had arrived on the scene. Chris had heard similar stories from other officers. Many became isolated because their children had moved away, and because of the demands by their children's families, the elderly parents were mostly forgotten. Chris had seen much of the hardening of America's soul during his short stint as a reserve deputy.

Chris approached his horse; the animal flared its nostrils and started to side step away from Chris. Chris walked away from the horse and approached him from the downwind side, quickly snatching the trailing rein. He turned the horse into the wind before he remounted. He sat thinking about what they both might run into in the future. After a while, he turned the horse away from the river and rode.

His thoughts returned to the tollbooth, and he wondered why there wasn't a rush of Mexicans crossing the Rio Grande into the United States. Perhaps the United States wasn't as attractive as it once had been. Chris noticed the tire tracks that paralleled his route the last mile. He followed them to the edge of a dry riverbed, planning a way down and across, when he saw a Chevy Suburban at the bottom. He wound his way along an old cattle path to the newer looking vehicle. Again, he smelled death and quickly backtracked, tying his horse to a fence post away from the truck. A closer look, after wiping some dust from the side of the truck, revealed the logo of Homeland Security. It looked like the truck had been purposely pushed over the edge. The footprints in the road told the story. One man was in the backseat dead, his seatbelt still holding him upright. He fit Jenny's description. His firearm was missing. Chris saw the man's radio on the ground, smashed by a rock. He searched the man's pants and didn't find his wallet. After a quick search of the area, he found it on the ground under the front of the truck. He checked the inside of the wallet and found only a picture of Jenny. He put it in his shirt. He went back to the truck and took the man's badge and nametag. He dragged the body out of the truck and put it alongside the creek bank. He used a tarp from inside the Bronco to wrap the remains. At the top of the creek bank, he kicked as much of the loose, dry soil as he could to cover the impromptu body bag. He hoped the body would stay covered and save it from scavengers. Back at the truck, he took the GPS receiver off the dashboard and stored the location in the memory. He made his way back to the horse. The horse was starting to get used to this; he only slightly flared his nostrils and blew the stink away, but he still had a wide-eyed look. Chris got on and rode along the bottom of the arroyo, looking for a way up and out.

He stopped at a UPS store outside of Eagle Pass, which the government had deemed "essential," and wrote a letter to Jenny expressing his regret at her loss and the circumstances of her husband's death. He added instructions on how to locate his body using the GPS. He put the badge, nametag, wallet, letter, and GPS receiver in a box addressed to her. He added a larger envelope, filled with as many fifty-dollar bills as he could without making it too obvious. Wiping a tear from his cheek, he left the store. He saw the faces of a few Hispanic children playing in the warm rain. He followed a riverbed westward, out of town. The children watched him slowly ride out of sight.

The next few days, Chris was riding through the scenic area along the Rio Grande. Outside of Del Rio, he passed Laughlin Air Force base. It was as secure as American tax dollars could make it. He stayed clear of the base and wasn't bothered. He skirted around the larger towns along his route. The Amistad Park and Reservoir was the largest he had ever seen. He camped at the Seminole Canyon Park and was left alone, except he did get to see his first nine-banded armadillo. He had heard they were common in Texas; it had taken long enough to see one.

He hadn't seen anyone for days. It looked dry toward the north; he decided to stay along the river, since it was cooler and the feed for the horse was better. He enjoyed the ride and felt safe since he was out of sight most of the time. He rode over the bridge at the mouth of the Pecos River and thought about the history of the west in this part of Texas during the end of the nineteenth century and the beginning of the twentieth century. Not quite ready to be sociable, he went north around Langtry.

The farther west he traveled, the drier the vegetation. The different species of oak changed as he changed elevation. He was getting higher, and the mountains to the north and west were impressive but on a smaller scale than anything found in Colorado. The San Francisco River ran straight west and looked inviting. Chris followed the bank of the watercourse.

The fine rain was being driven by a stiff wind. Eventually, he'd be soaked. He had passed ranches that were still occupied. He saw a copse of trees ahead and felt that it would make a good campsite until the rain and wind let up. He tied his horse's halter lead to a small tree among some larger trees. There was some sparse grass underfoot; he would have something to nibble on. He stripped off the saddle and blanket and carried the tack to a larger group of trees that was considerably drier and out of the way. After he gathered some dry wood and started a small fire, he warmed some coffee and ate one of the MREs. He noticed some creaking above him in the old tree but dismissed it. He settled in for the night and immediately fell asleep.

Chapter Thirteen
Grounded

The wind gradually increased in ferocity. Chris, sound asleep, failed to hear the changing sound. Unknown to him, the tree that he was under, started to sway in the gusting wind. The creaking that Chris had heard earlier grew louder. An old branch in the oak that should have fallen years ago had finally weakened to a point that allowed it to fall. The snap sounded like a gunshot. Chris's horse bolted and ran. Chris, in his sleep, was only aware of a crushing pressure across his chest.

He awoke and found he was under a large branch. It was as big around as his chest. A stub of the branch was lodged between his knees. His leg was numb. He couldn't move his arms; they were held fast to his sides by the old branches. The soil was soft, and Chris found that by moving his shoulders, he could work his way a little deeper into the dirt and breathe easier. He was stuck! After a while, the numbness left his leg and was replaced with excruciating pain. Chris was unaware how many times he passed from conscious to unconscious. He lay under the branch, totally helpless and in great pain. In his semiconscious state, he was aware of movement around him, but he failed to recognize the significance.

Chris heard music in the distance. He thought of a math class at school and Marcie on a horse. He saw Sarita smiling while she was holding a piece of cantaloupe. Nick kept staring at him across a hotel lobby. Jenny's sad face appeared and then faded. He watched himself slip an airplane to a landing. He was driving a car as fast as he could—at first on a highway and then along a dusty dirt road.

The flash of Evelyn's bathing. He was hiding behind bushes. He was sweating and stealing a car. He saw himself standing on a tall ladder, pulling a log to the top of a log cabin wall. He was standing in line during graduation. He was a small child, crying when he learned that he'd never see his parents again. He was alone, again. He woke up with a start.

Chris was lying on a bed. The sheets were crisp and clean. The room looked feminine and smelt as such. He heard music from a radio in a distant room. He heard someone moving about the house. His leg throbbed when he tried to move it. He felt a cast. There were footsteps outside the door. He closed his eyes. He felt a soft hand touch his cheek and then his forehead. A very soft voice said something in Spanish. Chris opened his eyes and saw a woman, bent over him, with the most beautiful gray eyes he had ever seen. He didn't blink, fearing she would disappear if he did. She had long, black hair, braided in a single coil hanging over her shoulder and out of sight past the edge of the bed. Her skin was fair and fine. She was wearing jeans and a light, colorful shirt. She looked at him, unblinking, and said, "You had me worried for a while. But, by the look of you, you seem to have done well."

Chris started to say something. She cut him off with, "Shush. You have to be starving. I'll get you something light to eat."

He closed his eyes, and settling back in the sheets, he waited for her return. She came back with a large cup of honeyed tea and a small plate of buttered rye toast. She put these on the bedside table. Chris could smell her perfume as she bent over. She helped Chris slide up, using the pillow against the carved headboard to support him in a semi-reclining position.

"You get started on that. Go slowly. It's been a few days that I know of, and possibly a few more since you've had a good meal." She left the room and came back carrying a chair. She placed it next to the bed and sat down, folding her hands on her lap. They sat in silence for a while. She was content to watch Chris eat.

After a while, she said, "You probably have many questions that I'll answer. My name is Patricia. Please call me Pat. Now, you save your energy and keep eating." She readjusted herself on the chair and continued. "A horse was in my front yard a few days ago. The night before was very windy. I assumed a rider had been thrown off. It wasn't too hard following the trail back to you. Your horse has cleats on its shoes and is easy to track. I found you unconscious, under an old oak branch. I came back to the house and loaded my truck with a chainsaw and some blankets. Cutting the tree off you wasn't too hard. You fought me a bit when I tried to get you into the bed of the truck.

"I called the hospital where I work and asked one of the doctors to come out and set your broken leg. For the last three days, you've been in this bed. I imagine you were having a whopper of a dream in your hysteria. I took care of your horse and gear. I cleaned your firearms, which were wet. Your clothes were muddy and torn. I washed and mended them. The money you have in the small bag is safe here. I have no need for it. I'm on vacation for two months, which is how long it will take that leg to heal, so I can tend to you." She sat back in the chair.

Chris checked under the sheets. He was naked. The little food he had eaten put him back to sleep. Pat rose from the chair and pulled the covers up. She grasped the chair back, and opening the door, she glanced back as she went out the door.

A few days later, Chris was feeling better and told her his name. She still had him stay in bed. Pat brought him some books to read. "Chris, you may find these interesting. They are from my father's collection. Read when you feel like it and rest when you can. I'll check in on you from time to time." He immersed himself in Hemingway, Steinbeck, a set of Louis L'Amour Westerns, a four-book set written by Winston Churchill, and Homer's *Iliad.* Pat checked in on him as promised. She took care of his needs and left him to himself.

One day he asked her a question, and a conversation began. Pat brought a chair to the side of the bed and leaned against the mattress while talking to him. They talked about their pasts and hopes for the future and their fears. The topics covered everything from politics to the changes since 9/11 and to Indian lore. They both loved history, music, and art. Pat was a classical cook, but her interests ranged from traditional to outright bizarre. Chris was a typical male; he would eat whatever was put in front of him and enjoyed it all.

Chris asked Pat if she had heard any new news about terrorists. Pat said, "There seems to be a division forming between Muslims and Christians in Europe. The Netherlands, Denmark and Belgium, since World War II, were thought of as being strong on internationalism, moderation, and social progress. Now, the citizens of those countries want the immigration laws looked into with an eye toward excluding Muslims. France, remember they were the ones that wouldn't back the US and Britain in Iraq, have banned head scarves in public schools."

Chris told Pat about Hisballah and how they viewed the world as either "Muslim" or "not Muslim."

"Looks like that bit them in the ass," said Pat, who at first blushed and then laughed at her outburst.

Their conversation continued well into the night. Eventually they were both talked out and fell asleep. Chris simply stopped talking and was asleep. Pat fell asleep seconds afterward, her head on the pillow next to his head.

She awoke the next morning, before Chris, and was surprised by her reaction. She smiled at her innermost thoughts and quietly walked from the room. With the stock fed and her other chores completed; she retreated to the shower. She became aware that she had been spending progressively longer periods in the shower. The warm water had never felt this good before. Life seemed to be more of a delight recently. She quickly changed her thoughts to breakfast. Still feeling lighthearted, she wrapped a towel around her wet hair and went into the kitchen. She liked being nude while working around the house, and she need not worry about Chris seeing her—he was sleeping and could not get out of bed. While waiting for the water to boil, she went to the living room coffee table for something to read. As she picked up a magazine, the open bedroom door caught her eye. She slowly turned her head and saw Chris watching her. There was something about his look that made her feel comfortable. They looked at each other without saying a word. She didn't feel self-conscious, which surprised her, since no man had seen her naked before. Still, she needed to maintain some form of modesty. She slowly stood up and went for a robe. Chris had never seen a more attractive woman in his life. He lay in bed waiting for his heart to stop hammering inside his chest.

Over a breakfast of poached eggs and toast, they talked more about philosophy and life. The eternal question about God and what happened after death. Both of them were unwilling to acknowledge Pat's nakedness, or their growing mutual attraction to each other. Both of them were feeling something neither had felt before. Nerves were becoming deliciously raw. They tried any subject they could think of to avoid it.

Pat picked up the dishes and went to the kitchen for coffee. She came back with a tray of two cups filled with coffee, a creamer, and sugar bowl. She told Chris they were her grandmother's and she couldn't remember when she had used them last. Chris was delighted that she decided to share these keepsakes with him. The warm morning sun made him drowsy. Pat noticed and quietly left the room.

Later that day, she looked in on him as he slept. He was on his back—the sheets had been thrown off. She started to pull them back over him and then stopped. The nurse in her took over, or so she thought. Looking at him clinically, she smiled a wistful smile. His fair complexion was taking a beating from the sun. She wondered how he'd look in a few years. Would he go bald? She didn't think so. Would he have the Western man's crow's feet? He should be wearing sunglasses. The next time she went into town, she'd get him a pair. His shoulders and arms looked strong. She liked his flat belly and small hips. She was glad he was blond with light body hair. She had worked with a doctor that was very hairy. His hair grew down his arms to the back of his hands. When he shaved, he had to continue down his neck to his chest. She remembered from nursing school that most hairy men went bald, but not all bald men were hairy. That was a long time ago, and she was sure it could have been the other way around. Continuing her inventory of Chris, his legs looked strong. He had good thighs that indicated good health. He would be able to walk long distances without much trouble. She'd be taking off the cast soon. Before she recovered him, she let the woman in her reappear; she glanced at his manhood. Laying the sheet down, she was smiling as she went out the door.

They both decided he needed a shave and a haircut. Pat was proud of her haircutting ability. She warned him about the sun on his white neck and told him of her plans for sunglasses. Chris told her he had a pair, but the night he broke his leg, he must have lost them. He asked her how she was getting to town. She explained she drove and could get gas; because of being a nurse, she was considered "essential." Chris laughed at that. He asked her, "If so many people are considered 'essential,' then what are the rest considered?"

Chris was fascinated when she stropped the straight razor on an old razor strap. She still had her grandfather's mug with soap and a shaving brush. Pat explained what they were, and she added some lore about how the strap was used for disciplining young boys in the old days. Chris winced at the thought. She lathered his face and went to work. She was careful shaving him with the old straight razor. She finished without a nick. Pat even had a bottle of Bay Rum. Chris was amazed the more he learned about her.

The day continued to be lazy, and they continued reading, him in the bed, and her in the chair. This pattern developed through the weeks. Chris fell asleep that night. He always slept soundly. She had noticed. He was catching up on much needed sleep. Pat waited awhile and then undressed, slipping in beside him. The next morning, she was out of bed before he woke. This pattern continued unnoticed.

He had gotten dressed. The pant leg had to be cut to accommodate the cast. Pat was glad to see him up and around. They had a quiet breakfast together. Chris offered to help with the dishes, but Pat chased him out of her kitchen. He hobbled out to the barn to check his horse. The weather was clear, and Chris heard the birds among the trees. He gingerly made his way to one of the corrals outside. He surprised a white-tailed doe as he came through the barn door. She ran a distance to the edge of the trees, looked back over her shoulder, and leaped over some unseen object into the brush. A small cotton-tailed rabbit thought it was hiding in the shadow of the water trough. A friend, or littermate of the rabbit, ran barreling around the corner of the barn and into the hiding rabbit. They both jumped around, sparred with each other like rabbits do, and ran off together in the direction of the barn.

Pat came walking through the barn and saw Chris leaning against the fence. She stood close to him, crossing her arms and putting her elbows on the top rail of the fence. She scratched her chin on her forearm and laid her cheek against an upper arm. She looked off into the distance. Chris could feel the warmth of her hip and thigh against his.

"Watching the wildlife?"

Chris slowly nodded.

Pat continued, "You can tell that I don't have any cats around here. The rabbits are thriving." Chris looked toward her with knit brows.

She continued. "Domestic cats are responsible for 80 percent of small game taken. I can't live strictly on beef. There's enough turkey and deer around here, but sometime I feel a need for, as they say, 'the other white meat.'" Chris laughed at that.

"Tell me more about cats and predation," Chris said.

"People see cats as harmless pets. The truth is that they are responsible for more small game taken than that taken by hunters. I'm not including songbirds and butterflies. Farmers have seen their own cats bring back, to the house, baby rabbits that were found in a warren. If the farmer were to take the young rabbit away from the cat, it would simply go back for another until they have cleaned it out. I won't buy into the balance of nature bit, simply because the cat is an artificially introduced European predator. They are different from other predatory felines in that the domestic cat has its needs taken care of, such as feeding and vet care. They live over ten years, and the females will give birth to over a hundred offspring during their lives. On the other hand, the wild cats have a short and rough life trying to survive. If the domestics were in the same situation, they would quickly find themselves on the bottom of the food chain. Coyotes find them particularly fun to eat. The bottom line is that I have no use for a creature that kills for no other reason than to kill. And that includes humans."

"That was the most thorough argument against domestic cats that I've ever heard. It's too bad that killing a cat has been elevated to a crime in many places around America. In addition, this is easily seen by the fact that many pets in cities are treated almost as humans. As an enlightened society, we sure have become lulled by emotional arguments." To change the subject and give himself time to think about what she had said, Chris asked, "I suppose you gig frogs in the evening with a flashlight?"

Pat snickered. "As a matter of fact, sometime I do. Frog legs are delicious with butter and garlic. A Chardonnay complements the meal."

Chris changed the subject again; he was getting a good idea about how she thought and what was important to her. "Pat, tell me why you're here alone."

"I'm here, alone, because I want to be. This is my parents' ranch. I joined the navy after nursing school and started to study to become a doctor. My tour was four years. My parents were murdered, and the sheriff of Brewster County notified the navy. They sent me back on a compassionate leave. I arrived after they were buried. The investigation is still pending. The sheriff stops by occasionally to bring me up to date. So far, it's been quite a few years, and nothing has come of it. I'm working toward becoming a coroner, but so far, I haven't completed the requirements for the job. Forensics has always interested me because of the depth of knowledge required. I would also like to find the answer to my parents' death.

"I've been busy at the hospital in Alpine and haven't had time for men in my life." She quickly noticed the look on Chris's face and corrected herself with, "I haven't let myself become involved with a man. Men do not know what to make of me. Most of them are too rough and crude. Even the refined ones are more interested in their selfish needs and can't seem to notice that I am more than they see."

It was Pat's turn to change the subject. She put her foot on the bottom rail of the fence and began, "My father and mother owned a few oil fields outside of Odessa and Midland. Farther east, they owned a rather large ranch and a few pecan groves that they leased. This was their retirement home. Everything my parents have accomplished has been left to me. I am all that's left of my family. I'm respected in this community and at my job. This is now my place and my life." Pat shuddered. Chris knew that is wasn't from the cooling air.

They slowly walked back through the barn and out to the sunny front porch. Pat walked slower to accommodate him. He had his arm over her shoulder and her arm around his waist. His face was in her hair, and she had her head against his chest, listening to the beating of his heart.

They sat together on a wide chair, using a smaller chair to elevate Chris's leg. Since they were on the subject of death, he felt comfortable talking about it. Chris told Pat about the episode at Jenny's house. Her face registered her surprise. She asked him how he felt about having to kill those men. He told her that it was something that needed to be done. He didn't feel happy or sad. They sat in silence for a while. Pat broke the silence. "Let's find something for dinner."

During dinner, they spoke about the native wildlife in the area. He told her about the first armadillo he saw. She chided him about his observation skills.

"They're everywhere!" she told him.

Chris commented about the mountains to the south and west. Pat volunteered by telling him they were the Davis Mountains and the house was between Mount Ord and Cathedral Mountain. She asked him about the attack on the oil platform. He told her the whole story up to the present. She listened intently. She offered her thoughts about Nick and Sarita. Her mouth opened as he described his meeting with the knife-wielding man in the brush. She laughed at the part about Evelyn. His trip through Central America and Mexico left her astonished. She fell in love with Cy, Josh, and Dan. She started to cry when he told her of Jenny, finding her husband's body, and sending his personal effects and the GPS back to her. Somehow the name stuck a chord in her, but she let it drop in the rapid dialog.

She wanted him to stay. Forever, if she could have her way. She enjoyed him in her home. In the little time she had come to know him, she felt he was an honest and trustworthy man. He was exciting and intelligent. The geology degree didn't seem to fit him; he was a man of action, and she was in love with him. Even knowing about Marcie, she felt like shamelessly throwing herself at him.

Chris again thanked Pat for saving his life, fixing his leg, and opening her house to him. He had no idea how to repay the debt. He saw her as an extremely intelligent, engaging, caring, and beautiful woman. She was talented, cultured, and he sensed there were more attributes that he hadn't discovered yet. The right man would eventually show up. If it were under any other circumstance, he could very easily fall in love with her. The way it was now, he would always carry her in his heart. Women like her were extremely rare. Chris could feel himself drawn to her. He wanted to respond to her love. He wanted to reach out and hold her. He felt unworthy. Something else was holding him back. The sense of duty was pulling him North toward Colorado.

Pat excused herself from the couch and retreated to the kitchen. She returned with a small plate of assorted cheese, fruit, and crackers. In her other hand, she carried an open bottle of Pinot Noir and two crystal glasses. Her hair was loose. When she bent over the back of the sofa, it cascaded over Chris's neck and shoulder. He could smell the fragrance of her shampoo and feel the weight of her hair. She put her cheek on his shoulder, softly kissing his neck. He could feel her full breast on his back. Chris reached over and held her head in his hands. He was living each precious moment, each second, on the edge of pure ecstasy. He turned his head. Their lips met in a sweet, soft embrace. He gently pulled her over the couch, holding her as he would hold the most precious thing in his life.

They stayed awake late that night. The owls were hooting in the night air. They were comfortable in each other's arms. They talked softly, at times a mere whisper, until well after midnight. Exhaustion eventually overcame Chris. When he was asleep, Pat lay awake thinking. There was one last thing that she needed to do. She gently disentangled herself from Chris and carefully slid from the couch. When she returned, there was a slight smile on her lips. He would be back. She just needed to be patient. She snuggled alongside him again. One of Pat's last thoughts was that Chris would be gone when she woke up. She hated the thought of waking up the next morning.

Chapter Fourteen
Kitty, a Good Friend

Chris backtracked to Langtry and decided to go north along the Pecos River. His leg was still sore, and he couldn't take a chance traveling through the mountains. During the last few days, Chris put many miles behind him. Pat had been on his mind. It was hard to leave a woman like her. Perhaps he was riding in the wrong direction. He had questions that needed answers. He kept riding relentlessly toward Colorado. The mountains were behind him. The swells of the plains seemed to be moving along with him. This beautiful, open country had an appeal that could grow on a man. He was starting to understand why Texans were so proud of their state and many died fighting for it.

He heard the bullet go by his head. He was off his horse before he heard the rifle report. Chris flipped the reins around the horse's head and over its neck. He pulled up the gelding's head while he pulled the neck down. The horse went down on its side. Chris pulled the rifle out of the scabbard and lay down in a nearby depression. He looked in the direction of the rifle report. He saw no one. He wasn't about to expose himself. He looked over at the horse. He was a good horse and easy to train. He didn't twitch a muscle. This latest stunt Chris had taught him a couple of weeks ago. Pat showed him how to do it. Chris would find out if it would save both their lives.

Two hundred yards away, he saw the wind tousle a head of hair. It was easy to spot since it wasn't as stiff as the grass. The man looked like he was losing patience and maybe a bit too eager to find out if he connected with his target. Chris had his hat off and lined up his barrel.

The man was now back on his horse and approaching straight on. He was coming in slowly, trying to be cautious. He may have thought he was, but Chris saw him as utterly stupid. When the man was within a hundred yards, Chris had his front sight on the center of the man's chest. The .30 caliber had a soft-point bullet normally used for deer hunting. It left a hole, no larger than the shirt button it replaced.

When Chris got to the man, he was face down. The hole between his shoulder blades was big enough for Chris's fist. Chris rounded up the man's horse, stripping off the gear, and let the horse free to enjoy life. Chris walked back to the man and looked around for identification. He found none and chalked him up as another lost soul that hadn't found a suitable niche in life. Chris didn't bother burying the man. The vultures, feral hogs, and coyotes would clean him up eventually. Occasionally, they too enjoyed "the other white meat."

While he was traveling across a particularly open area, a whimsical thought struck him. He got off the horse, walked around the dusty beast, and while holding the bridle in both hands, he looked him in the eye. He said, "Bud, we've been together quite a while now, and we're still not on a first-name basis. This has to change. Let me know what you want me to call you." Perhaps it was the afterglow of being with Pat, or he was just feeling good and decided to talk to his horse. There was nothing new about this since many a man had done this through the years.

With that said, he remounted and walked the horse along an old game trail. Chris had skirted around a bad section of the Big Canyon River. The normal residents of the area were out in full force. Squirrels, turkey, grouse, and some imported African species of which he couldn't recall the name. Chris walked his horse, who still hadn't given him a clue about what it wanted to be called, over to a roadside parking area. Chris didn't find any tire or horse tracks. It was nice to know he was alone.

Chris left the area and traveled into the trees looking for a safe campsite for the night. He found one, complete with a fireplace. It didn't take him long to gather up dead wood. He started a small fire, and when he was satisfied, he turned his attention to other matters. He took the saddle and blanket off his horse and tied the gelding to a tree surrounded by grass. This time, Chris would look up before he committed himself to a sleeping spot. He saw a group of turkeys roosting in the top of an old cedar.

He waited until they settled in for the night and carefully walked through the trees, in the dimming light, to get a better shot. He lined up on one of the smaller hens and proceeded to decapitate the bird. It was a great shot, but the bird hung upside down for a while, still holding on to the branch of the Cedar. Chris didn't want to broadcast his location, so he waited until the bird fell. Eventually, gravity won or leg muscle lost. Either way, Chris had a fine meal that night, complete with a bottle of Chablis that Pat had put in his backpack.

Chris was starting to feel the effects of the white wine. He thought about what could have happened between them if they had been under the influence of the grape. He was starting to feel silly. He looked over at the horse, and the horse looked back at him.

An idea came to Chris. "Chablis? Chabby? Shabby? Tabby? Kitty?" The horse looked at Chris with its ears pricked. "Kitty? Kitty! That's it! You are now Kitty. And you may call me Chris." They both agreed it was a fine name. "Kitty" snorted approval, and Chris rolled over to sleep. He had already checked the tree for large overhanging branches.

The next morning, Chris gathered up his belongings and saddled Kitty. He made sure the ashes were dead in the fireplace. He took a final leak and got up in the saddle. Kitty seemed to be a little more talkative this morning.

Continuing east, he came to Langtry. Looking at the town from a distance, he could see people moving around. For some odd reason, he didn't feel as threatened by the town this time. He chose to ride in. Across the street was the Judge Roy Bean Saloon and Museum. No one seemed to pay much attention to him. He looked just like they did. He decided to stop at the saloon and get something to eat. He looped the reins around the hitching post and walked into the saloon.

He walked over to the bar, looking out the window to make sure he could still see Kitty. The bartender asked him what he wanted.

Chris replied, "A Coke and a hamburger."

The man next to him snickered.

Chris looked the man straight in the eye and said, "What do you expect? I'm the designated driver."

With that, everyone within hearing distance started to laugh. He was left alone to eat. Chris heard some people talking about a multiple hanging this morning. He knew he was living in the twenty-first century, but now he felt that he had been time warped back into the nineteenth century.

Out on the street, Chris looked up and down, wondering where the action was this morning. He walked west to see what was on that side of town. As luck would have it, he found the undertaker's office and four wooden coffins propped up in front. It looked like an Old West picture. Four men in four boxes, each one still wearing a black sack on his head and a hand-printed sign pinned to his shirt. The first one was a horse thief. He was a short guy with dirty jeans and a torn shirt. The second man, with a pair of plain brown pants and a white shirt, wore a sign saying he had attempted to rape a woman. The third man, wearing black pants and a T-shirt, was wearing a sign proclaiming his claim to fame as killing someone while attempting a robbery. The fourth man, wearing blue jeans and a blue shirt, was said to be a burglar. None of the four men were wearing boots or shoes. Either they had come off when they hit the end of their rope, so to speak, or the undertaker had another side business going. Cy quickly came to mind.

Chris looked around and saw it across the street just visible and in a recess between two buildings. He walked toward it. In between the two buildings were the gallows. It was set up to handle six customers. A stout looking contraption, similar to what he had seen in the movies. Chris continued down the street and came to the county sheriff's office. On a billboard next to the door were the traditional wanted posters similar to what he had seen in his own sheriff's office as a deputy. They were well done. The reproduced photos most likely came from photos used by the motor vehicle division of the state. They were wanted for an assortment of reasons that covered everything from plain murder, to fraud, to wife beating and just about every listed felony in the state statutes. This was a serious community. Chris remembered where he was standing and checked to make sure his Colt was unnoticeable.

Just then, the sheriff walked out. He side-glanced Chris, stopped, turned at the hip, and asked, "You new in town?" His brow furrowed in the best Western tradition.

Chris almost laughed, but he knew this man was serious. Playing his part, he answered, "Just passing through." The sheriff, apparently satisfied with the answer, turned and walked down the sidewalk.

Chris started across the street. He idly scratched his cheek and felt he needed a shave. Looking around, he spotted the barbershop and headed that way. There wasn't much of a waiting line. He sat down in a chair along the wall. He listened to the various conversations, most of them boring. His attention was drawn to one man and a barber talking about a group of men causing trouble in the hills north of town. They had ganged up and were victimizing the outlying people. The sheriff in this county, Val Verde, couldn't do anything since it was out of his jurisdiction. The troublemakers were in Terrell County, and no one knew if there was a sheriff in that county.

Chris breathed a heavy sigh. That was exactly the way he was going to go. He couldn't go back to Alpine, which in itself was a very pleasant thought. He wanted to get back to Colorado as quickly as he could. He didn't have time to go around, and he certainly didn't have the patience to deal with those jerks in the hills. Would it ever end?

It was Chris's turn in the chair, and when the barber was finished, Chris looked as good as when Pat shaved him. He needed a bath. He asked the barber if there was one in town and was surprised when given directions. He paid the barber and was gone out the door. Chris walked back to the saloon, got on Kitty, and rode back to the other end of town, taking in the sights from a higher perspective.

The bathhouse, as it was, was a large army surplus tent from one of the Desert Wars in the Middle East. The inside was partitioned off for eight tubs. The proprietor of this Bath Emporium had it set up well. Chris stepped back outside to retrieve his saddlebags and rifle from Kitty. The sheriff was walking by and slowed as he passed Chris, watching him very closely.

Chris walked back in and put the backpack and rifle at the foot of a tub. His Colt, he put under a towel on a small table. Chris was in heaven in the warm water, and it helped his leg loosen up. He was undisturbed for an hour. When he felt clean and thoroughly relaxed, he got out and toweled off. He found clean clothes in the backpack and dressed. With his business done, he went outside and loaded Kitty.

Chapter Fifteen
Karen

Chris rode to the eastside of town and followed the road to the mouth of the Pecos River. When he rode up and over a set of railroad tracks, he saw a family of Harris hawks. He watched the birds. They were hunting as a group. These black birds with rust-colored shoulders and white under-tail coverts were unique in the world of birds. No other raptor in North America hunted like these hawks. The family group could be as large as a dozen birds. The group would constitute parent birds, young siblings, and those in transition from youngster to adults.

He watched as one bird dove toward a bush, forcing a jackrabbit to break cover. The other birds joined in the hunt by keeping the running hare moving. If one bird missed, another one took its place. Eventually the jack would be caught. The rest of the birds would join in the meal. Chris thought it fascinating that these birds had evolved to work together in such desolate surroundings.

As he rode up the Pecos River, he was amazed at what he saw. He was surrounded by hills on either side of the river. The Pecos was small and, at times, very wide. When the river was narrow, it wandered along the broad floor of the canyon. When it was dammed, the river took on an enormous size, and he had to ride around it. On occasion, he would see a large broad-winged hawk circling above him and then veer off downwind. The deer were evident. Sometimes he'd see some strange ungulate that had been imported to Texas from Africa. He spooked a small herd while they were drinking. He was constantly watching for someone lying in wait for him. It was definitely a great place to hide out.

Kitty was already used to walking on flat land and along mountain trails. Now, his education would continue in the wide valley. The hills loomed closer to them the deeper they traveled upstream. When Kitty first saw a river canyon, he hesitated, and Chris egged him on. The horse was game and continued. Chris watched him look back and forth at the hills. Ahead, there was a muddy spot, and Chris purposely walked Kitty through the deep mud. He navigated it carefully and didn't seem to get upset. Chris cantered Kitty through a shallow section of the river to wash the mud from his legs, belly, and cinch strap. He was learning well. After a time, Kitty was handling the deeper water quite well.

Chris recalled the conversation in the barbershop about a gang out here. Ahead was an abandoned house without any horses or livestock in the enclosed corral. Chris saw a nearby dirt runway but no sign of an airplane. He stopped a distance from the house, hailing it. There was no response. He nudged Kitty closer and got off. He cautiously walked toward the house.

After knocking on the door, mostly out of habit, he walked in the house. It was a mess and plain to see the original owners were gone and some slobs had moved in. Garbage was strewn everywhere. The kitchen was the worst. Frying pans, grease, and filthy dishes were scattered along the counter. He walked down the hallway, toward the bedrooms, passing by the bathroom. It stunk. Whoever had moved into this house hadn't enough decency to even flush the toilet. The bedroom carpeting and hallway were crusted with mud.

Chris went back through the house and out to the back. He scanned the backyard and saw a mound of dirt. It didn't warrant closer inspection. He knew the original occupants of the house were under the dirt. He quickly walked out of the house and looked for hoof prints. He found many. The main direction of travel was to and from the north. The same way Chris was heading. He'd been through a lot the last few months. His stubbornness had gotten him this far. He wasn't about to give up now.

Chris had an idea. He tied Kitty in the hangar and went to the garage and quickly looked around. He didn't find what he was looking for and headed back to the small airplane hangar. He found what he needed. A full five-gallon gas can was sitting next to a larger, partially filled tank. He took that and found a length of rope. He soaked the inside of the house with gas. Wetting the rope with the gas, he ran the rope out the door and along the sidewalk. He thought he hadn't used enough gas and went back to the hangar. With a hand pump, he refilled the can. When he was finished, the interior of the house reeked of gasoline. He re-soaked the rope again, at intervals, and lit it.

He ran to the hangar, quickly mounted Kitty, and spurred him into a canter away from the house, stopping when he thought he was safely away. Chris wasn't expecting what happened next. He had planned for the flame to travel along the rope slowly, and it almost did. What actually happened was the flame almost went out between the wet spots, but caught again at the next wet spot, which ignited the vapors collecting at the front of the building. It wasn't a bang but more of a deep whoosh that had enough force to be felt from as far away as he was on Kitty.

It wasn't long before he heard the sound of rapid hoof beats up the canyon. He quickly turned Kitty and headed up a smaller canyon. He made cover just as a small stampede rode by. When they passed, he walked Kitty back around the hill and watched six of them ride toward the now very vacant lot. It wouldn't be long before they figured out what had happened and come looking for him. He had purposely left an obvious trail. A blind man couldn't miss Kitty's shoe cleats.

Chris rode up the river canyon until he found a tributary leading into the hills. He quickly rode up the small stream, turned back into the hills, and left Kitty. He scrambled along the bank overlooking the creek and waited. He could hear the approaching horses.

Two men walked their horses along the creek looking nervous, thinking they were about to be bushwhacked. They were. Chris took them off their horses with two quick shots. He ran back from the edge and repositioned himself closer to the remaining men. He saw four grouped together at the mouth of the small canyon. They were having a heated discussion. Two men left the group on foot. Chris watched them carefully make their way toward the sound of his earlier gunfire. In his new position, he was behind them. His first shot took the farthest man. His second shot took the retreating man full in the chest. He looked over at the last two and saw them heading back toward the open valley. Chris ran down the low hill and back up a larger one. He caught a glimpse of the two riders heading north. He was willing to bet they were going to try to catch him in their crossfire. They would have a long wait.

It was a moonless night, and a stiff breeze blew out of the south. Hot and dry. Chris found a campsite out of the wind. Kitty was happy since he was picketed in the middle of what passed for lush grass.

Chris waited until well after midnight. He saddled Kitty and led him back up the valley, avoiding rocks and holes in the dark. It was slow going, but he had learned to be patient and cautious.

Up the valley, he heard the soft nicker of a horse. He quickly put his hand over Kitty's nostrils to muffle any reply from him. Kitty, being a gelding, didn't seem interested in socializing since those days were behind him. Chris smiled. Now he knew where the men's horses were, on the far side of the valley. He continued walking slowly for another thousand yards. Feeling he was past these men, he slowly got on Kitty and walked around a bend in the valley. Chris knew he was leaving an obvious trail. He continued up the valley.

It was just before sunrise when Chris spotted a road leading up out of the valley. He walked Kitty through soft dirt, making sure he left deep hoof prints. He left Kitty behind a hill farther down the road. Walking back along the dirt road, some bushes alongside the road caught his attention. He thought about it and then discarded the idea as being too obvious. He looked for another place to hide and saw a culvert under the road.

He was just starting to nod off when he heard the two men. They were obviously following his trail, one on either side of it. It was easy to see, and they kept their horses at a canter. Chris waited until they passed his position. They spotted the bushes on the other side of the road and stopped. They were getting wary. Chris eased out of the culvert. He had to sit up to see them. He braced his arms on his knees and took aim. One of the men was starting to get off his horse. The bullet took him in the spine, and his horse ran off with him hanging from the stirrup.

The last man turned and charged his horse toward Chris. Chris fired, and the mare dropped headfirst, flipping over on its back as it fell. The rider was crushed. The horse, dragging its rider, had run up the road and disappeared. The fallen horse and rider were dead. Chris had hit the horse between the eyes. The rider wasn't visible; the horse covered most of him.

Along his route, he passed a ranch on his left. There was some smoke coming out the chimney. Someone may be home. He saw a few farm vehicles alongside the house and a black and white dog barking from the front yard. It looked normal for a change. Chris wondered if these people had turned their homes into armed camps. Then he corrected himself; he was in Texas. He continued along the river, staying off the paved and gravel roads, favoring the dirt and fine gravel. They were too hard on Kitty's shoes, and he was tired of prying stones out that had lodged between the shoe and frog.

He was riding by another airstrip with a hangar. The large doors were open. Someone was working on an airplane inside. As Chris got closer, he saw it was an old yellow Stearman biplane. He walked Kitty closer to the hangar door and looked at it.

A voice from within asked, "Are you just going to sit on that horse and stare, cowboy?"

Chris was flabbergasted. He hadn't heard a friendly voice in days. The voice was female. He dismounted and stood there, waiting for the owner of the voice to appear from the dark hanger.

"C'mon inside and have a seat." A tall, honey-blonde woman walked out into the light. She offered her hand in a handshake and said, "Hi, y'all. My name as Karen." Chris shook her hand and told her his name. "Chris, you look like the man that's been helping us out."

Chris looked at her questioningly. She looked up and waved him inside, handed him a cup of coffee, and motioned him to sit down. He got comfortable, and she returned to her conversation.

"Most of us know what you've been doing, and we're mighty grateful." Chris continued to look innocent.

Karen reached in her pocket and took out a cell telephone. "The regular telephones work occasionally, but these little phones are still working. Long-distance calls can be a bitch, but occasionally we can get out of our local calling area."

Chris didn't smile. He waited to hear more.

"The sheriff of Val Verde County saw you go east out of Langtry and head north up the Pecos. He thought you were up to something. He followed your trail up to the Jackson Ranch. That's about the end of his jurisdiction. He called some of us up here in Terrell County and told us what he found. The local sheriff in this county has been dead for a few weeks. He didn't have any deputies to replace him, and the coroner said he'd be damned if he put on a badge, even if the law said he was next in line for the job. There hasn't been time for an election." She stopped talking. She looked like she was going to add something.

"You look a mess. You could stay here awhile. I could use some company." Chris followed her out the door.

Karen walked around to the shady side of the hangar. She came back around, leading her horse. Walking up to Chris, she looked at him squinting from the sun, and she seemed to be sizing him up. He could see the glimmer of a challenge in her eyes. She turned toward her horse, swung up to the saddle, said, "Follow me," and trotted casually away.

When Chris caught up to her, she glanced over at him, set her heels to her horse, and cantered briskly away. Chris pursued the fleeing blonde woman who ratcheted up to a hard gallop, her hair trailing behind her wildly. He was in pursuit. Kitty had his work cut out for him. They arrived neck and neck at her house. The black and white dog was barking happily. He sniffed his mistress and walked over to check out Kitty. Kitty dropped his head to smell the strange dog and blew, sending the dog on his way. When Chris got off Kitty, the dog walked back over to inspect his boot. Now satisfied, he walked under a nearby tree and lay down.

Karen motioned with her hand for Chris to follow her. They went around to the back door. She pulled off her boots and waited for Chris to struggle with his. Inside the kitchen, he noticed the lingering smell of bacon. "Smells good, don't it?" said Karen, with a smile on her windblown face. Chris nodded. She turned her back to him and said, "Let me get you some food. Go sit on the couch." Chris walked into the living room and sat on the overstuffed couch. He was asleep instantly.

Chris felt a warm nudge on the back of his head. He turned and saw a firm, round behind in a tight pair of jeans. "Foods ready. Let's get some in you." Chris walked into the kitchen and saw that only one place was set. He turned to Karen questioningly.

She answered, "I've already eaten breakfast. I'll sit with you while you eat." Chris tried to ask a question with his mouth full. Karen held up her hand for him to be still. "You keep eating, and I'll answer some questions you might have." Chris nodded. She continued, "You're probably wondering, what's a girl like me doing in a place like this?"

Chris nodded again.

"I was married once, but my husband left me. I guess he didn't like the loneliness, my flying, or the cattle. It really isn't lonely out here. That airplane you saw?" Chris nodded again. "I fly the airplane and visit folks all over. I even take trips to the big city." Karen stood taller and smiled as if proud of herself. Chris rolled his eyes and smiled. "Getting food around here isn't bad. Most of us go hunting. Those high-fenced ranches south of San Antone began to have too many deer. Since no one can drive, many of the owners cut their fences to let the deer roam. It worked out well for all since people need meat. It was a wise decision and a lot better than letting them overbreed and starve. More deer coming back too, since no one has been traveling these roads. The other food that we need, we either trade or grow. Did you notice the satellite dish outside?"

Chris nodded again.

"I watch the different news channels and see what's happening around the world. The financial troubles that they talk about and the problems with communications, both telephone and Internet, don't bother us too much. The bank in Langtry is good enough for us. The banker keeps money in the vault and does his banking the old-fashioned way. He hasn't modernized or joined with banking networks, which seems to have worked out well for us."

When Chris finished eating, he sat back in the chair and listened. Karen continued by bluntly asking, "Chris, how do you feel about those men?"

Chris thought for a while and sighed. "I've lived quietly all my life. I do understand why men prey on others, and I find it repugnant. I have always been respectful to others and simply expect the same in return."

She motioned for him to stay seated and disappeared around a corner. When she came back, she had some large bath towels under her arm. She quietly asked him to follow her. He was behind her out the door.

They traveled away from the house and around a smaller hill to a pool surrounded by stones. Karen knelt down and patted the ground next to her. "This pool is fed from a nearby artesian well. It's been here before the Indians. It's served me well through the years. I've always found it a great place to relax and let my mind wander. You get undressed and get in the water. I'll come back later for your clothes."

Chris watched her as she walked down the hill. He turned, undressed, and slipped into the cool water. He found a flat rock under the water. It was just right. He sat on the rock, his legs in the deeper, cooler water. He let his head fall back on the bank. He didn't recall falling asleep.

It was just after sunset when Chris felt someone next to him. He must have jumped a bit, because he heard Karen's soft voice reassure him, "It's all right, cowboy. It's just me." He felt her smooth leg slide slowly over his thigh. It was obvious she had removed her jeans. She pulled his arm across her belly. Her shirt was gone too. She began to idly scratch the inside of his forearm. They watched the darkening sky and the stars come out.

"Chris?" she said softly in a barely audible voice.

"Yes, Karen," answered Chris. A lone coyote called out in the distance.

"I lied," confessed Karen.

"How so?"

"When I told you I wasn't lonely."

Chris raised his arm and put it behind her head, pulling her toward him. Karen responded by turning to face him, straddling his thighs. Chris soon found that he was still a caring, sensitive human in spite of the death he had been forced to deal.

The next morning, Chris found Karen in the kitchen quietly humming a tune. Chris walked in the back door. He had just finished getting Kitty ready to travel. Karen turned and faced him. "I'll probably never see you again." It was more of a question than anything else.

Chris stood closer to her. They embraced for the last time. She turned away as he walked out the door. She changed her mind and ran out the door. She slowly waved as he rode away. The black and white dog ran up to his mistress. He sensed something was wrong in her life.

Chapter Sixteen
Strangers

It was close to dark when Chris set up camp in a group of broken limestone boulders. He made his campfire next to one of the largest and picketed Kitty a distance away in the shadows. He had taken a couple cans of fruit along with his rifle and heavy blanket to a secluded spot and began to eat in the darkness. His blanket was over his shoulders and the rifle across his knees. He had started to eat the fruit when he heard the sound of a loose rock and the shuffle of boots. Someone had stumbled in the dark. Chris was secure between a tree and boulder. He finished his fruit cocktail and drank the remaining juice. He quietly put the can behind him. His hand on the rifle stock, he waited.

The fire was still burning bright, and he saw a shadow moving on the far side of the rock. Another shadow joined it. Kitty softly nickered. Chris looked that way and saw a third man, just on the edge of the firelight. Chris raised the rifle, tightening his grip. Waiting. Two men appeared around the rock. They walked up to the blazing campfire and looked around. One was carrying a double-barreled shotgun. The other one had, what looked like, an old M-1 carbine. Chris's first shot took the carbine man in the neck. He levered another round and fired at the man carrying the shotgun. The third man ducked behind a rock. Kitty was behind the man. Chris repositioned himself by moving around a rock that let him get into a better position. He changed his mind and moved twenty feet closer to the man. Again, he waited.

The man charged the rock where he thought Chris was. He was

quickly firing a semi-automatic pistol. As he passed Chris's position, Chris fired at him. The bullet went through the man's chest, exploding his heart as it passed. Chris heard a swarm of lead pellets buzz past his head at the same time he heard the shotgun blast. He dove for the ground, abandoning the rifle and reaching for his Colt. He was on his belly with his head toward the gunman. After the man fired his shotgun, he stepped back to regain his balance and had his foot in the fire. He had lost his concentration during a gunfight. Chris rolled over on his back holding his Colt at arm length. He triggered three rounds in the man's direction. The first had hit the man in the pelvis, the second in the solar plexus, as he was bending, and the third in the top of the head as he was falling forward. Chris sat quietly in the failing firelight. Listening.

Early the next morning, Chris was on Kitty and heading up the canyon. Behind him lay three men lined up side by side. Their weapons were burning in the campfire. Chris had easily found their horses, took off the saddles and bridles, and let them loose. He wished he wouldn't meet any more like that. Reaching back into his saddlebag, he felt around until he found a piece of beef jerky. It wasn't much of a breakfast, but it would do for now.

A shot rang out behind him. The bullet went wide. Chris instinctively spurred Kitty, and the horse took off like a rocket. He wasn't too sure where the shot had come from, but after a quick glance behind him, he saw four men on horseback riding hard in his direction. The geologist and bay gelding rode across the flats and back toward the riverbed. He made the river and used the bank as cover.

Kitty stood in a foot of water. Chris lay belly down on the bank, his rifle parallel to the flat earth. The four men rode into sight, and Chris immediately took the lead man. His next shot hit the horse on the left, and it went down. The two mounted men retreated along with the one on foot. When the men reached some sparse cover, Chris could plainly see they had forgotten to hold on to their horse's reins. He fired a shot across the open area at the ground between the two horses. It immediately spooked them, giving the three men something to occupy their time—catching their horses.

He held on to his rifle, and with one hand, he swung up on Kitty. He traveled down the riverbed to an overpass. Chris tied Kitty to the far side of the overpass and took a position on the opposite bank of the river, closer to where he'd expect them. He waited for the two, possibly three remaining men to catch up. It didn't take them long to round up their horses and continue their pursuit. They were cautious this time. Chris could hear the three men talking above his position on the bridge. He realized his mistake and retreated to the far side of the overpass across from Kitty. He went up the bank and crawled along the roadside ditch. He was fifty yards from the river when he came to a driveway and the ditch stopped. He looked through the weeds and saw the three men amateurishly sneaking up to the overpass. He waited until they were out of sight and quickly crawled across the road to the other ditch. He went along that ditch until he came back to the bridge. There was tall grass along the safety rail. Chris crawled into the grass and found a depression to hide in. He could hear the men talking again. He put his rifle off to the side and pulled his .45 from the shoulder holster. The first man appeared on the far side of the road. Chris double tapped him with two rounds to the torso. Chris heard the other two running up the hill. He waited until he saw the top of the first man's head. One round to the head. He went limp. The third man had too much momentum and couldn't stop fast enough before he became visible. Chris was on his knees; he had to rise while he fired his remaining rounds. All four had hit in a vertical line from the crotch to the face. The man fell over backward, sliding down the hill. Chris looked back over the road at the first man. He didn't see him. He exchanged magazines before he moved from his position.

Chris got up and walked across the road, rechecking the first man and looking down to where he left Kitty. The horse was happily eating grass. He looked up at Chris and nickered. Chris chuckled. Chris rolled the bodies down the hill. He looked around for their horses and saw that they had run away. He was too tired to look for them. He walked down to Kitty and led him up the hill. He walked alongside the horse for a while. He needed to walk, even though his legs could hardly hold him up from the fatigue and nervous shaking.

Chris was at the end of the larger hills. A beautiful flat-faced bluff signaled the end. He had refilled his canteens in the river. He wasn't too happy about drinking the water, but it was wet. He thought again about Glenn Campbell's character drinking muddy water from a hoof print and laughed. He was heading toward Sheffield, and then he'd continue to Iraan.

As he rode along, covering mile after mile, he had much to think about. His thoughts drifted to Colorado and the mountains and plains. The smell of evergreens and sagebrush came to mind. It was an idyllic life. He hadn't a care in the world during school. Things had certainly changed since then. His life had become an emotional rollercoaster. Chris was getting a bit envious of Kitty. The horse had everything he needed and didn't expect anything else. Such was his simple, focused life. Chris needed a change in diet—from nothing to something. He turned Kitty up one of the tributaries and picketed him. He took his rifle and continued up the hill. It was still early in the morning; he might get lucky.

Chris caught a buck as it sprung from its bed. Chris was lucky with the snapshot—the whitetail hadn't had a chance to get hot. Chris rolled it over and zipped open the belly. It was easy sloshing the innards out. He slid the carcass up the hill a bit. He finished opening the thorax and pulled out the lungs and heart. He'd leave the "good stuff" for the coyotes. He didn't have a frying pan, so he couldn't cook the liver. *Too bad*, he thought, and left that too for the song dogs. He'd have to roast the meat over an open fire. Chris cut off the neck with the head, and the legs at the knee and elbow joints, leaving them in the growing pile for the scavengers. He found a stick and propped open the rib cage to help cool the deer.

Chris thought the whitetail was quite a bit smaller than the "mulies" back home. He dragged the buck downhill, headless end first. It was an easy drag going with the lay of the hair. When he got close to Kitty, the horse's eyes opened wide at the smell of blood. Chris looked at the horse and said, "After what we've been through, this scares you?"

Chris pulled the pin loose and led Kitty downhill to the river. He gathered enough wood and started a good-sized fire, letting it burn down to coals. By that time, he had the haunch skinned and on a branch, ready for roasting. While it was over the fire, he cut up the rest of the meat and prepared to jerk it. In his backpack, he found salt, sugar, garlic powder, and chili powder, along with some small packages of soy sauce. The only person that had been around his backpack was Pat. He smiled.

Chris went back to Kitty and lengthened the lead attached to him and then laid back against the saddle, slowly turning the roast venison. The jerky was hung from the stubs of small branches on a larger branch. He set the branch a distance from the fire and was letting it slowly dry.

He thought more pleasant thoughts about home. It really couldn't get better than this. Just then, he saw a man coming from upstream and walking his horse in the open. He was looking to the left and right, obviously looking for something. Chris watched as his head pivoted in his direction and stopped. The man walked his horse straight toward Chris without breaking stride.

Chris didn't see the man trying to arm himself, so he stayed on the ground. He did flip his serape over the shoulder holster but left it open enough that he would appear unarmed. His rifle was against a tree behind him. As the man came closer, Chris could tell he was wearing a uniform of some type. Chris spotted the glimmer of a badge. He waited.

When the man was a hundred yards out, he stopped and watched Chris for a while—obviously making sure he wasn't in danger, or to show that he posed no threat. He slowly approached Chris on horseback and stopped fifty feet out. He dismounted, dropped the reins to the ground, and raised his right hand in a greeting. Chris raised his hand and waved the man to come ahead. He was a sheriff, and most likely, Chris was in his county.

"Hi. I'd like to welcome you to Crockett County," said the sheriff. "I'm Sheriff Brad Martin."

Chris wasn't too sure where this conversation was going. He just said, "Hi," letting it go at that.

"So we don't waste any time, we'll skip the part about 'new in town' and 'just passing through.'" He reached into his shirt pocket and found a toothpick. Placing it in the corner of his mouth, he chewed it awhile. He was watching Chris, apparently looking for a reaction. He continued, "I've spoken to two people. One was the sheriff of Val Verde County, and the other a resident of Terrell County." Chris noticed the cellphone on his waist. He wondered what the man had heard. The officer continued, "I trust the sheriff at his word. The resident is a relative. I don't know whether to shake your hand or arrest you." Chris started to breathe again.

"That venison smells great. I haven't eaten for a while. Do you mind some company?" said Brad.

Chris was elated at his good luck. "Yes, I'd be happy to have company."

The sheriff brought his horse closer and stripped off the saddle, picketing his horse opposite the fire from Kitty. Chris was getting warm next to the fire. He took off his coat.

The sheriff noticed the Colt and said, "I had one of those in Operation Iraqi Freedom. It saved my life more than once. Damn good choice for a handgun, Chris."

Chris was not surprised that the sheriff knew his name. He was curious about what else the sheriff knew about him.

Both men feasted on the venison, and Brad shared some canned fruit that he had in his saddlebag. After dinner, Brad produced a bottle of wine. It was from California. *Oh God!*, thought Chris. He chuckled, and Brad looked at him questioningly. Chris told him how Kitty came by his name. The man laughed heartily and was full of life. They killed the bottle of wine and sat back. They were enjoying life in the night air.

After a while, Brad cleared his throat and said, "Chris, I won't ask, and I'm sure that you won't tell. Off the record. Many people are very proud of what you have done. I can't speak for myself, officially. Unofficially, you are one hell of a man!"

"Brad, I'm sure you've spoken to Karen. My best guess is that she told you how I feel about all this. I'm from Colorado, and I wasn't raised to expect what went on in the last few months. I'm a geologist, not a cowboy or a gun fighter. I've only done what I felt I needed to do to survive."

Brad nodded his head in agreement. He said, "Have you ever seen any of the John Wayne movies?" Chris nodded his head. "Do you remember the line, 'A man's got to do what a man's got to do'? It sounds corny now, but that simple wisdom has kept many of us going when others would quit. We don't have food lines out here. Every man, woman, and child has had to learn to stand on their own two feet. Pride is what they have, and it keeps the community solid. There's no hiding among others here, like in the big city where everyone is a stranger. The world sees you as you are."

The men soon pulled their bedrolls over themselves and fell asleep. The embers of the fire glowed in the night air. The moon rising in the east stirred a coyote to call out to its pack.

Chapter Seventeen
The Only Thing to Do

Chris heard the distant whinny first. He nudged Brad with his foot. Brad rolled over and whispered, "Yeah, I heard it." Both men got up. Each grabbed his rifle and saddle. Together they fetched their horses and retreated up the tributary.

There was enough moonlight to see where they were going and they both silently wondered if they could be seen as easily. They led their horses back around a smaller hill. Leaving them there, they climbed up a hill and waited for the approaching rider or riders. Brad was the first to see the riders. He heard them as their horses' hooves clopped over the asphalt road. There were three of them. They spread out after the road and approached the campfire from three directions. Brad noticed that and whispered to Chris that they weren't there to socialize. Chris noticed Brad's rifle was also a Model 94. *Damn good choice*, he thought.

Both men brought their rifles to bear. Brad told Chris to take the one on the left, and he would take the one on the right. The one in the center was fair game after that. Small clouds were intermittently obscuring the face of the moon. At times, it was hard to see the men. They watched intently, keeping track of them. The men had pistols in their hands. This eliminated the socializing question.

When they were within range, Brad whispered for Chris to fire when he did. He kept his front sight on his man. A moment later, Brad fired. Chris's report was a millisecond later. Two men fell, and neither Chris nor Brad got a clear shot at the center man. He disappeared.

Chris and Brad looked for the man, neither one wanting to move and give their position away. They waited.

A falling stone made a noise to their left; their heads turned in unison toward the noise. It was the oldest con in the world, and they fell for it. The third man was coming up the hill in front of them. All three men fired in the dark. Shots went wild, and some of them connected. The third man was down and moaning. Brad had been hit. He couldn't move, and Chris asked him where he'd been hit. Brad told him it was at the top of his shoulder. He couldn't move his left arm. Chris asked him if he could hold on for a while. Brad hissed through his teeth, "Yes."

Chris slid down the hill, searching for the wounded man. He found him trying to crawl away. He stiffly walked toward the man, Colt in his hand. As he approached the man, he raised the autoloader until it was level with the man's head. The man stopped crawling and rolled over to face Chris. When he started to soundlessly plead for his life, Chris pulled the trigger. The top of the man's head erupted in a black spray in the moonlight. Chris made his way back to Brad. Both men looked at each other. Nothing needed to be said.

Chris helped Brad down to their campfire and made him as comfortable as possible. He applied a makeshift pressure bandage to the wound and ran up the creek to get the horses and equipment. When he came back, Brad asked him to take his cellphone up one of the hills and call his office for help. Chris asked which number he should call. Brad told him how to scroll down to the directory entry labeled "Dispatch" and then hit "send." Chris asked Brad how anyone would know where they were. Brad told him the cellphone had GPS, and they would pick it up. Chris was off in the night to make a telephone call.

When Chris got back to Brad, he was unconscious, and his breathing was regular. Chris was sure there was quite a bit of blood loss. He lifted Brad's coat up over the wounded shoulder and cut open his shirt, looking for the wound. With the campfire burning brighter, he spotted it. The bullet had entered the top shoulder muscle next to the neck and exited under the shoulder blade. It was a small exit wound, so he assumed it must have been a solid jacketed bullet. Chris knew there'd be a lot of blood vessels and connective tissue between the ribs and shoulder blade. He had to stop the blood flow. He applied another pressure bandage to the exit wound and applied pressure with one hand to the entrance wound. He grabbed Brad's wrist and took a quick look at his watch. Three o'clock in the morning, two and a half hours to sunrise. Son of a bitch, he hoped they both would make it. He placed his other hand back on the entrance wound and squeezed.

Chris held that position until sunrise. He was dozing off when he heard the sound of an approaching helicopter. He checked Brad, and he was still breathing easily with just an occasional catch. His temperature was still warm, and by feeling his neck with his chin, he felt a normal pulse that was still strong. The helicopter spotted them and was settling into the grass. Brad was roused awake by the noise. He said something, and Chris moved his ear closer to Brad's mouth. Chris slipped the cellphone into Brad's pocket.

The paramedics ran up to them with a stretcher. Chris stepped aside and let them do their job. The sheriff raised his hand to Chris just before they slid him into the helicopter. The helicopter roared off up the canyon to the north. Chris hoped Brad would make it. He was a good, strong man. Chris rounded up the four horses, stripped the tack from three, and let them go. The fourth, he took the bridle off and tied it to the saddle horn, slipping the rifle into the scabbard. He gave the horse a resounding whack on the rear and sent it on its way. He gathered up the firearms from the three men and placed them in a pile that he would burn when he left. Right now, he needed sleep. He curled up in the shade of a hill.

Sheffield was a small town that did not pique his interest. He preferred to keep his distance. There was still daylight, so he kept on the trail to Iraan. Chris didn't know what to expect. When he came around a hill, he saw a sign. It was hand painted and said: Ain't No Terrorists Here. Chris laughed and walked Kitty toward the town. This time Kitty led him to the airport on the southeast side of town, where he munched on some grass. Looking around, Chris saw the helicopter that picked up Brad. He hoped he was doing well. He didn't see the yellow biplane parked out of sight between two hangers. It was as good a time as any for a short nap.

It didn't last very long. Kitty was nudging him to get up. He got up and walked beside Kitty into town. He learned quite a bit while leading Kitty around. The town was founded in 1926 after the discovery of oil. There was a contest, with a prize of one city lot. The winner was an entry naming the town after the owners of the nearby ranch where oil was discovered. Ira and Ann Yates. Chris quickly learned that the proper pronunciation was "Ira-Ann."

The town had seen its boom and bust cycles. It looked to be in good shape now. There were over 1,300 folks living there. When Chris was passing by a park, he saw a comic character from long before his youth. He walked closer and saw it was Alley Oop. The town was the birthplace of the cartoon's creator, Vincent T. Hamlin. His cartoon made its debut in 1932. Walking out of the park, he saw quite a few "road apples" along the street. Someone had started installing hitching rails. Some of the more affluent folk used the old "jockey holding a ring" model. Originally, the short jockey had a black face. The sixties changed that thinking, and the old black-faced jockeys started to sport white faces. Now, they all had dark brown faces and sinister looking eyebrows. One comedian had placed a turban on his jockey.

He walked farther toward the edge of town and saw an oil production facility. He watched a caravan of tankers leave. There were armored personnel carriers leading, and others following the group. A tanker was in the process of being filled, while another crew applied a plastic sign designating the truck as belonging to the US Army. Chris could smell the diesel fuel from where he was. He walked back around the corner toward the center of town. He was starting to feel the need for some friendly human contact. Kitty couldn't speak English—or anything else for that matter.

There was a nice-looking restaurant and bar on a corner with a brand-new hitching post. Country and Western music was playing softly in the background. There were quite a few good-looking horses tied at the post. It was becoming very obvious that these Texans had good taste when it came to women and horses. Depending on whom you talked to, it could be the other way around. Chris tied Kitty to the post and walked into the bar.

The exterior belied the interior. It was more than a roadside place. The bar was a showplace for the town. They had framed pictures of famous, and some not so famous, residents of the town. The entire seventy plus years of its existence was on display. He sat down. When the waiter walked over to his table, he ordered a Coke and a club sandwich.

While he was eating, a man in an orange jumpsuit walked over and asked him if he was the man that was down south along the Pecos with the sheriff. Chris nodded yes with his mouth full. The man excused himself and went back to the bar. A short time later, everyone that was at the bar was around Chris's table. People he had never seen tried to thank him. Everyone wanted to shake his hand. He was starting to feel like a politician.

He quickly learned that the whole community loved and respected their sheriff, Brad. They wanted to hear his version of the story, but Chris deferred. He said that since he was getting close to being as famous as Pecos Bill, he would let the story ride as it was. He did inquire about Brad and was told that his effort to stop the blood flow had saved Brad's life. There was a need for surgery. Brad had his arm in a sling and would be released in a week or two. Slowly, they went back to the bar and left him in peace.

When he was finished eating, he stepped outside. It was getting close to sunset, and he needed a place to sleep for the night. He got up on Kitty and walked down the street. As he passed the park, he paused to look at Alley Oop. A quiet voice asked from beneath a shadowed shade tree, "Are you just going to sit on that horse, cowboy?" Son of a bitch, it was Karen!

Chris was off Kitty and in Karen's arms. They acted like long-lost friends. "I was worried that you wouldn't get out of that valley. I heard what happened to you and my uncle. I almost died. I'm so happy you're all right. I thought I'd never see you again." She was breathless and crying.

Chris framed her face with his hands and gently kissed her. "Karen, how can we get to Ozona to see your uncle?"

"We could ride your horse." Chris sighed at that suggestion. "Or, we could take my airplane in the morning," smiled Karen with a big grin.

That night, they slept at her cousin's house. It was a long night for both of them. There were still more well-wishers showing up at the house after they had heard Chris was spending the night. It didn't take long for news to get around this town. The original plan was the proper one. The two of them would sleep in separate bedrooms.

When the house settled down and everyone was in bed, Chris thought he heard a floorboard creak somewhere in the house, and a short while later, he felt Karen's warm thighs and breasts against his back. He reached around behind him and felt her very firm, round behind. Much later, her gasping moan, even with her face buried between his neck and pillow, was a bit too loud.

The morning promised a beautiful day for flying. The air was clear and the sky a beautiful pale blue. After breakfast at Karen's cousin's house, they headed to the airport. Chris was surprised when he saw where the airplane was parked. He should have seen it when he was crossing the field with Kitty. He leaned against the wing while Karen was doing the pre-flight on the airplane. A thought crossed his mind about gas. He asked her how she managed to get gas. She told him her uncle was considered essential and had an unlimited supply of gas. He considered his niece essential, as he did her airplane. As she continued through her pre-flight, she released the tie-down ropes.

They got in the airplane, Karen in the rear seat, and Chris in the front. Chris was glad it worked out that way. As much as he had flown, he still felt airsick in the backseat of a tandem airplane. His macho pilot image needed to be maintained. He wouldn't share that with Karen. They serpentine taxied out to the run-up area. After her engine run-up and control check, Karen used Unicom to broadcast in the blind that she was taking off from this field.

Karen gradually increased power and applied some right rudder to counteract the gyroscopic effect as the tail came off the ground. When she had sufficient airspeed, she applied backpressure to the stick, and the airplane gracefully climbed into the sky. She turned east, heading toward Ozona. They climbed to 5,000 feet, which was roughly 2,000 feet above the ground. When she had the airplane trimmed out for level flight, she asked Chris if he would like to fly. Chris smiled and nodded.

He shook the stick to let her know he had it. He knew she would already have her feet and hands off the controls. Chris lowered the nose of the airplane and let the airspeed build up. He increased backpressure to the stick, pulling the nose up in a graceful arc. At the top of the arc, he reduced the power and continued the arc toward the ground. Close to the bottom of the arc, he started to reapply power and came out at the same altitude and heading that he started. He could hear Karen applauding him in the backseat. He flew straight for a while, letting the adrenaline rush ease. He dropped the nose a bit and started a bank. Using the elevator and rudder, he did a barrel roll. He could hear Karen breathing heavier on the intercom. He climbed up a thousand feet higher. Pulling the nose straight up, he waited for the airspeed to fall and ruddered the big yellow airplane over on its wing into a graceful hammerhead stall.

He let the airplane dive in a series of spirals. He was amusing himself with this aerial ballet. Smiling, he applied forward pressure and opposite rudder to stop the spin. The airplane started flying again, but he held it back from rising too fast and applied throttle. They were lower to the ground. He saw some deer in a clearing. Karen's breathing in the intercom sounded faster than it had before. Chris buzzed the deer, like all pilots would.

As they were getting closer to Ozona, karen called on Unicom, identifying the airplane and her intention. She chose a straight-in approach since she hadn't heard any other traffic in the pattern. Her voice sounded deeper and huskier. Karen asked Chris if he wanted to land it. He nodded again. Chris had the field in sight and corrected for the runway. He reduced power and rolled the trim wheel back to a slightly nose-up attitude. He kept the end of the runway centered in the bottom of the windscreen. He spotted the VASI lights next to the approach end of the runway and kept the red over the white all the way to the end of his approach. Over the numbers, he had the power off and the ship steady. He let the airspeed bleed off by holding the nose just above the horizon. As the speed bled off and he was coming out of ground effect, he raised the nose just a bit more and let it settle. He heard the tires whisper as they contacted the asphalt. He pulled the stick all the way back, making sure the tail wheel steering locked. They taxied over to the transient parking.

Karen did the shutdown procedure from her seat. They took off their harnesses and seat safety belts and climbed out of the airplane. Chris stepped onto the wing to get off. Karen stood on her seat and jumped over the side. Chris caught her, and they laughed like two kids. They stopped laughing and looked in each other's eyes. She was all over Chris. Her wild passion was visible by the look on her face. He had never seen her like this. She wanted to find a place; any place would do. The nearby hanger was close enough, where they could be alone for just "a little while longer."

Chris smiled to himself. *That must've been some air-o-plane ride.*

They walked to the hospital and found Karen's uncle. He was reclining in a hospital bed looking over some paperwork, probably from his office. When he looked up and saw his niece and Chris, his face softened. His shoulder was bandaged, and his arm was in a sling. He held out his arm, motioning Karen to come closer. When she did, they hugged each other. They caught up on the usual family gossip. When the conversation flagged, he asked his niece to walk across the street to the cafeteria and get them a few chocolate milkshakes. She looked at both men, keeping her thoughts to herself, and went out the door.

He looked at Chris. "While I've been in this hospital, I've gotten phone calls from many friends and relatives. The most interesting call that I received was from three cousins. Josh, Cy, and Dan. They had a lot to say." Chris stood there. He didn't know what to say.

Brad continued, "An interesting thing happened at this hospital. They stopped the bleeding. The EMTs had given me morphine, so I wasn't in much pain. The surgeon at this hospital was on vacation and couldn't be reached." Chris noticed the sheriff was carefully choosing his words and dragging the story out. "They needed a surgeon and an assistant. It took them awhile, but they found two in Alpine. The EMTs flew them back here to work on me. The surgeon and assistant stayed long enough to make sure I was stable. The surgical assistant seemed to know you. We had a very enlightening and long conversation."

Karen walked through the door with three shakes. The Sheriff changed the conversation. "Chris, I'm giving you an envelope to take with you to Colorado. Don't open it until you get there." Chris promised.

He took the envelope and put it in his back pocket. When the shakes were finished, they left the hospital.

"You really do like my uncle," said Karen.

"I'd trust him with my life," replied Chris.

Karen said, "That's interesting. He said the same thing about you."

They were soon in the air and headed toward Iraan. Karen suggested they go on a scenic tour along the Pecos. Chris said it was all right with him, so she cut across the hills and flew diagonally toward the Pecos. It looked like she was planning to intercept it south of Iraan. Chris looked out and below the airplane, watching the country pass by. The roar of the big radial engine was relaxing.

When they were over the river, she retarded the throttle, stood the airplane up on a wing tip, and gently slipped it into a slow spiral toward the ground. Closer to the ground, she returned the controls to neutral, added some throttle, and motored along the valley. They passed over the spot where Brad and Chris had their fight. Chris could still see the old campfire. The pile of guts was gone. He imagined a pack of coyotes lying under a bush, toothpicks sticking out of their mouths and very happy.

They passed another landing strip, and Karen did an impromptu touch and go. It was a three-point landing; she had timed it perfectly. Chris liked it and told her over the intercom. Chris noticed the spot where he ambushed the three men. He didn't see their bodies anywhere. Farther down the valley, Chris saw the three horses belonging to the dead men. They were patiently standing on the edge of a small tributary that fed the river. Karen spotted them at the same time. He didn't have to say anything. She pitched up and did a 180 turn and side-slipped it to a landing on the road.

When the biplane was shut down, they walked hand in hand toward the horses. It wasn't hard catching them. The lead horse had stepped through the loop of the rein. Together, they stripped off the tack, leaving it in a pile underneath a small tree. They turned the horses loose, none of them worse for wear. They trotted off a distance, stopped, looked back at the humans, and then walked off.

Karen and Chris stayed on the ground for a while, lying in the grass, head to head, next to the road. They talked about his coming trip back to Colorado. Karen asked him if was still going to follow the Pecos. He said he was going to follow the river up to New Mexico and then head north. She thought it a good choice and told him to the east, starting at the Pecos, was the Llano Estacado. The southwest corner started somewhere around Imperial, Texas. She explained a brief history of the area and told him it was pretty along the northwest corner. Karen rolled around into Chris's arms. They held each other for a long time. Chris could feel her quietly sobbing. He was starting to feel like the world's biggest asshole. Karen got herself together and tried to smile. In a bit, she shook her head and said, "Let's go flyin'!"

There were off and in the air in no time. Chris spotted the men he had left at the overpass. Either Karen didn't spot them or she decided to say nothing. They continued looking for lost horses but didn't see any. She did a low pass over her house, and when she pulled up, Chris saw the black and white dog bouncing around. Turning toward the northwest, she added power and started to climb.

There were small, puffy summer clouds at 10,000 feet. They climbed to meet them. They laughed together as she wove in and out of the clouds. Karen told Chris to watch behind them as she flew back and forth through a single cloud. She had disturbed it from the prop wash, and it soon took the shape of a giant doughnut. They both laughed at the sight.

She headed back to the northwest. She was clear of the clouds when they saw the end of the hill country. They both became quiet. Nothing was said on the way back to the airport at Iraan. The landing, taxiing, and shut down were mechanical. They quietly tied the biplane in its spot, and Chris waited while Karen put the control locks in place. It looked like rain, and she covered the engine cowl and the two cockpit openings. They walked silently back to town.

The rest of the afternoon was spent sitting in the park. Neither of them had much of an appetite to eat the hamburgers they bought. It was well after sunset when they walked back to her cousin's house. They quietly snuggled on the couch.

"Well, cowboy," Karen whispered. "I don't know if I can stand saying good-bye again."

"Let's not worry about tomorrow until then." Chris sighed. He was feeling weary from riding, driving, and constantly looking over his shoulder. He had to stop eventually. He had been too worn out from this trip, both emotionally and physically. He only had one more state to cross. They fell asleep in each other's arms.

Chris woke with a bolt. He looked around the room and saw he was alone. He caught the lingering fragrance of Karen's perfume. She was gone.

Chris packed up his things and went out to saddle Kitty. On the way, he remembered the envelope and put it safely away in the bottom of the backpack. With kitty packed, he saddled up and trotted out of town. Passing by the airport, he saw that Karen had left. He located the Pecos on the north side of town and followed it. He thought he heard an airplane and looked around. Seeing none, he hunched over his saddle and walked quietly along. He thought he heard it again and looked up to see it coming in low just over a hill. It was Karen! She waggled the wings as she passed overhead. Chris waved like a maniac. Then she was gone.

Chapter Eighteen
A Little Assistance

Chris took a renewed interest in his surroundings. He was more alert and less edgy. He noticed the short oil donkeys pumping endlessly. They looked like birds slowly dipping their heads. Up and down, up and down. They were everywhere. He was in the midst of a major oil field. He wondered how long the United States was going to depend on foreign oil. Perhaps the cutting of the gasoline use by civilians would encourage someone, or a corporation, to invent a better engine. He had heard much about the new hydrogen engines. No one seemed willing to go beyond a promise.

He always thought it would be cool to fill a car with water. He imagined a bunch of guys at a beer party recycling the beer that they had swilled. Most corporations, it seemed, would suck as much oil from the ground as they could before their commodity was replaced by water. There seemed to be a parallel between them and the old telephone company. A better idea and more choices put most of them out of business. Other companies suffered the same fate but on a lesser scale. There would always be a demand for diesel fuel, oil, and grease. The truckers, airlines, and military would see to that. The everyday auto would be the one to go. The insidious little things were everywhere on the planet. As long as they were here, there would always be a demand for more gas. Chris thought of a bumper sticker for Kitty's rear end: Kill the Automobile. Grow Grass.

Then he thought of the Middle East. Their economy was much like that of the States—only worse, the closer you looked. The difference between their "haves" and "have not's" was even more stark. The rest of the world had profited immensely from the Industrial Age and beyond. They sat there in what once was the Cradle of Civilization and wondered what happened. The world had passed them by. Not by choice. Corrupt, self-serving leaders had not allowed them to advance. Now, they felt humiliated and thought the rest of the world was looking down on them. Justification for what they did came in all shapes and sizes.

Then it hit Chris right between the eyes. They created law. The Law of Hammurabi! Chris thought he had it now. They grew up among corrupt leaders, and those societies saw that as the norm. Thus, they felt they could corrupt the rule of law via the religion they created, and the rest of the civilized world had to follow.

It was getting late, and storm clouds were closing in from the west. He needed a place to camp out of the coming weather. He was between Pecos and Barstow and just north of Interstate 20. He saw a small abandoned airfield and a steel hangar. He headed that way. The hangar doors were open and the interior deserted except for the resident pigeons and starlings. As isolated as it was, it was as good as any, he thought, as a place to stay the night.

He led Kitty around a corner of the corrugated building, and a cool gust of wind pushed them on their way. Kitty was getting nervous. Chris decided to put the halter on him and tie the end of the lead. He unsaddled Kitty and attempted to wipe the dust off him. They both heard thunder in the distance. He acknowledged it by turning his head toward the partially opened hanger doors. Kitty let it be known by flaring his nostrils and snorting. Chris heard sand hitting the side of the hangar. A flash of lightning lit up the inside of the building. They both flinched. Thunder echoed inside the building, vibrating it. Kitty sidestepped into Chris. Chris quickly took off his shirt and put it over Kitty's eyes, pulling the ends through the halter to hold it in place. This quieted Kitty somewhat, until the hail hit. Chris untied the lead and held onto it, so the near panicked horse wouldn't hurt himself throwing his head up. The sky had turned black as night. Chris watched the hail fall from the doors. They were the size of golf balls and sounded like hell when they hit the steel building.

The storm front quickly passed. The rain followed, falling continuously in sheets. The storm moved slowly east. Eventually, the downpour decreased to drizzle and finally to an occasional drop. Chris pulled the shirt off Kitty's eyes, and they both stood in the doorway watching the retreating storm. Kitty must've felt better. He shook, leaving a cloud of dust hanging over him. With the storm gone, Chris turned and led Kitty back to the corner of the hangar. He tied him there for the night. He pulled out his well-worn "bedroll" and put it along a wall. He lay there awhile, smelling the fresh ozone-laden air.

He would keep out of the Pecos basin the next few days. The fast-moving thunderstorm had caused flash floods along the river, and in many places, the banks had washed away. The river bank was too wet to ride Kitty. This wasn't the first thunderstorm he'd been through, but certainly the wildest. The storms of the South and Central Americas were heavier and lasted longer. Some had lasted for days. The plains storms were something else. It could best be described as the most amount of violence that you could cram in a small area. They weren't big like the other parts of America were used experiencing. These storms were fast-moving and scary.

He had worked his way north along Highway 285 and was traveling along a set of railroad tracks next to the Pecos River. At a small town, he bought some canned meat and candy. He decided it was a good time to stop. He put Kitty on the cooler east slope and sat on a small hill overlooking the river, railroad tracks, and highway. Occasionally, one of the fuel tankers would appear from down south and rumble by. It was nice to watch some semblance of civilization appear. The trucks were still labeled US Army, and he plainly saw the white GPS dome over the cab. He idly wondered why the armored personnel carriers were absent.

The sound of a vehicle woke him. Chris rolled over on his belly and watched as the driver went off the road, across the tracks, and took his time placing the vehicle for a fast departure. Five men got out of the large SUV and watched for traffic on the highway. They went back to the SUV, meeting the driver at the rear of the SUV, and each was given a weapon. Chris didn't like the look of this since they looked more civilian than military.

Chris slid back down the hill and got his rifle from the scabbard. He made his way back up the hill along an eroded culvert and observed the goings on. He saw two men with short tubes and recognized them as rocket launchers. The other four men split alongside the highway ditch and lay down out of sight. The men with the launchers took up positions to the north and south along the road, and they too hid in the ditch.

Before long, a loaded northbound tanker was cresting a hill. Chris saw the men crouch as the truck continued. The men were premature in their assault on the truck. They stepped out on the road too early.

The driver saw the men and shifted into reverse, backing down the road. The men had no choice but to run after the truck. They had over a quarter of a mile to get to the truck.

Chris thought he heard something behind him. He turned and saw two AH-64 Longbow Apache helicopters flying at full speed toward the truck. They wheeled in the air, behind the truck, and headed straight up the highway machine-gunning the three men. Two of the remaining three men, each with rocket launchers, fired on the helicopters and missed completely. One helicopter commander made short work of the two. They hovered alongside the highway and missed finding the sixth man.

Chris had long since slid down the dirt to the bottom of the culvert. He hoped to God that they didn't see him with their infrared equipment. They must have given the all clear to the driver. He started up the truck and continued north while the two helicopters loitered in the area. When the truck was out of sight, they headed back west toward Fort Bliss, sixty miles away. Chris waited until they were gone and then waited for the sixth man to move from the ditch. Then he finished the job for the army. Chris thought he had seen it all. This had to be one of the stupidest stunts he had ever seen. He slid another round into the tube magazine, replacing the spent around. He walked down to Kitty, who was happy in his world of grass and obviously used to the sound of gunfire, and rode north along the railroad tracks.

Chris had ridden around the east side of Roswell. The Pecos River ran through the Bitter Lake National Wildlife Refuge, which was a perfect place to be alone. He had run out of junk food and anything else to eat. Now he was seriously looking for something to eat. He staked Kitty among some trees. He hadn't tried still-hunting for years. He thought today was as good as any to try it. He found a nice place to sit, farther away from Kitty, among some trees. He waited for hours for deer, antelope, or anything edible to appear.

Just when he was about to give up, and mule deer stood up in the short grass. He was just inside rifle range for the .30/30. He slowly leveled the carbine at the deer. Just as he was squeezing the trigger, he heard a report from another rifle. The deer dropped back into the grass. Chris was not expecting anyone else to be around. He sat and watched slack-jawed as an Indian walked out of the trees fifty yards from him. The man walked down to the deer, checked it, and waved at Chris, signaling him to come down. Chris was in shock. He saw the Indian was carrying a .30/30, much like his. The Indian had made a shot that was from fifty yards farther than he would've taken.

"That was an excellent rifle shot," said Chris.

"Not bad for a white man. However, it was bad for an Indian. The shot was six inches lower than where I aimed," said the Indian.

"May I help?"

"If you help, you'll want some. Are you hungry, white man?" rumbled the Indian.

"Yes, I am."

"I imagine you are since you haven't eaten anything since Bentley Lake." Chris was surprised. It showed.

"Yes, I know you're hungry. I've been following you since the lake." The Indian smiled. "I'm on vacation. I had nothing to do, so I followed you. I need to keep up my Indian skills. I'm a bit out of practice, and you looked like the easiest thing to stalk out here."

Chris laughed. When he settled down, he asked the Indian his name. He said his name was Joe. Chris introduced himself. The two men stood around, joking about cowboys and Indians. They finally settled down and got to work on the deer. Chris thought that it was definitely bigger than the Texas whitetail.

The sun was just above the western mountains when the venison was ready. Joe had added some herbs, and Chris thought it smelled better than any deer he had in the past. The two men sat across the fire from each other and talked about what men talk about—the weather, politics, and current events around the world and the local news. Joe told Chris he managed a casino in Mescalero that the tribe owned.

"It's a tradition among Indians. We learned scalping from the white men in the past, when it wasn't a politically correct thing to do. And we'll continue to return the favor in the future, now that it's legal." He laughed so hard he had to leave the fire to take a leak.

Chris was well into telling Joe about himself and stopped.

"Why do you stop when you have just gotten to the good part?" Joe asked.

Chris explained that he wasn't proud of what he had done to get back home.

"Chris, listen to an old Indian for once. We all journey through life. What happens along the trail is what defines us as men. Some do nothing and become nothing. Others grow to become something. Tell me about your trail, my friend."

Chris told him about everything, including the money, since he felt Joe could be trusted. When he finished his story, Joe was quiet for a while. He searched around and found his cellphone. He called someone and spoke in a language Chris had never heard before. Joe hung up and looked at Chris without saying a word.

Joe said, "I called a cousin in Texas. He speaks Athabscan like I do, but it is a bitch to understand when he speaks. He has a west Texas twang, so he has to go slow enough for me to understand him. He belongs to the Lipan Apache tribe. You may have heard of them." Joe giggled. "I was making a joke, Chris," he deadpanned.

"He said you were in Texas, and they know about you. Some even saw you fight. Do you know what this means?" Chris looked clueless and shrugged his shoulders. Joe continued, "Some of those men were wanted by the tribe for crimes they committed against them. You are considered by the Apache to be a friend and a great warrior for what you did."

Chris sat there not quite understanding what Joe was telling him.

"No shit, Chris. My cousin said to thank you for getting the horses back. He was happy about the extra ones and the riding tack. He said not to worry about the old mare you shot. With the right seasoning, she tasted darn good. I'll have to give you his recipe." Chris rolled his eyes at Joe's humor. He quickly thought about it and wondered if he was serious about the recipe. Joe explained to Chris that he would call the tribal elders and let them know Chris was in the area.

The next day, Joe blindfolded Chris and led him to a secret location. The Apache were open to white people concerning their everyday lives and business. Nevertheless, Apache ceremonies were something else. They considered this part of their lives to be sacred and not privy to the whites. Chris was being led to a place away from the reservation. They would honor him on white man's land.

When the blindfold was taken off, Chris saw himself surrounded by nine Indians. Joe explained to Chris that they were the eight-member Tribal Council from the Mescalero Apache tribe and one representative from the Lipan Apache tribe. All the men, including Chris and Joe, sat in a circle. Joe listened as one of the men spoke in Athabscan. Joe explained to Chris that the elder speaking was recommending Chris to by honored by the tribes of the Apache. Other elders spoke. Joe said they were just adding their own thoughts to what the first elder had said. It was similar to the way white people seconded a motion at their meetings. The Indians just had more style, Joe added out the side of his mouth. White people lacked class and were boring.

When all the men were finished talking, their eyes turned to

Chris. Joe told Chris to stand up and walk over to the first elder that had spoken and sit down in front of him. Chris did as he was told. In front of the old elder, Chris looked in his eyes. He saw wisdom, strength, endurance, and gentleness. As the man spoke, Chris thought of Dan, Cy, Josh, and of course, the night with Brad. When the elder finished speaking, he presented Chris with four eagle feathers and an envelope. Chris thanked the man in English, since he didn't understand a word of Athabscan. The elder nodded and held out his hand. Chris grasped the man's hand with both of his. They sat there, looking into each other's eyes. Chris understood the meaning of this to the Apache. There was also a responsibility given to him.

The elder released Chris's hand and motioned to him to join Joe. All the elders, including Joe, joined in a prayer. Chris bowed his head as he would in any church. When they were finished, all the men stood and quietly dispersed. Without saying a word, they rode back to the west. Chris was curious; he asked Joe about the envelope.

"If an Indian sees those feathers, he will understand what they mean. A white man won't understand what they mean and may try to 'rat you out' to the Feds." Joe sighed. He knew the ways of the white man. He continued, "When an agent of the US Fish and Wildlife Service asks you about those feathers, you hand him the envelope. It will explain everything to him," Joe said, a bit sarcastically.

Joe started to laugh and said, "They also gave you a name."

Chris turned his head as if to ask a question.

Joe added, "It's 'One with Red Face.'" Chris shrugged his shoulders.

Joe pointed at Chris's face. "You've been without a hat too long. Your face is burned and peeling. When you take off your sunglasses, you look like a raccoon. Well, at least you won't get crow's feet and look like the elders. Not too good for a blonde, white man, Chris."

They stayed up late that night talking, while finishing the deer. The conversation turned to the life of Native Americans. Joe could not speak for all of the tribes in North America, so Chris asked him to tell about the history of the Apaches.

Joe began, "The word Apache comes from a Zuni word meaning enemy. There are six sub-tribes. We originally came from northwestern Canada and brought the Athabscan language with us. The Navajo came with us. Since then, we have gone our separate ways. They live in northwestern New Mexico, and we live here and to the south.

"We used to trade with the Pueblos and lived on the plains hunting buffalo. The Pueblos had pottery, corn, blankets, turquoise, and other things worth trading. Some of my tribe apparently did not like trading, so they took what they wanted. The Pueblos started to call my people 'Apachu'—the enemy. Apache guerrilla tactics came naturally, and we're good at it. We made the Pueblo tribes very nervous.

"The Spanish slave traders would capture my people and use them as slaves in the silver mines in northern Mexico. This was our opportunity to use our talents by raiding Spanish settlements for cattle, horses, guns, or sometimes people. Our warriors could run fifty miles nonstop. One American general, in the 1800s, called us the tigers of the human species. We just wanted to be left alone with our families. When push came to shove, we always tried to win.

"The whites have social, economic, and political units based on a male inherited leadership. Ours is the opposite, based on our mothers. The members of our tribe cannot marry within our own clan. So a man, when he marries, his obligations go to his mother-in-law.

"We moved freely like the geese, south in the winter and north in the summer. Our family groups followed the food supply. We did as we pleased. We owned nothing and yet everything. Our women are pure, and our leaders keep their promises. Today we have our own land and live alongside white society. I run a casino along with my brothers. We're doing well."

Chris thought about this well into the night. He woke up the next morning and hadn't heard Joe leave; his Indian skills were improving. He sat awhile, watching the sunrise in the eastern sky. He imagined how Pat or Karen had felt when he left. Quietly, he packed up his things and started north along the now dry Pecos River.

Chris saw he was gaining elevation the farther north he went in the plains. The river valley was continuing northwest toward the mountains. He would have to travel northeast to the flatter plains. He'd follow the Pecos up to Sumner Lake, just outside of Santa Rosa, and head northeast to the Columbia and then the Canadian River.

Chapter Nineteen
Meeting of the Minds

As he rode closer to Interstate 40, he saw the rising, sheer cliffs of the Mescalero Escarpment. Karen had spoken about these. He had been watching this formation rise along the eastside of the Pecos since he left Girvin, Texas. He was traveling along the western border of the Llano Estacado. He stopped Kitty at a roadside park to read about the area. To the east and south was high, dry desert that encompassed over 32,000 square miles, larger than New England. In the late Mesozoic Age, about 70,000,000 years ago, the uplift of the Rocky Mountains caused this area to lift and drain the inland sea from the land. The calcium carbonate carried from the mountains settled into the soil, creating the hard cap rock. The common name was caliche. The name, Llano Estacado translated into Staked Plain. The name originated from piles of stones and bones. The use of markers was common among the Indians, early explorers, and settlers. The vast area looked the same in every direction. Thus, the name was entirely plausible. Since that time, the southern area had grown to be a major oil production source. The water produced by the Ogallala Aquifer, which extended along the High Plains of the Rocky Mountains to the Llano Estacado, was rapidly being depleted and considered a finite resource. The plain, isolated by the Pecos and Canadian Rivers, could not be recharged by the larger aquifer to the north. Farmers still pumped water from the aquifer and grew cotton, sorghum, wheat, corn, melons, and vegetables. It seemed highly productive, and Chris was glad he stayed along the river.

He stopped at Conchas Dam. North of the reservoir, he found

a place to camp for the night. He unsaddled Kitty and led him down to one of the beaches. The horse looked nervous. With some encouragement, Kitty followed Chris into the deeper water. Chris got Kitty as wet as he could. The clear water was soon muddy. Kitty tried to shake off the water a couple of times, but Chris kept splashing water up on his back. He led the horse out of the water and back up to his campsite where he picketed him next to some grass. The bay gelding took the opportunity to roll himself dry in the grass.

Chris walked down to the water, away from where he had bathed the horse. Looking around, he found a quiet spot next to some large rocks and undressed, putting the Colt under his shirt. He waded into the cool water and sat on a submerged rock. It brought back memories of Karen. He sat there while thinking of her. The mood struck him to go for a swim. He paddled around and enjoyed himself. He was enjoying the opportunity to stretch; he had been in the saddle for months. Joe was right about his sunburn; the water stung his face. He paddled back to shore and sat on the same rock.

His thoughts turned to the remainder of his trip. He had about a third of New Mexico and half of Colorado left to travel. He wondered what he would say to Marcie. He hoped she and her father had built a nice cabin. He thought about what city life would be like closer to Denver. He wanted to avoid Denver, the Springs, and Pueblo as much as he could. Through the years, the major cities along the Front Range had run together much like one continuous suburban neighborhood. He thought it best to stay out on the eastern plains and then cut back to the west along a road through Franktown and up to the mountains. He felt better.

"Cowboy," said the whisper.

Chris looked around for the source of the voice.

"Cowboy," repeated the whisper.

Now Chris was sure he was losing his mind. "Who's there?" he demanded.

"Philipé Bouchét, and you are a very, very bad boy. Don't turn around."

"Huh?" Chris vaguely remembered the voice from the Central American restaurant. He would stall until he located this guy.

"The guy whose car and airplane you stole, you dumb mother fucker."

"I have a horse. No car. And, do I look like I'm flying an airplane? What do you want? I've better things to do than sit here in my birthday suit." Chris felt vulnerable being naked. He was glad he had his gun under the shirt. He just needed to know where Philipé was hiding.

"You know damn well what I'm talking about."

"Okay, Phil, refresh my memory." Chris knew that when people talk, they are less focused on violence. The trick was to keep him distracted long enough …

Since you're obviously a very slow cowboy, I'll speak slowly so you can understand."

"Okay, Phil." Chris let the words trickle from his mouth.

"The name is Sergei Maliqi. My parents immigrated to this country when we were three years old, fuck head!"

Chris knew he was getting to him. "Okay, Philly, Sergei, whatever you say." He wondered about the twin and asked, "Did your brother like his airplane ride?"

From an outcropping stepped another version of Phil or Sergei or whoever. This one had to be related, and he was missing the earlobe on the opposite ear from his brother. "I'm glad you asked about my brother Pavel. My name is Grigori."

Philipé, a.k.a. Pavel, picked up the conversation. "I know this is too much for your small American brain, so I will spell it out in detail before we kill you." He looked for a place to sit and lit a cigarette. It was obvious the story was going to take awhile since he had a lot of time to think about it.

"When you stole my Chrysler, that was the first insult. I had to find you to repay you for that insult. As time went by, I grew to hate you more. Driving up the Pan-American Highway was easy since it is the only highway going north to America. On the way, I met Nick and his lovely friend Sarita. As luck would have it, the money you stole from him was in an attaché case with a GPS beacon. Isn't technology wonderful? I still can't figure out how you managed to steal my airplane too."

Chris offered sarcastically, "Some of us are lucky?"

"Well, smart boy, that had a GPS in it too. The only problem we had was when you took that money out of the case and went cowboy on us." Sergei laughed at his attempt at humor. Grigori joined in with his nasal laugh. "But I'm getting ahead of myself."

The Maliqi brother waited while he regained his thoughts. Grigori seemed to be the mental midget of the twosome and started to fidget. Chris had a quick thought about his brother, Pavel, and how he was one to stay on target right up to the end. Apparently multitasking was not something that ran in the family gene pool. A smile crept across his face.

Sergei droned on, "We made a deal with La Palmeda to finance our operation. Oh, so now you look interested, eh?"

Chris was caught by surprise at the information, and Sergei caught his look. "Well, cowboy, I'll tell you before we kill you. Nick was a financier of various business, ahhh, opportunities. Smuggling people into the US has been very profitable. Usually the border people look for ways that have been used in the past. We change to what does work, and when that gets discovered, we go back to the old way for a while. NAFTA, you know the North American Free Trade deal that your President Clinton passed? That has been wonderful. Texas and Arizona have been building highways for the trucks. We have found many ways to get through Customs and the vehicle checks. It is almost as if the US and Mexico have added a freeway to South America. When you crossed at McAllen, Texas, do you remember the group that went across the river before you?"

Chris nodded.

"When the ICE people caught them and put them in their truck, no one was interested in looking for anyone else. You just walked over into Texas. That is the way the Americans are that work for the US government. A quick slam dunk and off to another coffee break. They don't ever look behind themselves. Over in the Big Bend area of Texas, the drug gangs are opening up the old routes into the US. No feds around there. Do you know why? Too hard, and they figure it won't make the news. The local sheriff hasn't enough deputies and no government help. Everyone seems to know this except the Americans. Cowboy, your country is going back to the Mexicans. And I'm going to get rich, and you will get dead."

Chris had been very slowly creeping toward his shirt and was now only a few feet from it. He needed a bit more time. "Sergei, what is the story about your ears?"

Sergei rolled his eyes and said, "Our father was a pig farmer in the old country. When we three were born, we looked exactly alike. Our father, being a practical man, left my ears alone since I was the first born, and then he removed the opposite ear lobes on my two brothers. I often wondered what he would have done if there were four of us. Okay, now let's get down to business. Where is the money?"

Just a little closer. "Sergei," Chris called, "why do you speak of Nick in the past tense?"

"He killed himself in the car wreck when he was chasing you. He whacked his head is what Sarita told us."

Almost to the gun. "What was that that you called Nick? La Palma? La whatto?"

"La Palmeda. Don't you hear too good? He likes to whack people in the back of their heads to get them to agree with him. Did you ever see the size of his hands? They scared me to death! Okay, now we get to business. Enough with all this talk."

Sergei called his brother, "Grigori! Do you want to take the first shot for Pavel?" Chris threw himself at the flat rock and grabbed for the shirt and gun. Ripping the shirt-draped gun free, he took aim at Sergei and took him midway through his kidneys as he turned in surprise. Grigori had more spunk than Chris expected. He flattened himself against the rocks and tried to get a clear shot at Chris. Ducking low in the water, Chris let loose with six quick shots, driving the man to the edge of the rocks, trying to get away from the flying lead and stone. The seventh shot found its mark, and he fell in a heap.

Chris stood in the water waiting for what else may come. He looked at his 1911 and saw that the slide was locked back. It was as empty as a politician's promise.

He stepped out of the water and up the knoll to reload. When he bent down to get a new magazine, he heard a car start up in the parking lot and drive slowly away. The Mercedes?

Chapter Twenty
Old Americans

Riding through the Kiowa National Grassland, he was amazed at the number of jackrabbits. Along a fence line, he saw a family of Harris hawks sitting on the posts. He knew they were happy, even if the jackrabbits and packrats were not. Ahead, to the north, he saw the Capulin Volcano National Monument. As he rode nearer the volcanoes, he saw chunks of lava scattered across the flat landscape. Soon he had to make a choice, to either go around the mountains east of Raton, or go over Raton Pass. He was far enough east; he'd go around the pass. He still didn't like the idea of being too close to any obvious travel route. There may not be many vehicles traveling the road, but there would be many opportunities for unobserved criminality within the confines of the pass. He had always preferred the openness and security of the plains. He could see someone from a great distance away, and he felt safer because of this. Sergei and his brother had proven that point.

Ahead of him was the black Mercedes off to the side of the road. As he rode closer, he could see the driver's door was ajar. No one was inside. He swung wide of the car and waited. Soon Sarita appeared walking toward the car. She looked at Chris and smiled. "Well, my handsome American man, you have traveled quite far and have been very lucky or talented in escaping from the Maliqi triplets." She caught Chris's questioning look and answered, "There are no places for women out here. You men can do things by just pulling it out, but not women—or at least refined women."

Chris nodded his head and changed the subject. "When I left you, Nick was unhurt and only dazed. Did you do something?"

"Yes."

"What?"

"I ended a relationship and regained my self-respect."

"What's the story with those brothers?"

"They were merely a means to an end."

"I was now independently wealthy since Nick left everything to me, and I could do whatever I wanted. They came along, and I decided to join in the chase to see how it ended. Chris, I was hoping you would get away from those three all along."

"So why are you here? Now?"

"The obvious answer is that I needed to see a plumber about a leak." They both laughed at that. "The other answer was that I wanted to see you one last time." She walked closer to Chris, still looking like the most beautiful woman he'd ever seen. She was close enough for him to smell her perfume. They embraced tightly, feeling in each other a passion that needed to stay under control, each with their mouths to the other's ear, waiting for an unspoken word. They stood that way listening to the other's breathing.

Perhaps the words never came or their patience ended, for they soon parted wordlessly, each to go their separate way. Sarita walked slowly to the Mercedes and drove off to her future, and Chris mounted Kitty and trotted northward.

Kitty was blowing and snorting. Chris looked around and saw nothing. Kitty continued to dance and not walk forward. Then it hit Chris! He quickly swung Kitty around and away from the area. How stupid could he be? The prairie rattlesnakes were starting to look for dens. Kitty had seen one and was not about to step on or near it. Beside the occasional rogue prairie dog hole, dug away from the main colony, these snakes were hard to see from a saddle. They were usually two to three feet long when young, but he had heard about the five-footers. They could be found lying in the sun warming their cold-blooded bodies in the early morning. During the heat of the day, the snake would seek shade either in a cool prairie dog hole, the shade of a tree, a bush, or even the overhang of a rock. Now, they were on the move, and he'd have to be more alert. He rubbed Kitty on the neck and told him he was okay. Kitty blew softly.

Southern Colorado was once part of Mexico. Many of the large ranches had land grants from the king of Spain. This was old country with much history. Chris had been in the southwest for months during this trip. He had come to love the people and their way of life. The pressures the white people had to endure in the northern cities and elsewhere didn't exist here. These people didn't have to account to someone for every moment of their time. These Hispanics took life as it came. The food was marvelous, and the beer was better than most.

Riding over a hill, he saw a wagon with a broken or slipped rear wheel. Chris rode over to the wagon and saw an old man standing next to the wagon, swearing in Spanish. He was so vehement in his cussing that he hadn't heard Chris's approach. Chris sat on Kitty and waited. When the man's rage subsided, he spit in the dirt and walked around the wagon for his canteen. He spotted Chris, who was smiling. The man stopped in his tracks and mumbled something. He went back to his canteen.

Chris attempted to ask the man if he needed help. It was obvious the old man couldn't understand English, and Chris knew nothing in Spanish. The two men were reduced to point-and-grunt dialogue. Chris understood the nut had come off the axle. The old man had a new nut but couldn't lift the wagon. Chris helped move the freight to the front of the wagon. Getting under the wagon, he raised it with his back while the old man slipped the wheel back on the axle. The old man was elated. He got his canteen and handed it to Chris. Chris deferred. The old man insisted. Chris tried it. Tequila! With lime!

Chris asked, or rather pointed and grunted, where the man was heading. He pointed north up the road. Chris asked if he could ride alongside him. The old man nodded his head yes, accentuating it with "*Si.*"

Chris rode alongside the wagon. The man coiled the leads around the hand brake handle and climbed over the seatback into the back of the wagon. He looked through some boxes and found another bottle of tequila. He got back in his seat, grabbed the leads, holding the bottle up for Chris to see, smiling. Chris nodded his head yes, and they shared the bottle.

The old man held up his hand, pointing to something in the distance. Chris understood that it must be the old man's house. Chris saw some saddle horses under a tree, across the road, without any riders. The old man noticed it but said nothing. They both heard a shot coming from the direction of the house. The two men looked at each other. The old man's face changed to one of horror. Chris instinctively spurred his horse toward the house.

He heard more gunfire coming from the trees east of the house. An arroyo ran from the road to the back of the house. He turned Kitty down it, riding as quietly as he could. When he thought he was behind the barn, he stopped Kitty and got off. He climbed up the crumbling side of the arroyo. As he made it to the edge, a chunk of crumbling earth broke off. He was lucky to have been standing on a solid piece of ground. He let the huge piece fall beside him. Kitty sidestepped it. He walked over to a few promising weeds. Chris slid back down the bank and looked for a cattle path. He found one. Pulling his auto loader from the shoulder holster, he quietly worked his way up the path.

At the top, he looked over the edge. Two men were behind the barn and another behind the trees. Looking toward the road, the old man was smart enough to stay back with the wagon. The trees where the men were hiding were closer to the arroyo. Chris went down the cattle path and back up the arroyo to the trees. Shit! No path up! He found another path toward the trees. He eased up the path, taking a quick look over the edge. He saw a man looking toward the house. He still wasn't aware of Chris's presence. He slid the .45 over the edge and took careful aim with two hands. Chris was concentrating on keeping the front sight on the back of the man's head. He must have sensed it and turned. The 230-grain hollow-point struck the cheek, removing part of his face. Chris ducked back down, knowing the others had heard the shot.

He ran back down the arroyo to a spot behind the barn. When he looked over the edge, they were waiting for him. Two slugs barely missed his face. Chris ducked back down into the arroyo, wiping the dirt from his eyes, and moved back to the west where there was a bend in the arroyo. He ran up to the edge and did not see the men. He ran toward the barn, making it to the wall. He knew standing next to the barn was deadly, so he quickly stepped away from the barn, about twenty feet, holding the auto-pistol in front of him, aiming chest high. He sidestepped to his right, watching the corner of the barn. Police referred to this as "cutting the pie." The odds were that he would see the other man before he was seen, if they were against the side of the barn. Chris sidestepped again. He saw nothing.

A few more steps to the right and he saw the muzzle of a rifle. He slowly inched his way to the right. The shoulder appeared. He was ready. Just a little more. The man moved a bit, and Chris saw the back of his ear. Chris stood there, his front sight on the man's ear, waiting. The man's patience failed him, and he was quickly rewarded with the back of his skull blown out.

Chris ran back to the barn before the other man could react. He ran around the corner and back around the barn. He waited, kneeling, knees wide apart, in the dirt. The other man came around the barn, his rifle held waist high. He saw Chris and fired more from reflex than fear. The shot went over Chris's head. Before he could lever in another round, Chris had three in his solar plexus.

Chris automatically reached for another magazine on his right side, replacing the partially spent magazine. He walked around the barn and saw no one. He went toward the front of the house, more cautiously, and saw the face of an old woman looking at him through the window. Chris turned to wave the old man in. He was already on his way.

The old man walked toward the house. His wife came out of the house. They saved the running part until they were within twenty feet of each other. All the while, they spoke so fast that if they spoke English, Chris still would not have understood them. They pointed at Chris, they pointed at the barn, they pointed at the trees, they pointed at the house, and they pointed back to Chris. Interspersed in their conversation were many "bang-bangs."

When they finally settled down, the old man motioned Chris to follow him. The old man led his horse and wagon to the dead men one at a time. They loaded the bodies into the back of the wagon. With that done, he drove the wagon across the road to another arroyo. He looked along the arroyo for a loose spot. He gestured for Chris to wait and went to the back of the wagon. He came back and signaled Chris to help him throw the three bodies into an eroded section.

With that done, he led the horse away from the arroyo. He took a stick of dynamite from his back pocket. Chris hadn't seen one of those since school. The old man found a crack next to the arroyo and forced the stick of dynamite into it. He lit the fuse and waved at Chris to follow him. They retreated to the wagon, and turned, waiting. It wasn't as loud as Chris would have expected. It was more like a dull boom. The old man went back to the arroyo, looked down, and took a gulp from his bottle. From where Chris was standing, it looked the old man was urinating into the arroyo. With a look of finality, he turned and walked toward the wagon.

That night, Chris was served the best Mexican dinner he had ever had, and he slept in a real bed, which he hadn't done since he left Iraan. He lay there awhile, thinking about Texas. Along with other things, that weighed on his mind.

When Chris awoke, he was amazed at what greeted him. His boots were polished, and Kitty had been curried, along with his mane and tail trimmed. Chris saw the eagle feathers, tied into his mane, weren't disturbed. The hocks, which were getting a little furry, had also been trimmed. Chris thought he saw newly clinched nails showing in the hooves. He picked up one of Kitty's hooves and saw new shoes, with cleats. His saddle and other tack looked new. His rifle and pistol had been cleaned. He was amazed at their show of gratitude. They were humble people of the earth. Chris only wished that he had known more people like them in his life. They fed him a light breakfast; he was still stuffed from the dinner. He rode away from their small house waving. He started to think about what he had seen. As old as they were, they still enjoyed each other. Their bodies may have looked as old as time itself, but they had a certain joie de vivre, and they were as animated as any twenty-year-old.

He was east of the Pueblo Airport and could see the army storage area farther to the east. He kept the low hills between him and the city. He soon found out that he needed to stay away from the cholla cactus. This was the worst he had seen in his life. The small, furry spines on top could hardly be seen, and they hurt like hell. The bigger spines, closer to the ground, would easily go through boots. He quickly learned to stay away from them. If he were wearing leather chaps, he may have been all right. He thought of Kitty, and he didn't want him in those damn things. Chris tried to stay in the grass and weeds.

East of Colorado Springs, he finally got clear of the cholla. It was flat, easy traveling, straight up to Peyton. To the north, it was rolling hills with many evergreens and open pasture. Many houses were built on secluded ranchettes in the area. Chris saw a few horses in an occasional paddock. He came to a meandering creek at the bottom of the broad valley. He sat under a cottonwood tree and let Kitty drink his fill. Among the evergreens, at the base of a butte, it looked inviting for a campsite.

Just after sunset, he heard a lone gunshot farther up the canyon to the northwest. He decided not to make a campfire. He slept a short distance away from Kitty. During the night, he heard another shot to the south. This went on throughout the evening. He didn't sleep much that night, so he thought he'd stay put most of the morning.

Later in the day, he started a small, smokeless campfire. The Hispanic couple had placed in one of his saddlebags some canned beans, a bag of soft cooked rice, and flour tortillas. They even gave him a small can opener and spoon. He warmed the beans next to the fire. When they started to bubble, he spooned some onto a warm tortilla and sprinkled some rice on top. He rolled it up and looked at the first burrito he ever made.

On the side of the hill, he had a nice view from his camp. He could see through the evergreens to the surrounding community. As the sun rose higher, people started to move about. This was as close to a community that he had been since he left Texas.

It was getting close to the fall migration. He watched a red-tailed hawk soaring in the rising air above the butte. Soon, others joined. Eventually, one would spot something in the trees and peel off from the group, diving through the evergreens after a fleeing meal. Chris never saw what they were after. Some would return above the butte while others wouldn't. Once in a while, he would see someone working around their house, either splitting logs in the backyard or feeding horses in a corral. As beautiful as it was, he decided not to go up the heavily timbered valley. He felt better going around the butte to the open plains. Around midday, he packed up and left.

He followed a dry creek bed shielded by cottonwoods. The plains were flat on either side of him. Some land had been planted with wheat that had been harvested. Other land was open pasture. It was simple to tell pasture from cut alfalfa; pasture was littered with cattle manure. He saw a man, on the far side of the pasture, sitting on a horse. Chris rode in that direction.

As he got closer, he saw that the man was unarmed and wearing jeans, boots, a down vest, and a baseball cap. Chris raised his hand in greeting. The man responded the same. Chris stopped ahead of the man's horse. The two animals and men were facing each other. Chris introduced himself, and the man said his name was Sam.

"You look pretty road worn. That's some sunburn you have," said Sam. The corner of his mouth turned up in a wry smile.

Chris sighed. "Yes, I've been traveling quite a bit. I'm on my way back home."

"Where's home?" asked Sam.

"Just north of Deckers." Chris replied, hoping he'd make it that far.

Sam cautioned him, "I'll bet you swung wide of the cities. It gets worse closer to Denver. Right now, you're halfway between Elbert and Kiowa."

Chris asked Sam, "Would it be better if I went along Highway 86 straight through Castle Rock or through the Black Forest along the Palmer Divide?"

Sam thought for a while. "Along the highway, there's a lot of people close to the road. They make me nervous. If you go straight west of here, the riding is a little more difficult, but you'll be able to stay in the trees longer. The closer you get to I-25, the thicker the homes. You'll be riding on the pea-graveled roads, which is easier on horseshoes. Not too bad. Whatever you do, be real cautious."

Chris thanked Joe for his time. Joe shrugged and said that's about all he had left. Chris turned Kitty and rode over a hill. He found traveling on the finely graveled roads easy. The pebbles were small enough not to lodge in Kitty's shoes. Once in a while, he would see a hoof print along the shoulder. The air was cooler at this elevation. The wind would blow through the evergreens, making a hissing sound.

He saw someone through the trees. It was obvious they were trying to stay away from the road and avoid strangers.

Chapter Twenty-One
Clueless

Chris rode over a small hill and saw a man walking along his driveway toward the road. Chris and the man met on the road. The man had a shotgun in the crook of his arm. They stopped, looked at each other. The man raised his hand and said hello. Chris nodded.

The man said, "It looks like you've been in the sun awhile."

Chris let it pass. He thought he'd fish a bit. "There doesn't seem to be much activity around."

"No, most people keep to themselves. Once in a while, I'll see someone, but most of the time they stay in their backyard or in their house. No one drives anymore. Many either moved away or died out." The man continued with other snippets of news, some interesting, some just neighborhood gossip. When he finally wound down, Chris bid him good-bye and left. Chris was thankful for the information and then realized he hadn't hit a wellspring of knowledge. Between Sam and this fellow, Chris was wondering about the effect isolation was having on people.

I-25 was used to haul fuel and many commodities for the cities. Formerly, the intersection of this road and I-70, in the heart of Denver, was the meeting of two major routes that were used to cross the United States with everything from everyday goods to illegal contraband and illegal people. Now it was all but empty.

The local kids had found a new use for the road. Skateboarders had a new paradise in the many hills south and west of Denver. The so-called flyovers were the biggest thrill. Chris watched them do their stunts and the high-fives being passed around. Things seemed to be getting back in order. Slowly, but it would be interesting to see the changes. Right now, his mind was on Marcie.

He turned Kitty around and walked him over a nearby overpass. The kids saw him and waved. He waved back. One of them said something that he couldn't hear, so he held his hand to his ear and shrugged his shoulders. The kid rolled down the hill. He said his horse was good looking. Chris thanked him and started again. He thought he also heard the kid say something about a bad sunburn.

He found a telephone at an old combination gas station and food store. He was all nerves by the time he picked up the pay telephone. The telephone rang twice and went to a recording saying the number had been disconnected. Dejected, Chris and Kitty headed toward the mountains and the cabin. He rode along a valley watching the rising hills and mountains.

Fall was beautiful in the Rockies. Most of the early light snow had already melted in the high country. Higher up, above timberline, the snow was starting to gather. The rivers still held enough water to be called babbling brooks. The aspen leaves were starting to turn yellow. The trunks accented the leaves with their stark white trunks. The route to the cabin looked different than he remembered. He dismissed that as just being too long since he was here.

As he and Kitty walked up the steep path to the cabin, it didn't look as well kept as in the past. As Chris got closer and when he could make out the details, he thought it looked abandoned. He walked Kitty up to the front porch and flipped his reins around one of the porch rails. Something was wrong. He looked in the big front window and saw the empty interior. He stepped back to the door and tried the knob. The door opened.

Inside, he looked around and saw a bird's nest near the ceiling. Closer inspection revealed rodent droppings in the corners and along the baseboards. Chris walked back to the front porch and looked over the area. He had to be at the wrong house or even on the wrong mountaintop. Chris rode back down the mountain. Some distance down the road, he saw a local resident at his mailbox. The man stood there, waiting for Chris to pass.

Chris stopped and said, "Good morning."

The man replied, "Good morning." Chris had heard longer conversations in Texas. He felt his bitterness turning to sarcasm.

Chris asked the man if he knew, or remembered, anyone in the cabin at the top of the mountain.

"Are you talking about the retired wildlife officer?"

Chris nodded yes.

"Are you the fellow his daughter used to date?" the man asked. He looked closer at the way Chris was dressed and armed. He also saw the eagle feathers. He looked nervous.

Chris was getting tired of this "woods wienie" and wasn't in the mood to play Twenty Questions. "Yes, my name is Chris. I've spent quite a bit of time getting back here. Do you know what happened to them?"

"I remember her father was ill. They had to move to a lower elevation, and she wanted to be closer to her father. They may be back in Denver or some other city down there," the man quickly offered. He paused and then added, "His daughter would show up once in a while to collect the mail and work on the house, but I haven't seen her for many months."

Heartbroken, Chris asked, "Did she say anything about where she or her dad were staying?"

"No, she didn't talk much," was his sobering reply.

Chris, now completely deflated, thanked the man and wished him good day. He hadn't any idea where to start. On his way down to Deckers, he stopped at another convenience store with a pay phone outside. He thought he'd try Marcie's number again. It was the same result. He pulled out the wallet and remembered it had belonged to Philipé, a.k.a. Sergei. Nothing in there but receipts and bills. He put the fat wallet back in his pants. He turned to the telephone book hanging under the telephone. He paged through the book trying to remember Trish's last name. He finally remembered it. He turned back to the telephone and called her. Chris let the telephone ring; he had nothing else to do. A female voice answered the telephone, "Trish here. It's your quarter."

Chris was relieved when he heard a familiar voice. "Hello, Trish. This is Chris."

There was a long pause. Chris was about to speak, when he heard her voice again. "Chris. Is this really you?"

"Yes it is. I'm south of Denver, not too far from your place. I apologize for being late." He was amazed it had been that long.

"It's good to know you're really alive and still have a sense of humor." Trish was quiet for a moment. "You're probably wondering where Marcie and her dad are."

"Yes," he said, wishing she would get on with it.

Marcie continued cautiously, "I'd like to meet you somewhere. Where are you?"

Chris picked a spot close to her house, since no one was driving. He told her to look for a brown horse and a man needing a shave. She laughed a shallow laugh at that. He hung up the telephone and did some mental math. He had just enough time to meet her.

He was waiting in the park. It felt like an unusually warm fall. He remembered that it could continue well into November and possibly December. The grass and trees would become dry and brown. The trees would lose their leaves, and everything would stay brown until December when it may or may not snow. The mountains would collect snow in variable amounts. That depended on whether it was a wet or dry year. Chris was feeling a bit sour. He sat on a bench, and Kitty's reins trailed from his hand. Kitty was in grass. At least he was happy.

Trish was walking across the park. She walked faster when she spotted Chris. They hugged each other and asked how each was doing. She stepped back and looked at him. She commented on how thin and worn he looked and said he should be doing something about his sunburn.

She told Chris how things were going around Denver. Chris told her about his trip, in abbreviated form, from Santiago. He had a feeling she was being distant. Chris couldn't stand it anymore. He was tired of her dancing around and avoiding a question he knew she was expecting. He had learned that city people, in their attempt to be polite, will verbally dance and not get to the point. He wanted to know, flat out, "What happened to Marcie?"

Trish finally settled down and took a deep breath before she unloaded. "Chris, when you didn't arrive on your flight, we didn't know what had happened to you. A few days later, a representative from Eco-oil visited Marcie and told her you were missing from the oil platform. We found out much later that it had been attacked by terrorists. She was the beneficiary on your insurance policy, and they gave her the money. She mourned your loss for months. When she finally came to terms about your death, she decided to move on."

Trish got to the hard part. "She took an interest in another man, and the relationship took off. Her father became ill while working on the cabin. He came down with chronic bronchitis from the sawdust. Marcie finally realized that he was much older and could no longer do what he always wanted. I hardly see her now. I do know that she is happy where she is. I don't know what else to tell you."

Chris was quiet for a moment. He told Trish that it was all right. There was simply no possible way for him to call, and now he did not want to interfere in her new life. He was sorry about Marcie's father. He asked Trish to tell Marcie he wished her well. Chris got up on Kitty. He looked at her one more time and nudged Kitty with his leg, walking slowly out of sight. Chris felt he had been doing a lot of walking away this year.

He traveled south, riding Kitty along I-25. He found a comfortable place among some old cottonwood trees. There was enough dead wood around to start a small fire. After a quick meal, he thought it a good time to take inventory of his things. It would be a long trip to where he thought he was going to go. He put the bundles from the backpack in neat piles of $10,000 each. He remembered the fat wallet. That would take him farther yet. He opened it and pulled out the wad. He added that cash to the pile and totaled it. His thoughts turned to South Dakota. He had enough for a small ranch and could do what he wanted. Maybe he'd travel through the Black Hills during the summer and take Kitty with him following the geese south like the Apaches. He was, after all, One with Red face! He smiled at that and snapped out of his depression. He had an idea, and it was something that interested him.

He gathered up the bills and started to put some of the money back in the wallet. Something was catching on the money. He pulled out a folded piece of paper with two fingers, and the money slipped back into the wallet. He held his hand up, looking at the paper, trying to remember what it was from. He opened it, curious about what it was.

> *Chris,*
>
> *When you find this, I hope you are well and have found the answers for your many questions.*
>
> *All my life I have been waiting for the right man to enter my life. You were here, but left for Colorado with my heart in your hands. I will be waiting for your return, no matter how long it takes.*
>
> *I will always love you.*
>
> *Pat*

She had included her address and the numbers for her house, cell phone, and the hospital.

So much for South Dakota! Chris hardly slept that night. The next morning, he was a flurry of activity. Kitty was ready to go before he was. He was eager to get back to Texas. It was his birthplace, and he had many friends to visit.

Chris was reorganizing the backpack when he felt something in the bottom. The letter! And another folded wad of papers. He opened the envelope and found three sheets of paper. The first was a partially completed application form for the Sheriff's Department in Brewster County for the position of deputy sheriff. The second sheet was the copy of a recommendation sent by Brad. The third was a personal letter to Chris.

> *Chris,*
>
> *I hope, when you read this letter, you will be in Colorado, and all is well. I suspect you will have found many of the answers about life and human relations. I, along with others, think you will be coming back.*
>
> *I chose Brewster County for three reasons. The first, because one of my brothers (the third best looking) is the sheriff of that county. The second, because it is the largest county in the state, and the county seat is Alpine. The third must be obvious to you by now.*
>
> *Brad*

He looked up at Kitty. He was dancing around, acting like he wanted to go somewhere. The two of them rode along I-25, looking for a place to cross. He would take the route back that was first suggested by Josh. At least this time, he would be heading south like a migrating bird. In a way, he would be migrating to a new life. He chuckled and then laughed out loud. The months of tension and anxiety were beginning to lift from him.

He was still laughing when he saw a parked semi-trailer alongside the interstate. He was on the same side. As he rode closer, the driver got out and walked toward the back of the truck. Chris felt his Colt with his left elbow and felt a little more secure. There was something familiar about the truck driver, but he just couldn't place it. When Chris got closer, the driver called out, "Chris? Chris, is that you?"

Chris hadn't heard that voice in a long time. "Bob?"

It was Bob Nelson. Chris got off Kitty and tied the reins to the truck bumper. They hugged each other as hard as they could. Each needed to hold a friendly human. Chris started to tell Bob about his experiences. He told him everything from the day they had graduated from school, up to his meeting with Trish. Bob asked Chris where

Pat lived. Chris told him she lived outside Alpine and gave him an idea where it was. Bob told him he was hauling some freight to Fort Stockton for the army. He would be glad to put his horse in the back of the truck and take Chris to Texas. He would be safer on the return trip. It was also faster.

Chris stripped Kitty for the trip. He asked Bob if he could put the saddlebags in the truck cab. Chris noticed the laptop computer and the wire going to the roof. He knew that there was a GPS on the roof. He smiled, knowing that he would be safe with Bob. When they opened the back of the truck to load Kitty, Chris laughed so hard he had to lean against the doorframe. The truck was loaded with mules. Bob suggested that Chris read the logo on the door. Chris walked to the front door logo.

Robert Nelson— I Haul Ass for the US Army

Chris couldn't stop laughing until they came to Pueblo, Colorado. By then, it was just an occasional giggle.

"Bob?"

"Yeah, Chris."

"Can we stop somewhere to buy a cellphone?"

PART TWO

Chapter Twenty-Two
New in Town?

Paulo was window shopping around the town of Terlingua, Texas. A few hours earlier, he was helping some customers cross the US-Mexican border. With the extra cash, it seemed like as good a time as any to do some shopping for his wife. He felt secure, knowing that he fit in with the other Hispanics and could speak English as fluently as they could. It seldom occurred to him that an American cop would think of questioning him.

"Sir," came a voice from behind him.

"Yes?" Paulo turned and saw a tall, blond deputy wearing Oakley sunglasses.

"Sir, may I see some identification?"

Paulo had none. He began to sweat. "I left my wallet at home." He wasn't lying; he just didn't want to say he left it on his dresser in Ciudad Acuna, Mexico. He thought he'd try to dissuade the cop by using verbal judo he had learned from his friends that worked in California.

"Officer, do you usually stop people without a reason?" Being a Mexican National, Paulo was aware of the American Constitutional protection against unreasonable search and seizure. In Mexico, he had no constitutional guarantees. The Mexican police routinely ran rampant over what Americans would consider their constitutional freedoms.

"I believe I have a reason to detain you, sir. Would you please step over to the car? This will only take a moment." The deputy was now holding Paulo's upper arm, and he could feel the firmness of the officer's grip. He now wished his bowels were as firm as that grip. Paulo's defiant stance was rapidly crumbling. He reluctantly walked with the officer to the patrol car. The officer had a perfectly valid reason for stopping Paulo, which he would state in his report. He wasn't ready to tell the Mexican yet at this stage.

The officer pulled a device resembling small cellphone from his duty belt. He flipped open the lid and asked Paulo for his right hand. He rolled Paulo's thumb across the screen and said, "Sir, if you'll wait in the backseat of the car, we'll quickly have an answer to my question." The arrest was proceeding well. His report would state that the suspect was detained while waiting for information regarding the status of the detainee.

"But, officer ..." He was escorted, gently, into the backseat of the cruiser. The caged backseat reminded Paulo of the ICE, more officially known as the Immigration and Customs Enforcement bus. The name had been formerly known as U.S. Immigration Service but was changed following the terrorist attack in New York by the newly enacted Homeland Security Act.

What Paulo was witnessing was radical, new technology. The "cellphone device" was a transmitter that sent the digitized image of the fingerprint to his onboard laptop computer, and then the digitized information was forwarded via the sheriff's office data link to the National Crime Information Center and Homeland Security computers. The encrypted information was processed through the massive files, and a match was quickly found. A new file was automatically computer generated with subsequent information added and the complete file delivered back to the officer. The whole transaction took just under three minutes. Paulo was an illegal alien. The illegal immigrant phrase was dropped years ago since a new, tougher president was voted into office along with a very competent staff. Someone in charge finally realized that people were or weren't citizens and were or weren't in this country legally.

"Sir, you are an illegal alien. You've been caught two other times by the INS and ICE. Your name is Paulo Roberto Molena; you were born on June 23, 1978, in Ciudad Camargo, Chihuahua, Mexico. Paulo, do you want me to continue, or have you heard enough?"

Paulo sat in the backseat, reflecting on his piss-poor luck. For the last ten years, he had been making a good living as a *coyote*. His family was living well, and his wife had grown used to the extra money and his disappearing at odd hours. She didn't question his activities—not wanting to jeopardize their only means of support for her family.

Now some deputy sheriff, not too far from the Mexican border, had caught him. He wasn't sure what the future held for him. Usually, the Immigration and Customs Service would find him, and any others that had been caught along the border, and quickly load them into a white bus for a trip back to their own country. Twice ICE had caught him, and now he had been caught in a small Texas town he had never heard of.

Paulo was thoroughly deflated. He slid down in the seat. He already knew what was coming—or so he thought. On the way to the ICE boarding point, the deputy informed Paulo that there had been an agreement between the United States and Mexico, expanding the American version of the "Three Strikes and You're Out" policy, along with a huge aid package and an "understanding" to continue the North American Free Trade Agreement (NAFTA). Only now the United States had the option to raise or lower the importation of goods as they saw fit. Another agreement was necessary about how foreign nationals found illegally in the United States were to be handled. Mexico, when they received the detainees, would keep close tabs on them in the future. They would become, in essence, a prisoner in their own country.

The trip to Presidio, Texas, took just over an hour along Highway 120. As they passed a deputy coming from Presidio County, the two converging officers casually waved at each other with four fingers, signifying a "Code Four," meaning everything was okay. Paulo wanted to find out who this officer was by trying to engage him in a conversation. The man was as closed mouth as any he had run across. His voice, or lack of it, and some mannerisms seemed familiar, but he couldn't place him.

They drove straight up to a white bus emblazoned with the logo of Homeland Security and US Immigration and Customs Enforcement boldly painted along the side. Paulo was placed next to the bus and re-fingerprinted for a positive match. His personal information was compiled from the NCIC computer and a hard copy produced. The paper was collected by an ICE officer and added to a growing binder. As each "illegal" was processed, they were escorted aboard the bus. Paulo took a seat near the rear so he could see the police officers standing outside.

As the bus began its trip to the border, the deputy that had arrested him tuned toward the bus and took off his sunglasses. It was the same man he had seen under the bridge in Reynosa, Mexico. The blond guy that had a reward on him. If only the men he was taking to America hadn't been in such a hurry. He could have waited in the weeds and gotten this guy. A million American dollars would have put his family on easy street for the rest of their lives. He wondered what would have happened if he told his companions of the reward. Then, on the other hand, he wasn't the sharing kind.

Paulo half-stood as the realization hit him. His mouth was open and his eyes wide. He stared at Chris, who smiled and waved at Paulo while the bus pulled away.

Chris chuckled while watching the antics of Paulo. He had remembered him from their meeting under the bridge years ago. And now, watching the man's actions, he understood that Paulo wasn't interested in helping him; rather, he would like to have helped himself.

Chris walked back to his cruiser, a new Chrysler-Daimler Jeep that was vastly superior to the old Ford Crown Vic that had a reputation for folding in the middle when driven over very bumpy roads. America had finally come to terms with the fuel problems. The US Army had led the way with a complete conversion to diesel fuel in the early part of the twenty-first century. The other armed services had followed, and in time, the entire United States was using diesel and the new vegetable oil fuel.

The farming community had been conned into ethanol made from corn at the urging of speculators, which had cut into the food supply and skyrocketed the price of corn. Diversification led to more soybeans being planted, and finding an alga that produced sufficient oil caused a worldwide switch in priorities. America was now substituting veg-oil in place of diesel. More nuclear plants were going online each year along with a massive amount of communities going solar. The silicon plates were a thing of the past since a new film was being covered with a product that could be colored any way the customer wanted. Camouflage was the current rage. Third-world countries could afford the cheap oil, and many countries still used it for lubrication. The industrialized countries had finally seen the light and were in the process of reorganizing energy priorities.

All the restaurants in town had contracts with various veg-oil refiners that carted the oil away to recycle it. Two such companies had a contract with the sheriff's office. There was also a wizard in Kansas that had a very good reputation for getting double the mpg from a supercharged large block diesel. His personal wealth was starting to get close to the legendary Bill Gates.

The improved Jeep had equipment that was user friendly. Gone was the gun rack that stood astride the center floor hump. The .223 carbine and the short barreled, 12-gauge shotgun were stored in an enclosed overhead rack that was accessed by a hidden switch under the dash. The overhead light/siren control panel had been replaced by a newer and smaller touch panel in the dashboard. The radar readout was now part of the widened instrument panel and could be used forward and backward along with the police vehicle being in motion. The computer screen had the capability to switch to GPS readout for his location or his intended destination.

A larger, master terminal was at the sheriff's office for staff to keep track of where the deputies were. The deputies were linked through this base and could see where their brother or sister officers were. They were particularly fond of the feature that allowed them to send information, either written or voice, to each other. Also, the terminal didn't need the keyboard; it was voice operated and easily trained by the principal user. Chris didn't need a mouse, as it had an improved touch screen. The radio stack, once a major space problem, had also been incorporated into the dashboard. The manufacturer had also replaced the window glass with more substantial glazing, not bulletproof, but very close. The side doors were reinforced with a new wonder ballistic ceramic that would stop anything up to a .30 caliber, solid point, rifle bullet. (The long since banned .50 caliber ammunition was seen as a military weapon and had absolutely no use in the civilian world.) The ceramic material was also used on the presidential limousine and the other Secret Service vehicles. It was much lighter and less expensive than the old, heavier titanium plating. The trunk was packed with survival and rescue gear along with extra ammunition and remote battery chargers for his field radio, flashlight, and remote GPS.

Chris Nelson had been hired by the Brewster County Sheriff's Office five years earlier. He was highly recommended by Brad Martin, the sheriff's brother and sheriff of Crockett County. He kept a low profile, and nothing was said about his past, but rumors still persisted about how he had saved Sheriff Martin's life. Chris had applied himself to the coursework with the same drive as he had at the Colorado School of Mines. Criminal Justice had been his second major in college, and the police academy added to his personal reservoir of knowledge. He enjoyed the firearm training, but not with the same desire as he previously had.

Since his trip back to Colorado, he had started to have a dislike for guns. That changed when he started his new job and realized that they were still tools, in the law enforcement officer's tool bag. And with that reconciled in his mind, he had the highest scores during the impromptu, fun matches the deputies put on. Chris suspected that the deputies had these matches as a way to see him shoot. Occasionally, he would see one of them try a method or procedure that he had used. He took this as a compliment and kept quiet. He wanted to keep learning and wasn't comfortable being a teacher or confidant. He still didn't feel as confident as he did with his old firearm instructor from years ago.

Chapter Twenty-Three
Just Like the Old Days

After his tour, he was to meet Pat at a quiet restaurant for a light dinner. She had finished her work at the hospital and was waiting for him in a corner table. He immediately spotted her and nodded. She looked fantastic, as she always did. How she managed, after a long day, continued to amaze him.

"Busy day at the office?" he asked as he was taking a seat next to Pat. He made sure his thigh was touching hers. If it wasn't, Pat would make sure they were somehow touching before the meal was served.

"A bit slow. I did an autopsy on an elderly man. The old gentleman finally met his end with emphysema. We had his medical history at the hospital. It was a given. His physician had noted how he had counseled his patient through the years.

"So, my darling husband, what adventure did you have today?" Her thigh was slightly moving against his, in anticipation of a thrilling cop story. Pat liked the stories but would never knowingly put herself in harm's way. She knew the nature of policemen, adrenaline junkies. She was more cerebral, and that's what appealed to Chris's other side.

"I ran across Paulo today." Chris would always monotone the beginning of these stories. It was his best impersonation of Sergeant Friday from the old television series *Dragnet*. Pat's leg stopped moving.

"What happened?"

Just then, their order arrived. A beautiful, pan-fried beef filet cooked in a delightful mustard and peppercorn sauce. They both asked that their ice tea be refilled. The glass of wine would come later—at home.

Chris told her the story. He included his observations and the reactions of Paulo during the time that Chris had him in custody and when he finally remembered Chris.

"Do you think he'll decide on retribution or something as equally stupid?" Pat's leg returned to its slow motion against his leg.

"I really don't know. The Mexican authorities will be keeping an eye on him." He reached under the table and ran his fingers along her inner thigh. He knew he was getting to her when he saw her eyes narrow and she swallowed hard. They had discovered this game shortly after he had come back from Colorado. In reality, it was a more active version of the subtle game they had played before he left. Right now, he was glad that he was wearing loose-fitting street clothes. The game seemed to increase in intensity the longer they played.

"It would be best to keep him in mind."

"I have—for years."

After dinner, they decided to stroll along the streets of Alpine before the drive home. The shops were still open, and even though they had nothing in mind to buy, it was nice to walk and look. Chris never knew when Pat would find something that interested her. He'd take her interest as a clue to what she wanted for her birthday or just on the spur of the moment.

After their stroll, they ended up back at his car and headed home. Pat usually left her car at the hospital and preferred to drive home with Chris after work. When she was on call, the plan changed to accommodate the schedule. If something unplanned came up, there was always the trusty "blue bomb," an old Chevy truck that had belonged to her father, the one she had used to help save Chris on that rainy night long ago.

The eighty-mile stretch of Highway 118, between Alpine and the Big Bend National Park, wasn't busy this time of year. More people were starting to venture farther from home, since the Unites States had recently undergone a terrific engine exchange to diesel from gasoline engines. Many companies were producing the venerable engine that lasted three times longer than the engines they replaced. A national effort by government and automotive companies eclipsed any effort approaching that of the WWII effort to win that war. Oil was no longer an issue, and many Middle Easterners had gone back to goat herding when the oil money ran out. The congressional hearings and subsequent court cases ferreted out the speculators, price fixers, and gougers and did much to restore faith in the corporate business structure and the working man and woman in America. In essence, equilibrium had returned to the world.

The next morning while Chris was driving his cruiser south he passed a faded blue Chevy van going northbound. At first, he didn't think much about it. He watched it recede in his rearview mirror and noticed the van having a severe lean to the right. He turned his car around and caught up to the vehicle. He flashed his overhead lights and watched the driver in the van's mirror. He noticed movement through the rear window of the van. He saw the driver look at him in surprise and start to slow down. He seemed to be looking for a safe place to pull off or may have been stalling for time. Chris toggled the release switch for the access door to the shotgun and rifle overhead. He pulled the shotgun free and placed it on the passenger seat. After cycling the action on the old pump gun, it was loaded.

The driver was taking too long to pull off, and Chris tooted him with the siren again. The driver pulled off onto a side road and maybe a bit too far from the main road. Instead of pulling up behind the van, he decided to stop ahead on an angle with the passenger side exposed to the van. If the driver decided to "rabbit," he'd have to be very skillful at driving in reverse. Chris wrote the license number on a pad and left it on the center console. This was good officer safety practice, since it would give someone a clue if something nasty happened to him.

Chris walked up to the passenger side of the van and motioned for the driver to roll own the window. He watched the driver and looked for a hidden gun or anything else dangerous around the man. Chris had his hand against the van to detect movement. When the driver had the window down, Chris asked him for his license, proof of insurance, and registration. While the man was rummaging through the glove box, Chris detected movement in the van. He stepped back toward the front corner of the van. When the man produced his license and said he was still looking for the rest, Chris took it and went back to his police car. He chose the mini-terminal and put it on the roof of the car and moved the shotgun to the driver's seat. When he accessed NCIC, he had an immediate hit that the driver was wanted for a felony. He had escaped custody and was wanted for murder, trafficking, and other crimes. Chris saw a man's feet and legs appear at the back of the van and grabbed the shotgun.

He had just made it to the left side of the cruiser's trunk when the second man came around the van. He had a shotgun and was bringing it to bear on Chris. The Remington model 870 roared—the nine .32

lead pellets hadn't enough distance to spread apart at twenty feet. The load had hit the man in the neck and exposed most of his spine. He fell backward like a rag doll. The driver had his hands against the window, making sure Chris didn't think of him as a threat. Chris ordered him out of the van and handcuffed him while he was face down on the graveled road.

Once the man was in the backseat and belted in, Chris accessed his computer to summon aid for the fallen man. Going back to the van, he looked to see if anyone else was hiding in the back. Even in the aftermath of 9/11 and all the problems afterward, the pot business was alive and doing very well. This had to be the biggest haul he had personally witnessed.

He knew the "shooting team" would be on their way to collect evidence and testimony from Chris and the wanted man, to determine if the shooting was justified. He sent another message to the substation requesting a large truck to transport contraband.

The arrested man tried to engage Chris in a conversation. Chris told him that anything he said could be used against him in a court of law. If he could not afford legal representation, then one would be appointed for him. The man thought about what Chris had said and decided to shut up, which was quite all right with Chris! He stood at the front of the car to use the satellite desktop and keep tabs of his prisoner. He had a long report to write and didn't need the distraction. That was the beauty of the newly equipped cars; reports could be written sooner after the incident, while everything was fresh in the officer's mind. It was a good thing he had packed a lunch.

That evening, while he and Pat were sitting on the couch, she asked, "How'd the inquiry go?"

"Justified. And the other guy will be attending court for his previous felony and the current charge of drug trafficking along with being an accomplice during the attempted murder of a law enforcement officer. Sheriff Martin would also like to add pre-meditated murder, but he'll let the district attorney make that call. The DA got excited when he saw the load of grass from the van. Heck, everyone from the sheriff on down thought it was something to see. There will be calls from the DEA, INS, Homeland Security, and who knows what else."

"Nice. Good job, Deputy Nelson. Speaking of jobs, you did a nasty one on the guy that was delivered to me."

"I tried to get him center of mass, but I was rushed for time."

Chris knew that Pat understood that he took no pride in shooting another. He did what had to be done and tried his best to live with it. The braggadocio was just a cop's way of glossing over the internal hurt while he dealt with it. She cuddled next to him while they looked out the large picture window at the setting moon. They slowly drifted off to sleep, Pat's hand on his belly, and Chris's hand wound in her heavy, black hair.

Chapter Twenty-Four
A Promotion of Sorts

Chris was called into the sheriff's office for an interview. Sheriff Martin asked, "Deputy Nelson, could you investigate a crime involving someone close to you and still be objective?"

Chris stiffened, fearing for the worse. "How close?"

"Not someone you ever knew personally. But, there's a reason why I'm asking the question this way. I would like to consider you for the new lead investigator for the still-open case regarding the murder of your wife's parents. The investigator in charge of that case, Chuck, is retiring, and I haven't another detective available. You may possibly find something he missed. Heaven knows, it's kept him awake for many nights."

The sheriff sat back in his chair and took on a more reflective look. "I knew the Doctor and Mrs. O'Reilly well. Both were respected and looked up to by many. I'm Pat's godfather, and I feel a responsibility to bring this case to an end. It's been years since that murder, and as they say, enough is enough. I'll support you with whatever you need to get this done. You can use your present vehicle, or any other, and go wherever the proverbial finger of fate points. That goes without saying. Meet with Chuck, and he'll give the case to you along with the files. The evidence, what there is of it, is in the evidence holding area. Good luck, Chris. And, say hi to Pat for me."

Chris was shocked, or amazed, at the trust the sheriff had placed in him. He hadn't known that Pat was the sheriff's goddaughter. There was still much that Pat hadn't told him. He believed that the hurt was still painful, and she simply had tried to put it to rest the best she could.

He visited the detective and picked up the paperwork, photos, and notes on the evidence. He found himself a quiet desk and carefully went through the information. The file was thick; Chuck had done a fine job keeping notes along with his own thoughts and comments regarding the interviewed people. The list was frightfully short. The pictures of the couple showed them to look remarkably young in spite of their ages.

Pat's father, Dr. Robert Allen O'Reilly, was a surgeon at the Alpine hospital. His specialty was thoracic surgery. He looked robust and every bit a man's man. If he weren't a surgeon, Chris would have thought him to be a mountain man during the opening of the West. Pat's mom was Angelica Patricia Martinez. She was the looker that had caught Dad's eye. *And her daughter did the same to me*, thought Chris.

Mrs. Murphy was a respected teacher at the local school. She taught history and had her master's from Princeton University. She was working toward her doctorate when she met her untimely death. Her specialty was Hispanic Culture in the Americas. So far, they seemed quite normal and without an enemy, mulled Chris. He read further. Chris flipped over the crime scene and autopsy pictures. He'd deal with those in time.

The financial findings were stated with no credit problems. Dr. and Mrs. Murphy apparently had no credit cards, and all the vehicles were without a lender's lien. The good doctor preferred to pay with cash, or a check that was as good as gold. The list included his financial holdings of oil-producing wells, the ranch that Chris now lived on with Pat, along with cattle and land holdings outside of Carrizo Springs in Dimmit County.

The transcribed statements were there, along with more of Chuck's notes. Chris read through the folder again and decided to call it a day. He gathered the paperwork and headed out the door. He ran into Chuck in the hallway. "Chris, there was always something that bothered me about that case."

"What's that, Chuck?"

"When you go through the evidentiary pictures, you'll find one of a shoe print that was found on the front door. The heel print, above the doorknob, was well defined since the shoe, or boot, stopped sliding at the knob. Looking for one shoe or boot, out of millions, is beyond anyone's limit."

"Do you have any information about anyone out of the ordinary contacting either the doctor or his wife?"

"None. Pat didn't know of anyone strange or different being around the house."

"That's all right, Chuck. I'll be seeing Pat in a while. I'm not too sure how she'll take this."

"I hope she doesn't get as upset as she did back then. You didn't know her then, Chris, but I'll tell you that she damn near went nuts."

"Thanks, Chuck. If I don't see you at your retirement party, good luck and have a great retirement."

"Thanks, Chris. If you have any questions, you know where I live. Stop by, if not for any other reason than to shoot the shit."

Chris thought about how he would break the news to Pat about his new role as an investigator in this case. He had time to think about it before she came home. He carefully laid the paperwork out on the coffee table in the living room. He sorted the paper out to some semblance of order. He decided to start at the beginning and work through Chuck's footsteps. He heard Pat's car approaching and put the crime scene photos back in the envelope.

Pat came in the door and said, "Hi, hon. What's new?"

He already had the chilled Chablis opened and greeted her at the door with a full glass and a smile. His guts were in an uproar. "Pat, I have a new assignment."

"Wine and a guilty look?" Her smile faded. She took the glass and walked over to the couch. Noticing the file, she said, "Mom and Dad?"

"Sheriff Martin gave me the case since Chuck's retiring. He also said that you were devastated by the death of your parents. Are you up for this?"

"Honey, let me sit here and gather my emotions. I'll explain in a minute."

They held hands while Chris waited for her to gather her wits. "Chris, I can go forward with this. The only thing I want you to do is not let me see the crime scene or autopsy photos of my folks. Anything else is okay with me. You can't imagine what it did to me back then. Both the sheriff and Chuck were too kind to me back then. Sheriff Martin is my godfather; I'm sure he told you that." Chris nodded the affirmative. "He identified Mom and Dad at the scene, trying to save me the later trauma."

They talked about the double murder, and Pat tried to remember anything that could help with the investigation. Nothing came to mind. Tomorrow was Saturday; Chris would continue again in the morning. He lived on the crime scene. At least he wouldn't have to drive very far to get there. "Pat, let's go watch the rabbits."

"Chris, I thought you'd never ask."

They strolled out to the barn and around to the horse paddock. Kitty had his head up, anticipating their arrival. "Hey, old boy, I bet you missed me. I've been busy the last few weeks. For some reason, you don't look like you're getting fat. Have you been working out?"

Pat laughed. "I've been riding him. He's like a rocking chair. You never told me likes to bathe."

"Huh?"

"When I get near a pond or a bend in a river, he walks in up to his belly and turns his head as if asking to take a bath. So, I take off his saddle and blanket and lead him back to the water. He goes nuts like a little kid."

"I'll be damned. I think that started in New Mexico. It was dry, and we were both feeling like dried prunes."

"Riding him is almost surreal. He anticipates what you're going to do, and the same with his gaits. I never asked you, but did that trick I taught you two, the one that teaches him to play dead, help at all?"

"Yes," was all he said. Pat could tell that he wasn't going to answer in depth. It must have been bad, she thought. He had told her much about the trip back to Colorado, but she was sure he hadn't told her everything. Judging his self-control when she first met him, under the tree and later around her house, she was sure that he had handled himself well after he left. She just wished she could share some of the pain in his life.

"Pat?"

"Yes, love of my life?"

"Do you remember telling me how you felt about cats and the needless killing they do? And you finished with a reference to humans that do the same."

"Yes, I do."

"Where you referring to the man, or men, that killed your parents?"

"Exactly."

"Pat, If I solve this case or if I reach a dead end, I'll tell you what happened on the trip to Colorado. You're wondering about the bad men I met?"

"Yes." She raised her eyebrows in surprise, thinking that he was starting to read her mind.

They were standing with their thighs touching, his arm protectively around her waist. She had her arm over his shoulder when the two rabbits appeared. They scampered over to the feed trough and rummaged through the fines that had sifted through the bottom. Chris and Pat laughed at the scene, remembering the antics of the rabbits years ago.

"Chris, why is it that when we get back here, I feel exactly the same as I did the first time we were here?"

"I'm not too sure why, but I do remember that from here we retreated to the front porch ... for another glass of wine."

Pat pushed him away in mock shock. "Chris, you know that's not what happened!" Turning her back on him, she walked over to a loose hay bale.

He laughed as he threw another flake of hay into the bin. Pat tackled him when he bent over the hay pile for another bundle. The night was warm enough for them to stay outside. They didn't get to sleep until much later. Kitty politely walked back into the barn.

The morning sun woke them both too early. After lying in the strewn hay, Pat was the first to suggest a morning shower together. Chris was up for that! Much later, Chris sat at the kitchen counter going through the case while Pat prepared one of her wonderful light breakfasts.

"What's changed around here in the years since your parents' death?"

Pat thought hard and said, "It's been a long time since I've thought about any of this. You must have knocked a few brain cells loose last night." She demurred when Chris looked at her. She continued. "I didn't think of this before, so I couldn't tell Doug or Sheriff Martin. My dad was always worried about a house fire. He kept important papers in a small room, in the corner of the barn. I forgot about the room and have since covered the corner and the doorway with hay and grain.

Chris could hardly wait to see the room. Before breakfast, he fetched the file from the cruiser along with a camera and left them outside the front door. Next on his growing mental list came the halogen work lights in the garage.

After breakfast, they headed for the barn and started to move ten tons of hay and thirty-one very full bags of grain. With the doorway cleared, they both donned latex gloves and checked the doorknob for fingerprints. Chris dusted all the exterior, smooth wood for latent prints. Pat operated the camera and photographed the prints while Chris transferred them using clear plastic tape, which he the fastened to a white glossy card. They carefully opened the door and saw some boot prints in the dust.

Chris turned to face Pat, and she said, “My dad always thought of himself as a doctor and not a cowboy. My mom persuaded him to try a Stetson, and that was as far as he’d go. Chris, did you notice that the Cat’s Paw logo is still visible?” She photographed them using a ruler alongside for comparison, and then Chris transferred the prints to another sheet of Mylar. The boxes of paper were too many to go through. They elected to check the opened boxes first. Chris carefully loaded the opened boxes into the backseat of the police car. He’d have the forensic lab, Pat, go over the boxes and each sheet of paper for fingerprints. Then they would continue to research the documents and hopefully find the beginning of a paper trail. Pat was elated that the investigation finally had feet and was going somewhere.

In her office at the hospital, Pat checked for fingerprints on the three boxes and the contents. She ran the prints through the FBI’s NCIC database. The majority of the latent prints were her father’s. She researched the other prints and found that they belonged to a banker, his secretary, a court clerk, and, on some, her mother. The boxes yielded three partial prints from different people. One matched her father; another came from a court clerk, and the third from a man named Claude Salton in Dimmit County. When she started on the individual sheets of paper, she found the prints belonging to the Salton man on different sheets. Pat laid out the sheets containing the Salton prints and tried to think of a commonality between them. Pat called Chris and asked him to come to her office. She went to the break room for a fresh cup of coffee and something to eat while she waited for him.

The two of them sat in high-backed chairs looking at the paper. “Pat, most of these were from the box with the land titles. If you look through these documents, will you be able to see if any one document is missing?”

“No. Dad pretty much did his thing solo. Mom and I were happy to be living comfortably, and she rarely said anything about his dealings. She preferred to let him do what he was doing. We looked at it as his hobby.”

“Let’s go through these and see if we can find a sense of order.”

They both chose a box and went through the papers. Pat was the first to hit pay dirt. “I’ll be dipped!” She exclaimed.

“What’s up?”

“I just found a master sheet, of sorts.”

“No shit, babe.”

It was just a matter of time until they found, or didn’t find, the missing title for a parcel in Dimmit County. “It looks like we’re going to Dimmit County to visit Mr. Claude Salton.”

Chapter Twenty-Five

Meet Neil, Harry, and Sam

While Pat was getting her field equipment ready, Chris drove to the sheriff's office to exchange his cruiser for the more stoutly built Jeep Grand Cherokee powered by a supercharged diesel that had been modified by Mr. Jonathan Goodwin in Kansas. The trailer hitch was needed to haul Kitty, and the roominess would allow for the extra equipment. The interior of the SUV was equipped as a larger version of his cruiser. Checking one last time, he was satisfied and drove back to the hospital for Pat.

With Kitty in tow and Pat securely aboard, they headed east on Highway 90. En route, Pat queried the computer about Mr. Salton. The information was kept in an ongoing log, which she kept updated with notes on the investigation. They both knew that Sheriff Martin would be watching the progress from his office computer. They had Salton's address, and Pat set the GPS for the route. With that done, she lay back in her seat and started some small talk to wile away the time.

"Do you remember our honeymoon?" said Pat, out of the clear blue.

"Which part? Some parts are more vivid than others."

Pat moved closer to Chris and put her head on his shoulder. Passing motorists did a double take when they noticed the two. Pat had her hair tied up with a ball cap on her head. A first glance, she would look like a very affectionate deputy. Chris smiled at the thought. Pat moved her hand to his thigh, saying, "This almost feels the same as when we started that trip, complete with Kitty in tow."

"Yup, I couldn't leave him behind. He was my closest friend during half my trip. At times my only friend."

"We were going in the same direction and on the same road. We didn't get much farther than Marathon before we needed to stop. Do you remember the place?"

Chris did, indeed, remember the place and time. He looked at the GPS on the dash and thought it was definitely close. He spotted the place and turned off the road. By the time he had the SUV turned off, Pat was already loosening her clothes. It was awhile until they were back on the road.

As they got closer to Carrizo Springs, Chris was starting to recognize the landscape since it was flatter than the hills around her home. Pat noticed the look on his face and asked him what was going through his mind. He told her, "We're close to Jenny's place." When they drove up to the address, he remembered that it was the home of the three brothers that he had killed. Chris sighed, and Pat looked at him questioningly. "The three brothers lived here, and they're buried at the next ranch to the west."

They went into the house and saw that it had been vacant for years. Pat went over the house to search for anything that looked as if it held DNA evidence. When she finished, they walked among the out buildings for anything that seemed of interest. Finding nothing, they drove to Jenny's house. She wasn't home. In fact, it looked as if she hadn't been there for years. It was starting to look like a wasted trip and a very dead end. They drove back to Carrizo Springs and stopped at a restaurant for lunch.

When they entered the restaurant, they saw that they were alone. They stood at the entrance, since a sign said to wait to be seated. They waited and heard someone busy in the back. There was a ringer at the cash register, so the obvious choice was to ring it. The waitress came out and asked where they wanted to sit. Chris recognized Jenny. It was obvious that she didn't recognize Chris. He looked quite different from when she last saw him. Jenny brought two water glasses and two menus. Chris introduced himself and his wife, Pat. Jenny wrapped her arms around Chris, thanking him for what he had done. When she settled down, Chris asked her to join them at the table. She pulled up a chair.

"Jenny, how are things? We were at your house, and it looked deserted."

"I was told by a banker that it was no longer mine, and I had to get off the property. I've been working here so I could afford an apartment."

Tell me more about this "banker."

Jenny told him about how she and her husband had leased the property and were in the process of buying it. After the death of her husband, she had to deal with his burial and had lost track of the pending deal. "A banker paid me a personal visit and informed me that the property was no longer under my control and had been sold to someone else. He wouldn't tell me who it was and strongly suggested I move within the month."

"Do you know who the owner was while you were leasing the property?" asked Pat.

"Yes, he was a very kind man. I met him once when he visited the place, and I asked him if he would consider selling it to us. The price he asked was the same as he had paid a long time ago." Chris looked at Pat and saw a tear running down her cheek. "Excuse me, ma'am, did you know that man?" asked Jenny.

Pat picked up her head and said, "Yes. He was my father."

"I'm so sorry."

"Chris had told me about your husband and your plans for the future. I saw your house, and I realize that you've undergone a tremendous loss too," said Pat, who had herself under control now.

Chris asked, "Jenny, what were those three brothers up to?"

"They apparently had heard that I had lost the house and wanted to 'help' me out. I wonder if they also knew my husband was dead."

"Why do you think they acted that way?"

"I don't know."

"Pat and I are going to go to the sheriff's office and tell him what happened to the three men. I was the one that shot them in your defense. I'm sure he's a reasonable man, and it will be cleared up immediately. After that, we will be going to the house of those three men to collect evidence, and we will exhume the three men for more evidence."

Jenny wished them well and thanked Chris again for helping her with her husband. She bid them both good-bye and returned to the rear of the restaurant.

On the way to the sheriff's office, Chris mentioned that they had forgotten to eat. Pat said, "I lost my appetite. Did you notice the look on her face? She looked so forlorn."

"That was the same look I saw when I first met her."

They arrived at the sheriff's office and headed for the door. The sheriff seemed to be expecting them and asked them into his office. He extended his hand to each and told them he was Sheriff Dave Powell.

Chris explained their investigation, his involvement with the three men, and wrote a statement about what had happened that day. The statement was easy to write; the memory was still fresh. The sheriff told them that the three men were probably the Adkins brothers—Neil, Harry and Sam.

When they prepared to leave, the sheriff thanked them for stopping. He had seen the Brewster County logo on the SUV and was wondering when they'd be paying him a courtesy call.

In the SUV heading back to the house, Chris blew out his breath. "Whew, I thought I'd be in deep shit. Sheriff Powell acted as if I had cleaned house for him."

"You did, love. I'll bet he knew those guys back in grammar school, and I'd bet they were the school bullies well into high school, if they got that far.

"Well, now that we have official permission to search the house, what do we do that we haven't done already?" asked Pat.

"Let's go through it again and look for something relevant—like paper."

Try as they might, they couldn't find any documents, or anything else for that matter, that would help their investigation. The decided that they had reached the end there and drove to Jenny's house, or whoever owned it now. They would check the county office on Monday for the current owner.

When they arrived at Jenny's house they saw that the front-loader was still behind the barn. To Chris's amazement, it started on the third try. He drove it to the next field, while Pat followed in the Jeep. Chris dug to within inches of the bodies. They both used shovels to clear the dirt down to the bodies. The soil was soft and easy to dig. They pulled the exposed bodies out. Chris was glad he had had the foresight to use tarps to wrap them.

With the three bodies unearthed, they transported them back to the privacy of the barn, behind Jenny's house. Each of the corpses were processed in turn, with a sample of DNA collected from each. The first one turned out to be Harry Adkins; he looked good, considering the decomposition. He had his wallet in his pocket, which helped immensely. Pat photographed him and did a commendable job getting some of his fingerprints. His rifle was also dusted and the prints lifted. The same was done on the next body, which was Sam Adkins, who also had a wallet with a driver's license. Next up, obviously the third brother, was Tom Adkins. His wallet, rifle, and fingers were processed, and while Pat was reloading the digital camera with a fresh battery and memory chip, Chris went through the huge trucker's wallet. The first thing he noticed was that "DB" (dead body) Harry, was a proverbial packrat. His wallet was stuffed with receipts.

Chris walked over to the workbench and laid the paper out in a row. He studied each aged piece of paper. He picked up one and did some mental math. Turning to Pat, he said, "I think this receipt is dated a few days before I got here." Pat started to walk over to him. "It's a receipt from the Dimmit County Clerk's office for a transfer of deed."

Chapter Twenty-Six
Marvelous Marv

When they had finished with the bodies, they decided to rebury the "Three Stinker's" in the same hole, only deeper this time. Chris felt that Sheriff Powell would have wanted it that way. The county offices were closed on Sunday, and they decided to take the day off.

The hour drive to Laredo was quiet. The traffic was beginning to increase, as more veg-oil was being produced in the United States along with the massive engine replacement program. The newest cars, which ran entirely on hydrogen, were starting to appear. The Holy Grail of the automotive world had been found. The earlier hybrid models used a combination of gas and electricity, but that idea had been quickly tossed into the dustbin of history when the batteries needed could no longer be produced in the quantity needed. The new models, introduced earlier this year, were about the same size as a Toyota Corolla and used a pure hydrogen engine along with a sufficient dynamo. This combination allowed enough water to be electrolyzed to produce hydrogen in quantity for high-speed cruising, and at lower speeds, enough for storage. General Motors was advertising the new Cadillac Escalade would be available in two years, with a super long-distance version of the hydrogen system. Chris was wondering when the sheriff would change over to the new technology. It would be nice when the service stations of today, which only allowed you to pump your own gas and buy high-priced junk food, changed to a service station that actually provided more service.

Chris remembered when he had thought the technology was more fantasy than fact. America had enough petroleum to meet its needs, which was mostly bio-diesel and lubricating oil and grease, and now there were many synthetics becoming available.

Along the main highway, they found a grocery store and loaded up with what they'd need for an impromptu picnic. They chose Lake Casa Blanca International State Park because they thought the view of Laredo from the far side of the lake was a nice change from the dry, cactus-studded area around Carrizo Springs. This would also give them an opportunity to think about the case.

Chris busied himself starting a slow fire for the barbecue. Pat mixed a hot, dry rub for the meat and set out the potato salad, chips, fruit, and a bottle of Chardonnay that she placed in a bag of ice. One she was finished, Pat lay back on the grass and watched Chris.

"Are you really going to use one match?" questioned Pat. She already knew that he could, since he had had enough practice a few years ago. He was better in fire-starting than an Eagle Scout and could have earned his merit badge hands down.

He looked over his shoulder at her and smiled. He knew she would say that when he started to make a few fuzz-sticks for tinder. He would have this baby going with one match. He loved the challenge, and the process brought back some pleasant thoughts from the past. He was glad he only had to make fires for cooking, since he was mostly traveling during the time of the year that it was warm. He was definitely glad that he hadn't had to make a fire for warmth. That would have been a back breaker since he hadn't had a saw or axe at the time.

The fire pit had a grill in place, which he used to sear the beef and pork ribs. As the fire turned to coals, he put the meat back on and retreated to where Pat was waiting for him with a cold glass of wine. "I don't know if we're on or off the time clock, but here's to y'all," said Pat. They settled back to watch the fire and reflect.

"Okay, so what have we accomplished?"

"We know that Harry Adkins, the Third Stinker, had a receipt we need to look into. Jenny seemed to feel that the three had some urgent need to get her off the property. The Dimmit County Sheriff, Powell, is obviously new and may not have been aware of what went on. Then on the other hand …" Pat let the thought drift off.

"Good thought. We can e-mail Sheriff Martin and ask for a background report about Sheriff Powell."

"What do you think about the mysterious banker?"

"It would be in our favor to approach him, if only to feel him out."

They ate their lunch and looked for a movie that piqued their interest. They settled on an older film called *Assassination Tango*, starring Robert Duvall. Afterward, Chris made a mental note that they would have to learn to dance the tango. He sensed that Pat enjoyed it; she had kept her hand on Chris's leg during the dance scenes. The sheriff's office paid for a rather nice motel that night, along with room service.

They arrived at Carrizo Springs State Bank and Trust at 10:00 a.m. sharp. They asked a bank officer, John Tyler, if he had known an employee that had dealt with a property that had belonged to Pat. He asked for a description of the property, excused himself, and disappeared into the file vault. When he came back, he was carrying a sheaf of paper. He sat between Chris and Pat and opened the file. Pat asked him to wear latex gloves.

Picking through the pages, he found the first form, from the South Texas Land and Title Company, with the original owner's name, Michael D. Griffen. The property was sold just after Pat's parents were killed. The buyer was Jason T. Johnson. Pat and Chris looked at each other in shock. They asked Mr. Tyler if he could find the name of the bank's representative at the closing. He went through the paperwork and found a name, Mark Hanson. Mr. Tyler said that he had been at the bank for over twenty years and had never heard that name. Pat asked if she could take the documents outside for a while. Mr. Tyler gave a nod.

Outside in the SUV, Pat photographed all the documents, with close-ups of all the signatures. The old method of fuming in a large tank had been changed with an enclosure that held a single sheet of paper. Much less cyanoacrylate fumes were used. She developed the prints and photographed them. The two investigators thanked Mr. Tyler and left the bank.

In their vehicle, Pat was stewing. "Chris, do you smell fraud?"

"Oh, yes I do. I'll e-mail the sheriff, update him, and request a check on Griffen, Johnson, and Hansen. We have no DOB, so it will be a shot in the dark."

"Any news about Sheriff Powell?"

Chris hummed as he booted the terminal. He read through the report and told Pat, "It looks like Sheriff Powell is a new boy in town. He came from Arkansas, two years ago, as an undersheriff in that state. Since Dimmit County is small, as far as population, and the fact that they needed a sheriff, he easily won a one-sided election. His credentials are impeccable, as is his background. It looks like he was just burned out from Arkansas and decided to move to the country. The old war horse just can't seem to quit being a cop." Chris wondered if he'd be able to hang up his star when he reached that point in his life.

"Well, the sheriff of Dimmit County is one of the good guys." Chris sighed. "That leaves us with—oh shit!"

"What's up?" Pat had been lost in her thoughts, and Chris's sudden start brought her back.

"The three, Griffen, Johnson, and Hansen, are not in any database. It's safe to assume that they are fictitious names. Do you have the prints ready for transmission?"

Pat helped to upload all the fingerprints found on the documents. They went back to the restaurant for lunch and a chat with Jenny while waiting the results. Jenny was working a table when they arrived. She quickly sat them and took their order. The other customers finished and left, leaving them free to speak to Jenny.

Chris was the first to speak. "Jenny, can you think of anything about the three brothers or any bank official that you hadn't thought of before?"

"I always wondered why I wasn't mailed anything officially. I thought the post office was having problems and the banker decided to deliver the news firsthand. Still, I wondered why I wasn't given anything in writing." Chris and Pat both agreed that it was unheard of since the Great Depression in the thirties. Jenny recalled that the three had kept to themselves. Neither she nor her late husband had anything to do with them. The neighbors hardly mentioned them, except in passing, and not much was said by them either. She recalled once, when driving down the road, she did see a well-dressed man coming out of their house. She had caught a glimpse of him, but couldn't remember specifics, but she did remember that he was about in his thirties and stared at her as she drove by.

Chris's cell went off with an e-mail message. The results were back from the prints. Chris and Pat excused themselves and went to the SUV.

Chris read the report with Pat. A number of prints were from past employees of the bank. This was verified by employment records when someone from the Brewster County Sheriff's Office had called the bank and verified the names with Mr. Tyler personally. Most likely, Sheriff Martin had made the call. Another print belonged to

Marvin Gessler of Del Rio, Texas. The DOB, address, and personal description followed. Chris turned his head toward Pat. They stared at each other, and Pat shook her head in disbelief. They continued to read the screen. Neil and Harry Adkins were two other prints found on the paper. Chris answered the e-mail and notified the office that they'd be going to Del Rio. He also requested that inquiries be made about the natural resources around Carrizo Springs.

"It seems that two of the Stinkers were present at the closing. I'm very interested in what Marv has to say. Judging by his DOB, he's seventy years old now. I sure hope we don't have to interview him at a cemetery." He looked at Pat from the corner of his eye.

Pat smiled grimly. "Chris, we're about fifty-fifty, counting the stiffs and live ones."

When they found the address, it wasn't as big a surprise as they thought. It was called Shady Acres Rest Home. They introduced themselves to the manager and requested to see Mr. Gessler. The staff let them use a private office for the interview. Old Marv was wheeled in. He looked up at the two and smiled. "It took you awhile to find me."

The two introduced themselves and asked Mr. Gessler what he meant by his comment.

"Aren't you here about some phony checks?"

"No. But what can you tell us about some other documents? Like a land transaction?"

"As you can see, I'm getting a bit old. How long ago?"

Chris told him the date of the closing and who was present. He also mentioned the bank and what was being sold.

"I don't remember the bank or the property. About that time, I was paid to ..." He stopped in mid-sentence and asked if the statute of limitations was still in effect. Chris told him that it wasn't; if he was involved in a murder, then it didn't expire. "Nope, I didn't kill nobody." He started to cough and took an offered drink of water. Wiping his mouth with his sleeve, he continued. "Some guy wanted me to forge some names."

"Do you know who he was?"

"I never seen him before. He found me."

"Do you remember the names he wanted forged?

"Yup, a Griffen and a Johnson. I can't remember the first names."

"Were there any other names?"

Pat was sitting on the edge of her chair. Chris couldn't tell if she was breathing or not. The three of them sat there until the fog of old age parted.

"Do you remember any Irish names?" Pat couldn't take the tension any longer; she had to break it.

"No. Not back then. I do remember some job with an Irish name. It was about three months earlier. The name started with an O like that guy on Fox news."

"O'Reilly," offered Pat.

"Yup, that's the one."

"Who did you deal with back then?" Pat asked. The last time Chris saw this look on her face, he was healing from a broken leg when she told him of her parents' death.

"He was a young guy, maybe in his thirties. Well-dressed and drove a nice car. He never told me his name. He just gave me the samples and showed up a week later to pick up the paper. He paid me cash." Marv lapsed into a coughing fit. No one offered him a drink.

"What was the paper about? Did you read it?" asked Chris.

"Nope, I wasn't being paid to read, just write."

"Do you remember anything about it?"

"It was an official-looking document. Maybe it was a land title or something like it. I duplicated two names. One was a man, and the other a woman. I charged him double. I don't do women's names too well."

They thanked Marvin and told him that they'd be in touch if they had more questions. He nodded okay and waved for an intern to help him. Chris left a business card at the front desk. The husband and wife team left and headed for the Jeep to continue back to Dimmit County. "Pat, we need to get our hands, or rather latex gloves, on that land title."

"I was thinking the same, lover. How about something to eat?" The tension was easing from her voice.

Chapter Twenty-Seven

XXX

They had to keep themselves from running into the Dimmit County Recorder's Office. Chris handed the surprised clerk a pair of latex gloves and asked her to find the original property recording for Jenny's ranch. As an afterthought, Chris asked if he could also see the property recording for the Adkins place. When the clerk returned, Chris produced the receipt taken from Harry Adkin's wallet.

"Ma'am, could you verify that this is a proper receipt and what was it for?"

She turned to check her records, and Chris and Pat went to work processing the documents for prints. The clerk returned and told them that it was valid and the date in question was correct. The transaction was for filing a change of ownership for the property that a Mr. and Mrs. O'Reilly had owned, to a new owner, Mr. Michael D. Griffen. She explained that during that time, there was hardly anyone working for the county. Many properties were changing hands because of the fear of a dismal future. Many just wanted to get out, and others had simply defaulted on their loans. The banks called in their notes either by a representative going out or by official registered mail. She started to giggle and then stopped and excused herself, explaining, "I just remembered something that I saw that day."

"What could that be?" questioned Chris.

"I watched a lone cowboy walk out of the UPS store, across the street, and ride west out of town, in the rain."

"Why was that so funny?" asked Pat.

"Well," she started, "it wasn't so funny as how I felt."

"Yes?" prompted Pat.

She kept her voice low and continued her thought. "He was the sexiest man I had ever seen. No one before and no one since has fired my jets like that man did."

Pat glanced over at Chris, who was trying his best to act like he hadn't heard a thing. He was cleaning up and was about ready to leave. Pat thanked the clerk and bid her good day as they left.

"She was talking about you?"

"Yes."

"Well, Detective Nelson, let's get these prints loaded and find a motel. It's about time you fired my jets, Mr. Sexiest Man I Ever Saw!"

Chris had already started the uploading. Pat noticed a slight tremor in his hands after she had spoken. When he finished, he looked at her with a large grin and said, "Let's go."

It was very early in the morning when Chris heard his cellphone. Looking at it, he had seen that it had gone off at least ten times before he pushed the cancel button. He turned to Pat and suggested that they get back to work. They both had the distinctive look of the proverbial horse that had been ridden hard and put away wet. "Babe, let's do a cool shower first." Pat led the way into the shower. Chris turned it back to warm, and the water renewed their passion. Eventually, the hot water supply ran low, and they quickly finished rinsing off.

Chris was the first out and he went to the Jeep to get the laptop. When he came back, Pat had her trousers and shirt on and was in the process of wrapping a towel around her still damp hair. She was ready to work.

The prints they sent had been identified and a report returned. They had found prints matching Marvin, the clerk, and one index fingerprint belonging to a Mr. Roger Tucker. The last known address was included. An enquiry had been made regarding the natural resources, and the reply had stated that there were mineral deposits similar to that found in areas where Kimberlite was mined. This deposit was beneath the property belonging to her parents or Jenny's place and the Three Stinkers, the brothers Adkins.

"Oh boy! Now is Roger Tucker really Michael D. Griffen or the one that hired Marvin to do the forgeries?" Chris was getting exasperated. "What is Kimberlite?" Then it hit him … hard. "Pat, in my geology class, we each had to pick a project to pass that class. I chose Kimberlite because that's where diamonds are mined. The South

African, Canadian, and Arkansas sites are all diamond-producing sites. It was an exciting class, and I did find some other sites, though closed to the public, south of Boulder in the state park, and another just south of the Wyoming state line." Chris rolled over and shut the light off. "Where did we leave off?" Pat giggled as she stepped over to the bed while letting her trousers fall free.

Later that morning, Chris received a cellphone call from the rest home. Marvin had succumbed to advanced age. He had died peacefully in his sleep. The secretary making the call had a hesitancy in her voice that Chris picked up on. He asked her if something was wrong. She said Marvin had made a phone call, and during the conversation, he was very upset. He had raised his voice and hadn't mentioned what had upset him. He was highly agitated until he took his medication.

Chris hoped he wouldn't last as long as Marvin did. Being stuck in a chair, with the best years gone, didn't suit him. Chris told Pat the news and his thought about his future. Pat thought awhile and said, "My father had said the same thing. Once his vision was gone and he couldn't practice medicine, his reason to live would quickly fade. What is it with men? Is working your only reason to live? Chris, have you ever wondered why I have interests that are very far removed from what I do for a living?"

Chris got the message and hugged her while they lingered in each other's embrace. He was hoping their future would hold more tango and less cop and doctor stuff. But, to get there, they needed to see Roger Tucker, a.k.a. Michael D. Griffen. His last known address was in Sheffield, Texas. Chris remembered that Sheffield was in Pecos County. The memories of Karen flooded back on him. "Pat, I'll feed Kitty. It looks like we've got a drive ahead of us."

The drive to Sheffield was back up Highway 90. Chris gave Pat a running commentary of what it had been like along the road. The turn to the north was at Highway 349, which was west of the Pecos River and parallel to his old route. He retold her parts of his trip north as bits came back to him. Sheffield looked exactly as it had the last time Chris saw it. The town was small, so they drove around looking for the address. When they spotted it, they drove around the corner and parked the marked car out of sight from the house. They waited, making sure they hadn't been spotted. They walked to the front of the house, and Chris rang the doorbell. There was movement from within as someone walked toward the front door. A pleasant-looking middle-aged woman answered the door.

"Goodness, may I help you?" She looked surprised to see the deputy and Pat.

"Yes, ma'am, were looking for a Mr. Roger Tucker. Does he live here?"

"Roger has gone hunting. Is there something I can help you with?"

"We have some questions to ask Roger. Is there some place where we can find him?"

"Roger went hunting with his friend, Jason Johnson, east of Pandale. Do you know where that is?" she asked.

Chris answered, "I'm very familiar with the area, ma'am."

"The last time I spoke to him, he said they would probably be there for another two weeks."

"Thank you very much."

Chris and Pat walked back to the car. "Pat, let's take a drive up to Iraan. I know a pretty good restaurant."

They drove through the small town, and Chris pointed out the highlights and history. They stopped at the same restaurant he had been at before. With the food ordered, they set to business.

"Pat, I have a feeling that Kitty and I are going to do a bit of riding. I'd like to talk to the sheriffs of Crockett and Val Verde Counties and ask for their help. That will be our next stop." After a quick lunch, they headed for Ozona, the county seat.

"Who? You've got to be kidding!" Chris heard Sheriff Martin's voice from his office in the back, from the front of the building. His steps grew louder as he came closer. Pat looked at Chris with a look of feigned fear. As the good friend rounded a corner and saw Chris, he burst into laughter.

"Chris, if you aren't a sight. You sure look better without a sunburned face. Dr. Patricia O'Reilly and I have met on occasion, as you know. You might have guessed that she was the major reason for my letter."

Shaking Brad's hand, she said, "I'd like to thank you for saving my husband-to-be. Is your shoulder better? I've always wondered about it."

Brad swung his arm in a circle and said, "Couldn't be better. What brings you two out here? I don't think it's a social call. You're in uniform, and I saw the brand-new sheriff's Jeep outside."

"Brad, we have a problem, and we need your help and the sheriff of Val Verde."

"Let's sit in my office." He called over his shoulder, "Deputy Miller, could you bring three chocolate shakes to my office? And get one for yourself." Brad smiled on his way to the office. His brother, Sheriff Martin in Brewster County, had already called him, as a courtesy.

Chris informed Brad of his ongoing investigation. The different people involved and the paper trail leading to two men, Tucker and Johnson, both of them hunting somewhere south of there. Brad thought about it and said, "Chris, the Pecos has flooded this year. Using your vehicle is out of the question. You'll have to pack it in by horse. How's Kitty?"

Chris gave a thumb's up.

"Good. Using the county's helicopter is out. It's in for an overhaul. Pat, you'll stay with Mary and me at the house." Pat was about to object when Brad held his hand up. He reminded her, "Pat, you're a doctor. Your safety can't be guaranteed in the field. This is probably only a quick pick-up of two guys. I'll send Deputy Miller with Chris as a representative of our county. Miller's very good at police work and has just come back from the FBI Academy. Miller also knows the back country around here." Pat shrugged her shoulders in resignation as the back of a deputy pushed open the door to the office. The three shakes had arrived. Chris was just about to turn back toward Brad when he caught sight of the deputy's hips and hair pulled up into a tight bun. He quickly turned and looked Deputy Miller in the eye. Karen Miller was now a deputy sheriff.

Chapter Twenty-Eight
Deputy Miller

"Deputy Miller, you drive a cruiser up to your place and change clothes for the road. Chris, I'm sure you have clothes. Get ready and put your hitch on the back of our car. Then, you two find these guys for questioning and bring them back." Sheriff Martin spoke to them from his personal car. Almost as an afterthought, he added, "Deputy Miller, you have my permission to use your aircraft for the initial search. After you find these guys, use ground transportation."

Pat was in the other seat, and they both wished them well. Then they were gone down the road to Brad's house. Chris knew Pat would be safe with the sheriff.

Chris turned to Deputy Miller. "Well, how have you been, Karen?" It was about the lamest thing he had ever said.

Silence.

"Why did you want to be a cop?"

More silence.

"Let's get the rig hitched up." Deputy Miller walked stiff-legged to her car. As she backed up to the trailer, Chris thought she was trying to run him over.

They drove away in silence. Chris watched the scenery pass as they drove along the freshly paved road. He remembered the narrow tributary where Brad and he had a gunfight with the three men and how he had saved Brad's life. He thought he saw the remains of the old fire pit. He slid down in the seat, closed his eyes, and recalled the long ride and the danger he had faced. Many times, he faced danger alone and the fear he had felt during the aftermath. At other times, while in trouble, he had help, either from Pat, Joe, Brad, or the three brothers, Dan, Cy, and Josh. He even remembered his school chum, Dave Nelson, who was always asked if he was related to Chris, and the same happened to Chris. He was eternally grateful that he had come across Dave. He had made life easy at a time when it was beginning to wear him down. Chris had thought his world was at an end when he had traveled north from South America to find that his girlfriend, Marcie, had thought him dead and begun a new life. A letter from Brad, and a note, later found deep in his bag, from Pat, kept him going. And then there was Karen, now Deputy Miller.

Chris had met her after he had met Pat. He had to retrace his route after his accident, since his leg had been broken and was still sore. Rather than riding north through the mountains, he chose to ride along the Pecos River where he met Karen, and later, Brad. He had run across a number of bad men along the river. The physical and emotional strain on him had been terrible. He had thought he had died emotionally. When he was at his lowest and feeling like an empty shell, he ran into Karen, who had been alone since her husband had deserted her for an easier life. The night in the natural pool, behind her house, had started him to think of living again. Over the next few days, he realized that, through Karen's freely given love, he had to keep going. When he reached the end of his journey, he realized that life had played a cruel trick on him. The rest, as they say, is history. Now, he didn't know what to do. He still had feelings for Karen, but not the same as when he had first met her. He was madly in love with Pat, since she had touched his very soul in ways no one had before. This is what he discovered in himself during the ride north. Marcie had unknowingly helped Chris down a new path by closing the door on the existing one.

He was sleeping when they reached Deputy Miller's house. The black and white dog's happy barking woke Chris. He opened his eyes to watch Karen as she walked stiffly toward her house. He grunted and got out of the car. Since he hadn't been invited inside, he decided to look around the place. It hadn't changed a bit. He walked up the hill behind the house to the natural pool. He stood there awhile, remembering that night.

He didn't hear her behind him. "That was a beautiful night. I still think of it; it helps me at night when I'm feeling lonely. I still haven't met a man like you. I don't know if I ever will. I'm so envious of Pat. My uncle told me that you two were getting married. I thought about going, but I didn't want to interfere with your new life. I asked my uncle for help getting into police work. I think he understood how I felt. He's been a strong supporter and mentor."

Chris turned toward her, hugging her with his head on hers. He looked off in the distance and said, "Karen, if I had any idea how I really affected you. If I had had more sense, or sensitivity to what was really going on. If I hadn't been so goal oriented. I can go on with ifs until the cows come home. Karen, honey, baby, I don't know what to say to you. We both know where my heart is." They held each other like two scared and lonely people. The same way they did years ago.

"Chris?"

"Yes, Karen."

"Do you still love me?"

"I can't answer that question. It will jeopardize my marriage and give you false hope," replied Chris, as sober as anything he had ever said.

"Well, cowboy, I'll always love you." She was defiant as he'd ever seen her. "And if that causes you concern, tough shit!" She stormed off toward the car. Chris thought he heard her crying. When he caught up to her at the corral, she had red eyes and was busy with her horse.

Chris had a confession to make. "I never knew your last name before today."

"That's right. I never told you."

They drove to her hanger and readied the airplane. It was still well taken care of and as beautiful a Stearman as any he had seen.

They taxied out to the short grass and began their take-off roll. Once airborne, Karen asked Chris if he would want to fly while she looked over the sectional. He nodded and wiggled the stick to let her know that he had it. The last time he had flown was with Karen in this same aircraft. Since then, his life had changed, and he had immersed himself in Pat and the business of being a cop.

As they flew south along the Pecos River, Chris watched forward and to the right. Karen scanned the map and looked to the left. Cutting to the east, they saw Pandale in the distance. They overflew the town and saw a lone set of fresh truck tracks east of town. On a hunch, they agreed to follow them and see what they could find. The tracks became hard to see at a distance, but they didn't want to spook whoever made them. The gained altitude and reduced power to keep the old Stearman as quiet as possible. They had a larger area to scan and tried to appear like a passing airplane to anyone on the ground.

At the end of a wide canyon, they spotted the end of the truck tracks. A tent and truck with a horse trailer along with two ATVs.

It looked like they were planning on staying for a while. Chris asked Karen to further reduce power, fly on their present course, and gently lose altitude. He had seen a broad valley just over the crest of a ridge to the east. He asked Karen if she could land in that spot using a dead-stick approach.

She nodded the affirmative and banked slightly away from the men on the ground. Her intention was to deceive those on the ground that they were a passing aircraft with no interest in them. When they had lost enough altitude to put them lower than the surrounding hills, Karen flew back toward the valley Chris had told her about. She approached with the power almost at idle while maintaining a constant rate of descent. She cleared the easternmost ridge and pulled the power back to idle. Side-slipping the yellow biplane, she allowed it to sink further below the ridgeline. The landing was perfect with hardly a bump, save for the occasional animal burrow. Deputy Miller, Karen, had the engine off as they rolled to a stop.

"Ready for a hike?" Chris smiled and reached for the hiking water packs. Karen was standing in front of the propeller hub, looking up the hill, when he walked up behind her. He recalled the last time he had seen her in jeans. She was still a sight to see. "Well, let's hump."

Karen wondered if he could guess how much she wanted to. She was wearing a pair of binoculars and started ahead toward the top. The walking was gradual since they went up the hill at an angle. Once on top, they lay side by side watching for movement around the campsite.

"Chris?"

"Yup?"

"So what if we see two guys. How will we know who they are? We don't know what they look like."

"Shit. We're too far away from a radio repeater and can't even use our police radios or cellphones."

"Let's check the vehicle registration. At least we can find if it matches one of them."

"Hmm, more sneaking around in the bush. Okay, let's wander down there and find out."

They tried to stay out of sight and keep their movements unnoticed. They hadn't seen the two men and started to wonder how far they had gone from camp. When they approached the truck, it was getting toward sunset, and they saw that the horses were gone. Checking the truck, they found the paperwork, and the registered owner was Roger

Tucker. They were on the right track. They waited in the shadow of some bushes for the two men to return.

As the night grew long, and much cooler, they found they could be waiting in vain, along with a need to keep warm. Neither one wanted to start a fire, which would give them away. Instead, Karen snuggled alongside Chris, as he lay on the ground. Chris kept awake as Karen fell asleep.

At sunrise, as the darkness barely turned to a dark gray, Chris could have sworn he saw something move a hundred yards to the north. He watched as the grayness lightened and turned into daylight. Karen stirred, and Chris cautioned her to keep still. She slowly rolled onto her belly and looked in the direction he pointed. He whispered that he had been watching for movement before dawn and had seen nothing since. They waited awhile longer, until the air warmed, and then set out to find the twosome.

Tracking the two men was easy on the dry ground. They followed two sets of hoof prints northward about a half mile and saw the tracks continuing to the hills. They stopped searching and decided to exchange the airplane for the Jeep and horses. They quickly trotted up and over the hill. The airplane looked secure.

Karen readied the engine settings while Chris pulled the external control locks. He stowed them in the front cockpit with him. They were both belted in by the time Karen yelled, "Clear!" They looked among the ridges and valleys to the north, and Chris spotted something among the brush. Karen spiraled down for a closer look. There wasn't room to land, so Chris hit the GPS for the location and stored it in memory. They continued to Karen's place, stored the plane in the hangar, and headed out to the GPS location with the Jeep, Kitty, and Karen's horse.

Using the saved GPS bearings took them longer than they expected. The route they traveled was much different than the straight course depicted on the GPS screen. Some valleys were too steep and had to be ridden around, while some of the hills had faces too steep to climb. What normally would have been an easy day's ride now looked like it would take half the next day. They had anticipated this and had enough food for themselves. They picked a sheltered spot alongside a small stream. The water was clear and cool. Karen decided to clean up while Chris set up for a quick meal of canned beef stew with canned German potato salad on the side. It was nothing like the food Pat served him, but this was work in the field.

Karen walked up as the stew was boiling. "Hmmm, looks like we're roughing it."

"This, Deputy, is as good as it gets, even if it is pretty disappointing stuff. I think we've been working along the roads and in the cities too long. Scarcity of food has become a thing of the past, and we've forgotten what hungry is really like. This being a short trip, I thought I'd grab whatever came to mind. It looks like I was in a hurry and didn't give it much thought. Maybe I should pay more attention when Pat's in the kitchen."

"It's not your fault. You're too much of a guy to think about cooking. I remember when you could live on beef jerky. You really pushed yourself back then."

"I'm getting soft?"

"No. You haven't been pushed like you were then. We've all settled into the comfortable lives we led before the gas and money shortages. Bad people tried to take advantage of what they saw as weakness or vulnerability in others."

"Yes. You're right about that on both counts." Chris talked around a mouth of potato salad.

They finished in quiet and soon stretched out to sleep. The horses had been taken care of and stood in the shadows along the stream. Chris was the first to speak. "Karen? What did you name your horse?"

"I thought about names but finally gave up. I just call him Horse."

"What about your dog? Dog?"

"No. It's Butch."

"Okay. Good night."

"G'nite."

The next morning, Karen was up heating water for coffee and frying bacon. The smell always seemed better when he was out in the sticks. Karen saw him watching her. "The stew just didn't cut it, cowboy. I'll take a crack at cooking this morning."

After a quick and delicious breakfast, they rode east toward the GPS heading. It was just over ten miles away. Along the way, they saw a single set of hoof prints heading toward and then away from their destination. They followed the tracks single file with Chris in the lead. The buzz of the bullet passed Chris's ear. He subconsciously heard the slap of the bullet as he jumped off Kitty. Taking cover in a shallow depression, he looked over his shoulder in the direction they had come. Karen's horse was running back down the path. She was on her side and motioned for Chris to keep moving up the hill toward their attacker. Chris looked to his right and saw a rocky shelf he could use to keep out of the line of fire. At the end of this protection, he would have to continue his way diagonally up the hill—duty gun in his hand. He estimated that the shot had been fired from some distance away. The shooter was most likely using a deer rifle with a scope.

Another shot rang out. Chris quickly moved up the hill, keeping as quiet as he could. As he was just about to crest the top of the hill, he paused to gather his legs under him.

"Don't move. Sheriff's Department!" called out Chris.

Chris had caught the two men prone and looking downhill. He handcuffed them in that prone position. Walking down the hill with his prisoners, he stopped at Karen.

"Karen? Are you okay? Karen ... Oh, God!"

Chris hustled the two men further downhill and freed Karen's lasso as he passed her horse to use for tying the two men to a tree so he could watch them from a distance. With that done, he ran to Kitty and found his first aid kit in the saddlebags. He ran back to Karen with tears running down his cheeks. Rolling her over and shielding her face from the sun with his body, he checked her pulse and breathing. He saw the bullet hole in her shirt just over the pocket.

Karen whispered, "Hey, cowboy, did we get 'em?"

"Yeah."

"Good. Hey, Chris ... well ..." deep sigh, "you know ..."

And just as smoothly as she had entered his life, she now departed his world.

Chapter Twenty-Nine
Confession Is Good for the Soul

The two men were put inside the horse trailer with the animals. Chris wrapped Karen's body with his old woolen blankets and placed her body in the back of the truck.

The men were placed in separate cells out of earshot of each other. The truck they were driving was placed in a secure area, and Chris began the investigation. He started with the truck and quickly saw a map on the front seat with a location marked in red marker. It was the ranch outside of Carrizo Springs. There was also a folded map of mineral deposits throughout the world. Looking at the legend, Chris saw areas around the globe, but nothing around Texas. Looking closer, Chris remembered his Colorado School of Mines days, and one hot topic was the Kimberlite find in Canada. Other "Kimberlite pipes," as they were known, were found in Arkansas, Colorado, Wyoming, South Africa, Russia, and Canada. No one had found anything in Texas except oil and gas. Or so it was thought.

Kimberlite pipes were as old as the earth. Pressure beneath the earth's crust would force magma from deep within the earth to break free to the surface. These so-called pipes were rich in carbon-bearing minerals. It was said that when these pipes erupted, the material was spewed at supersonic speeds and traveled many miles. Chris had a sample that he found east of Boulder out past Greeley from an ancient Kimberlite pipe. A farmer had given him the strange rock during a field trip of his. He had also found a "pipe" in northern Colorado. It couldn't be developed because the Union Pacific Railroad still maintained the mineral rights for twenty miles on either side of the railroad. Congress had used this easement as motivation for the railroads to increase the westward expansion of the United States. The railroads quickly capitalized on this and created communities to use their service. It was a rigged deal, but westward movement and the colonization of North America moved forward.

The interrogation of Jason Johnson started.

"Jason, it's pretty obvious that Griffen had you involved in some land deal. Do you care to share?" Chris said dryly.

"No."

"Let me tell you what I've found out," Chris said in a monotone. "You and Tucker, also known as Griffen, were scheming to control a parcel of land outside Chorizzo Springs. I'm not too sure how Tucker found out about the diamonds …"

"What diamonds?" barked Jason, his eyes wide at the revealed information.

"He didn't tell you?"

"No. I was just a name on a piece of paper."

"Well, my friend, in Tucker's world, you were nothing more than a brown stain on a piece of paper."

Calling to the detention facility deputy, Chris said, "You can take him away now."

Now it was Tucker's turn in the chair.

"Roger Tucker. I know that you killed Doctor and Mrs. O'Reilly. You also left a paper trail of forged names and a very clumsy Deed Assignment for a piece of land. What goads my curiosity is how you found a Kimberlite pipe in Texas."

Tucker's eyebrows shot into his hairline. "How did you know about that?"

"Roger, I get to ask questions in this room. Right now, all the evidence points to you. Fingerprints on receipts, deeds, and we can even place you in a small room on a ranch outside Alpine. Plus you shot and killed a sheriff's deputy. Need I go on?"

"He was planning on selling part of that property to the couple that rented the parcel. A border cop and his wife. When I was looking the property over for the doctor, I found a dark colored rock out in a field a ways off from the house. I put the rock in my pocket and forgot about it. Later, out of curiosity I took it to a geologist, and he told me about Kimberlite and diamonds. The doctor surprised me when I was going through his files in the barn, so to keep him quiet, I had to kill him. He put up one helluva fight for an old guy. His wife heard the commotion and came out to the barn. She was just as tough. Surprisingly, she fought me harder than he did. I guess you figured out the rest." Chris nodded his head in relief and fatigue.

Chapter Thirty
Peace

Later that week, Chris attended Karen's funeral. Many people at graveside lost their composure. He did quite well until the lone bugler played "Taps." Josh's hand was on his shoulder, and the other two brothers, Dan and Cy, stood on either side of Chris and Pat.

Pat understood and stood at her husband's side. She knew about Chris's passage along the Pecos and his friendship with Karen. What Chris didn't know was that Karen had accidentally befriended Pat at the hospital when Chris was on his northward journey. Women being women, they had compared notes and decided that Chris would make the final decision if and when he returned. They both had realized that he was undergoing an extreme physical and emotional burden. Nature would indeed have to take its course.

That evening, a breeze swept along the summer flowers, and the air held a hint of rain. Idly watching the rabbits, Chris asked Pat, "Now that you're the owner of a possible diamond mine, what are your thoughts for the future?"

"Chris, it goes beyond imagination the wealth that may be in that land. My father and mother were always concerned about this community. Perhaps we can do something for others as well as ourselves. I know Jenny will be pleased with what we have planned for her. We'll have lots of time since you'll be spending more time around the home. Perhaps we both need a break from work and should pursue something loftier in our lives."

Chris looked at her over his sunglasses questioningly.

"I do know that you are going to have a son in just over seven months," Pat said with a sly grin on her face. "We have many plans to make."

Epilogue

When Chris and Dave drove back to Texas, the president of the United States announced that there would be a massive effort to grow soy, safflower, canola, peanut, and other like crops to produce vegetable oil. Also mandated was the conversion of all gas-powered engines to diesel. The automotive industry was compelled by an Act of Congress to facilitate the change with as little disruption of the citizenry as possible.

Secondly, oil companies were put on notice that their product would be gradually phased out as a primary motor fuel. Environmentalists around the world went wild. The Mid-East oil cartel understood its place in the sun was quickly disappearing, and terrorists would find no more support within that failing society.

Thirdly, ethanol plants were converted to oil-separation centrifuges running on the electricity produced by their in-house diesel plants. This was later mandated for all new plants with an eye toward self-sufficiency.

Fourth, starting with new homes and brought forward to existing homes was a national re-electrification project that started with individual homes creating electricity and the feeding into the grid. This reversed the concept of feeding from into feeding to. People were much more prone to become part of something willingly than to be forced to "give" in the form of increasingly higher prices.

Lastly, all American auto manufacturers and engine manufacturers were mandated to immediately stop production of the common internal engine, known as a gas engine, and become licensed to build diesel engines. Everything down to the lowly weed whacker was converted.

The American farmer was now a respected part of the US economy. Enough pressure was put on fertilizer and seed companies to cut their profits in half since a congressional probe discovered gouging, profiteering, and unfair market practices. As a mea culpa, they turned their attention to improving the olive in an attempt to allow that plant to grow in various climates in the United States. Jordan had opened the door to its citizens to plant and harvest olives alongside their highways.

As more baby boomers retired and moved out of the city, they quickly discovered that farming for American veg-oil could be fun, and farm equipment became a community resource, allowing the ownership and maintenance to be spread over many instead of a sole burden. America's citizens were rapidly heading toward becoming the future oil barons of the West.

In a subsequent court order, the property offered for sale by Pat's father and the adjacent property owned by the Adkins brothers, fondly remembered by Chris and Pat as the Three Stinkers, was awarded to Jenny, who decided to develop the potential of the Kimberlite and started many shelters for widows and children of fallen law enforcement officers. She remarried and spent the rest of her life with her new husband, whom she had been introduced to by Chris. Dave Nelson kept his mules on a small part of the property to remember his past and keep himself focused on his roots.

About the Author

Richard Hultén has traveled and flown over much of the United States and abroad to the Middle East. He retired from a large communications company and spent twelve years as a reserve deputy sheriff outside of Denver, Colorado. He is a private pilot and has a homebuilt airplane that he has flown over much of the western United States. He has been a falconer and has an eight-year Quarter Horse named Sophie. His double-major degree was a combination of criminal justice and philosophy. Having seen the building of the Internet and seeing the possibility for mayhem, this story is a look into future troubles.